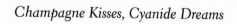

Champagne Kisses, Cyanide Dreams

CHAMPAGNE KISSES
CYANIDE DREAMS

a mystery by

RALPH GRAVES

Ralph Graves

DAVID R. GODINE

Publisher · Boston

First published in 2001 by
DAVID R. GODINE · *Publisher*
Post Office Box 450
Jaffrey, New Hampshire 03452
www.godine.com

LIBRARY OF CONGRESS
CATALOGING-IN-PUBLICATION DATA

Graves, Ralph.
Champagne kisses, cyanide dreams / by Ralph Graves.—1st ed.
p. cm.
ISBN 1-56792-179-5 (hardcover : alk. paper)
1. Martha's Vineyard (Mass.)—Fiction. I. Title.
PS3557.R2887 C48 2001
813'.54–dc21 2001023569

FIRST EDITION 2001
Printed in the United States of America

To Eleanor

53 years of friendship
46 years of love
43 years of marriage
36 years of a Vineyard home
— and still counting

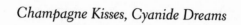

Champagne Kisses, Cyanide Dreams

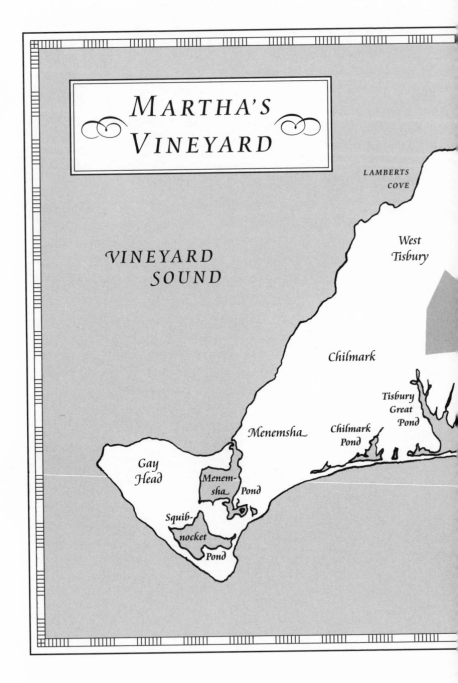

MARTHA'S VINEYARD

LAMBERTS
COVE

VINEYARD
SOUND

West
Tisbury

Chilmark

Tisbury
Great
Pond

Menemsha

Chilmark
Pond

Gay
Head

Menem-
sha

Pond

Squib-
nocket

Pond

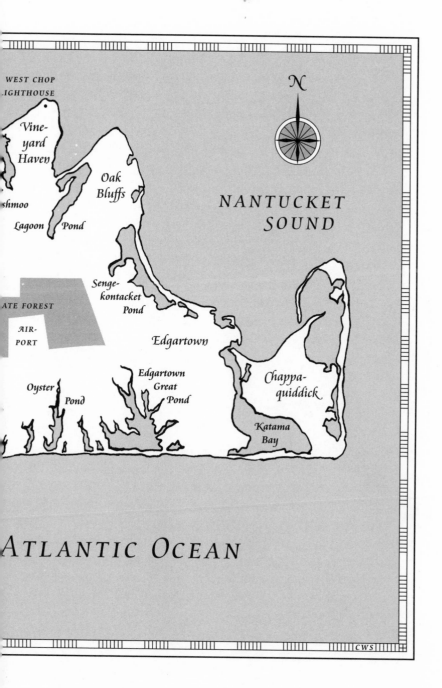

All the victims and suspects in this story
are imaginary characters.

But the celebrity invasion of
Martha's Vineyard
is all too real.

There Goes Millie

GROWING UP in Manhattan and attending Groton and Harvard, I learned to tolerate many frightful people. But you have to draw the line somewhere. I drew the line at Mildred Silk.

Millie. Silky. Like almost everybody I called her Millie, but she liked to say that her lovers called her Silky "for personal reasons." This phrase was accompanied by a lifted eyebrow, an airy puff of her cigarette and a small twist of her mouth that said, *I know more than you do.*

I'm sure she had many lovers, although not as many as she claimed in her conversation and her writing. She was a born storyteller and a congenital liar. The distinction between her fiction and her nonfiction was invisible. I had read most of her books in both categories, and the tone was always the same: supercilious and self-serving, with occasional unconvincing touches of humility, as if to say, *Look, I'm not quite as perfect as you think.* She was often venomous, never dull. The critics loved her, and although she was too intellectual to be a giant bestseller, all her books were still in print, still selling, still admired. She was the star property of Okapi Press, one of the last independent publishers.

Whether or not he called her Silky, by far her most important lover was Harry Harkness, the developer of suburban shopping malls. They got married at the height of her literary fame and at the height of his wealth. It was a marriage made in heaven, to which he soon ascended, leaving Millie a townhouse in Manhattan, a waterfront property on Martha's Vineyard, and ample funds to maintain both. She lived well and dressed well but spent no money on jewelry, having previously accumulated all the impressive pieces she could possibly wear, most of them pried out of Harry.

I had no problem avoiding Millie in New York. I was twenty-five years younger, and we moved in different circles. Her circle was the celebrity-intellectual world of books, theater, art, opera and know-it-all conversation. I had no circle. I could get through an entire winter with no more than a few glimpses of her in a theater lobby or restaurant or at a museum benefit. She could not be mistaken for anyone else. She was tall, with rather short red-gold hair — short enough so that one could always see what glorious earrings she was wearing. Her face was handsome, arresting, with strong, striking vertical lines. In evening dress she was regal. If you did not know her, you would probably want to meet her. If you did know her, you would avoid her. At our random winter encounters we rarely spoke and seldom nodded.

But summer at the Vineyard was different. Millie had made herself the doyenne of the celebrity crowd, a group that was, alas, growing every year. Even though the celebrities came from different fields, they all knew each other and liked to cluster together. Celebrity incest is incurable. Millie had the credentials, the stature, the house, the money, the chef and the self-importance to rule a summer salon.

Her dinner parties were more than famous, they were obligatory. One did not dare refuse an invitation on the grounds of a prior engagement. Since, to Millie, that excuse was not acceptable, one ran the danger of not being invited back — ever. She could hold a grudge for years. She also had a savage tongue and used it generously to flay anyone who disappointed her. The Vineyard's most important artist, the up-Island recluse Caleb Stone, would have nothing to do with her world or with her invitations.

She therefore referred to him as "that rustic boob." She pitilessly disparaged his work and patronized the Island's second-best artist, Jeremy Gaines, who faithfully responded whenever she pushed his button. Everybody did.

But I don't want to be too unfair. Her invitations were much sought after. She held the dinners in her grand open dining room, with its parade of windows overlooking the ocean. Two round tables of eight and a single table of six, where Millie presided. Always twenty-two people with, as a point of pride, never a vacant seat. In an interview with the *Vineyard Gazette* she explained that she found her arrangement "more interesting" than three tables of eight, which she said would be not only boring but vulgar. My own interpretation was that a table for six was easier for Millie to dominate conversationally than a table for eight. It also provided a fillip of exclusivity. If you made it to Millie's head table, you must really be somebody.

She gave one dinner on Memorial Day weekend to open the season, then one in June, two in July, as many as three or four in the super month of August. She ended with a season-closer on the Labor Day weekend. Last year she added a Columbus Day dinner because so many people came back for that weekend. In Millie's earlier years on the Island my parents were sometimes invited to a dinner in the shoulders of the season, but once the celebrity invasion occurred, they were dropped. They did not mind. My mother disliked Millie and was glad to escape.

My social standing and my accomplishments as a very now-and-then writer did not qualify me for Millie's twenty-two person dinner cut. But as a quite presentable single male with life-long Vineyard summer status and with respectable parents who lived in a respectable waterfront house, I was twice invited — at the very last minute — to fill a gap.

On the first occasion the call came from Millie's New York secretary, Miss Quinn, a totally subjugated woman who did all Millie's typing, all her social scheduling and anything else that her demanding boss demanded. Miss Quinn was never rewarded with a trip to the Vineyard. She phoned on the morning of the dinner. I'm embarrassed to say that I accepted, but I swore I would never accept again.

I was, however, highly qualified for Millie's cocktail parties. These took place on her mammoth deck and her wide green lawn, both with a splendid view overlooking the Atlantic. The hors d'œuvres, varied and excellent, were distributed by catering girls in white blouses, black skirts and black bow ties. Being far less exclusive than her dinner parties, her cocktail parties included Island newcomers, promising authors, rich young Wall Streeters and similar riffraff. I admit that I always went. The fact that I felt I had to accept did not make me like Millie any better, although they were excellent parties. I shared my mother's view.

For several years Millie had let it be known she was working on a book that was, to the many Island celebrities, both thrilling and threatening. Thanks to Millie's enthusiasm for talking about herself, we all knew the book's title, *Celebrity Watch*. The scuttlebutt, spread by Millie herself, was that her book would be the definitive portrait of this segment of Island society. "You're all in it," she told her friends and guests and enemies, "warts and all." Then came that big airy puff on her cigarette, blowing the smoke into the sky, and that ruthless smile. "Especially the warts."

I thought this was just smoke from an extinct volcano. She was sixty-something and hadn't published a book in five years. But now, apparently, it was finished and due out within the year. Tonight's dinner was the opening salvo. Her longtime editor and publisher, Leonard Marsden of Okapi Press, had flown up from New York to be the guest of honor and chief flack.

One hour and forty minutes before cocktails were scheduled to begin, I got my second dinner summons from the New York secretary. "Mr. Arnold? I know this is rather short notice, but — "

Having sworn I would never, never again accept the role of last-minute substitute, I played a little hard to get before I succumbed. "If this is only 'rather short notice,'" I said, "what would you consider very short notice?"

"I beg your pardon?"

"Who canceled this time?"

"I beg your pardon?" she said again, her voice still polite but stiffening a bit.

"This is very late for a cancellation," I said. "I just wondered who I was replacing." I also wondered how many other possibilities Millie might have tried before getting around to me. Not much time to spare, any port in a storm.

"Oh," Miss Quinn said, pausing to think that over. Apparently she decided it was permissible to answer. "Mr. Hergesheimer suddenly got called away on an assignment."

Bob Hergesheimer, head man of ABC's weekly *News Magazine*, was an Island devotee. Most weekends all year long he and his wife flew up to their Edgartown house right after he taped his show. Millie could usually count on him, but every once in a while he had to do a special story on short notice. I didn't think Miss Quinn's leash would let her tell me what this story was. Probably she didn't know.

"Tell Miss Silk I'll be glad to come," I said, giving in once again. For the last time, as it turned out.

If Mildred Silk had been murdered at one of her cocktail parties, I would have been a legitimate suspect, but only one among many. Since she was murdered at dinner, I was promoted to the role of serious suspect — one among a handful.

* * *

I was once a serious suspect in a Manhattan murder case. I suppose if I had actually done the deed, I would have enjoyed it less. In fact, I'm sure I would have been terrified. But since I was innocent, I had a wonderful time. I knew the victim, Eliot Simms. Two weeks earlier he and I had a rousing public argument that many witnesses remembered. Since we'd had several drinks, we threatened each other loudly and extravagantly. Curses were thrown, along with a couple of harmless punches.

I was questioned at length by a gray-haired homicide detective named Dirk Schultz. A sharp-faced slender man with extremely bright eyes, he was polite but skeptical. He addressed me as Mr. Arnold and never raised his voice, but apparently my answers did not satisfy him. My alibi, although true, was not ironclad. After that interview I got the works. I was read my Miranda rights, just like in the TV cop shows. I refused a lawyer because I knew a lawyer would interfere with the personal attention I was getting. Fingerprints. A saliva sample and a blood sample. My friends were questioned. My cleaning lady was questioned so rigorously that she got the notion that she herself was a suspect and burst into hysterical tears. Her mother wanted to sue the city for police brutality.

Lieutenant Schultz interviewed me again, this time with a hefty homicide sergeant in tow. I don't know whether the lieutenant wanted physical protection from a possible maniac, or whether he wanted a witness to my answers. The sergeant never said a word.

My estranged wife at last got to talk to someone who was not only willing to listen to her but even took notes on what she said. Doris described my habits, character and principal short-comings. It made her year. Her long happy afternoon with the detectives was so therapeutic that it put her in a good mood to reach a reasonable divorce settlement.

The next time I saw Dirk Schultz, he didn't bring the sergeant. He asked if I would be willing to take a lie detector test.

A lie detector test! Nobody I knew had ever taken one. I was so tickled that it was difficult to keep my face straight. Of course I wanted to say yes, yes, hook me up, but I had to uphold my role as a serious suspect. I pretended to think for a long agonizing moment. I stared down at the floor, my brow appropriately furrowed. Finally I said, as though to myself, "No. No, I don't think so."

When I looked up, Schultz was grinning at me. "You're having a good time, aren't you, Jason?"

It was the first time he had called me Jason instead of Mr. Arnold, so I knew something had changed. "How do you mean?"

"The lab says you're out of the loop. You're clear. I was just curious to see what you'd say."

So we enjoyed a laugh, and I thanked him for the entire experience. I asked him if I could take the lie detector test anyway, but he said now that I was officially cleared, that could get him in trouble.

I didn't stay out of the loop. All the questioning I had gone through had forced me to devote a lot of thought to Eliot Simms and to the people he knew — and then to remember something odd, something that struck me as quite possibly important. And then, as a result, I figured out something even more important.

I called Dirk Schultz and told him what I knew and what I had concluded.

A long pause at his end. Then he said in a quiet voice,

almost to himself, "That's very interesting." Then after another long pause he asked, "Could you testify to that?"

"Yes. Definitely."

I turned out to be right. My father said it was the most useful thing I had ever done, which I think was meant to be praise.

Dirk Schultz got a special commendation for closing the case and was grateful.

He bought me a few drinks, and later I bought him a long lunch. We got along very well. I had a great time learning about homicide. He liked talking about his work, and he enjoyed a layman's acute interest in his experiences. Long lunches — sometimes Italian, sometimes Chinese — became a regular habit. I bought all the lunches. A year later he invited me to his retirement party. I was the only former suspect so honored. Everybody else was family or police.

I love murder. I've spent many, many happy hours with Holmes and Hercule Poirot and Nero Wolfe and their colleagues. But murder in real life is even better, especially when the victim is someone I dislike. Who did it? And why? Of course in real life, Dirk Schultz told me, the answers to those questions are usually straightforward, often obvious. There usually isn't much mystery to it. It's usually a question, Dirk said, of collecting accurate proof to support what you already know. But once in a while you get lucky, and then it's very interesting indeed. Like Eliot Simms — or Millie Silk.

* * *

By the time I had showered, put on the proper uniform of a summer-weight blazer and tie and arrived on Millie's aircraft-carrier deck, little remained of the cocktail hour. The other guests were already there, standing around in small groups, glasses in hand.

I knew several and recognized most, but first I had to report in.

Millie was on her favorite throne, an old-fashioned porch swing with a tassel-fringed canopy, a lovers' swing but wide enough for three. In windy weather it had to be carried inside lest it be lifted off the deck, swept across the lawn and down into the Atlantic. Only two sat there now. Leonard Marsden, her publisher and editor for many books and many years, looked ruddily British with his guardsman's mustache. Millie, as was her custom, wore a long skirt, this one with big swirls of bright blue and bright green. Tonight her earrings were small sapphires surrounded by a flock of little diamonds — her summer jewelry.

Millie did not apologize for asking me on such incredibly short notice. Apologies were not her style. But she did thank me for coming, which was as far as her courtesy could stretch. She introduced me to Marsden as "an occasional writer, but no books as yet." Perfectly true but rather stingy, I thought.

I barely had time to ask for and receive a vodka on the rocks before Millie looked at her watch, rose from the swing and announced, "Please come in to dinner. We mustn't keep Marcel waiting."

As an occasional writer with no books as yet, I did not rate an outstanding dinner partner. My handwritten place card set me between the absent Bob Hergesheimer's dowdy but intelligent wife Mary, and Everett Munk's third wife, the blonde, sexy, but featherheaded, Nancy. Everett was a serious older writer who had once won a National Book Award and thought he deserved a Pulitzer and much more money than any of his books had earned. It was difficult to imagine what he and Nancy talked about. Sex, I suppose.

I was seated at the more distant table for eight and had been placed with my back to the view. Just because I had agreed to fill in at the last minute didn't mean that Millie Silk was going to change her social priorities and put me in a special seat. However, at Millie's dinners there was never a bad table. On the other side of Nancy Munk was a real live United States senator, silver-haired Max Washburn of Connecticut. He was a handsome but not very good senator, best known for his womanizing, especially when it came to young women. Millie had mischievously put him next to the young, pretty Nancy, of whom Everett was profoundly jealous. Millie rarely seated couples or lovers next to each other or even at the same table. As she explained, "They can talk to each other during cocktails or after dinner, or even in bed, but my concern is to arrange my tables in the most interesting way." This included making trouble if possible. From the next table, close enough to see but not to hear, Everett Munk slighted his dinner partners and kept peering our way to see how his young wife and Max Washburn were getting along. They were getting along just fine.

Looking at the other tables, I saw that Millie had seated only one couple next to each other. Sam Cone, who owned a national string of scurrilous tabloids and thought of himself as a press lord, sat beside his wife Bebe. Everybody, very much including Millie, knew they hated each other. Bebe Cone, once a whiz real estate agent in Fairfield, Connecticut, had moved to the Vineyard full-time to get away from her press lord and to ply her trade among the Island rich. Sam Cone came to the Vineyard only for occasional weekends — mostly to fight with Bebe, the gossips said. Millie's seating arrangement enabled them to fight during dinner.

In my opinion, Senator Washburn, with his youth fetish, was concentrating on the wrong dinner partner. On his left was a still beautiful, still marvelous creature. I could not believe I was sitting right across from one of the Vineyard's most dazzling new celebrities, the movie actress Elena Bronze. All right, at mid-fifty-something she was a little old for Senator Washburn, but she looked wonderful. Although she had built her trophy house on Edgartown Great Pond a year ago, I had never caught sight of her. Now that she was only six feet away, I tried not to stare at her world-famous chest.

Born Elena Bronzini, she and her agent and her studio shortened her name as soon as it became obvious that she was going to be a star. Thirty years ago she had been a good serious young actress when she first appeared in a bare-breasted scene. Back then, serious actresses never did that. In fact, no respectable actress, serious or not, dared to — certainly not Katherine Hepburn, not even Elizabeth Taylor. In an interview during the ensuing uproar she said, "Nakedness is a natural part of life, often a very good part. I have nothing to be ashamed of." Certainly not her breasts. After her third consecutive movie display, *Time's* movie reviewer reverently christened them "the bronzinis." Tonight she wore a discreet flowered blouse, mostly pale green, with long sleeves and a quite high neck, but I still found it hard not to stare. Her dinner partner was Danny Rothman, another newcomer to the Island, a pudgy fellow who was C E O and principal owner of the third largest cable company and movie channel. I expected them to talk shop, but as near as I could follow from across the table, they were trading horror stories about the difficulty of getting Island builders and electricians and plumbers during the summer months. Those of us who have been here for years no longer find this topic riveting.

The last two at my table were Jill Klein, the wealthy defense attorney whose specialty was crimes of sexual violence, the more violent and kinky the better, and Harris Lawford, the noisy and wealthy Boston proponent of gay and lesbian rights. Millie had been right in thinking they would have a lot to fight about.

A pretty good right-field table, I had to admit, but to put it in perspective I had only to look at Millie's smaller table where, in addition to her editor-publisher Leonard Marsden, she could talk to Jane Millhouse, the black soprano diva, Chick Bird, the young California software king who flew his own jet to the Vineyard several times a month, Lulu Waring, the plump beloved hostess of the network gossip show *Celeb/Celeb*, and Rufus Mainbocher, who owned almost as much of Wall Street as Warren Buffett. Chick Bird's real name was Byron Bird, and the business press called him Lord Byron, both for eminence and arrogance, but everybody else called him by his childhood nickname, Chickie or Chick. He was the inventor and the owner of the popular HumDinger software system. He was the only man in the room not wearing a tie and jacket, but his embroidered suede shirt — whirly white silk pattern against dark brown — cost more than all the other jackets in the room put together.

At the other eight-person table, from which Everett Munk was keeping his wife under surveillance, sat a sad contrast to Elena Bronze's preserved perfection. Betsy Pope, our most popular singer for the last two decades, was a wreck. In her earliest days, when she was a very young country singer and then a very young movie star, she was tiny enough and lovable enough to be called Bitsy Betsy. Bitsy Betsy, the little girl with the big voice, as they used to say. The great voice was still there, at least now and then in a recording studio. But the hit movies and the packed concerts and the vibrant TV appearances had vanished. She had burgeoned into a lumpy, dumpy figure with a puffy, bloated face. Drugs, booze, sex, glandular problems, five thousand brandy alexanders, her favorite drink. Looking at that thick-necked, heavy-shouldered figure at the next table, I calculated that she was fifteen years younger than Elena Bronze. Millie had, with what I assumed was deliberate cruelty, placed Bitsy between the hotshot young sitcom star Jiggs Cooley and the serious, serious novelist Everett Munk. A sad dinner, part of a sad life.

After a superb lobster bisque, and grilled swordfish with capers and lemon sauce, and a bibb lettuce and avocado salad, the maids cleared our tables for the dessert course.

But before the dessert presentation came Millie's customary champagne flurry. This consisted of frosted ice-cold flutes placed before each guest into which was poured Charles Heidsieck Blanc des Millenaires, 1983 vintage. As she had once explained in a *Vanity Fair* interview, she could of course afford to serve Cristal, but that would be foolish ostentation, since she had the good taste to prefer "what the British call Champagne Charlie."

When the last flute was full, in came Marcel himself, a roly-poly figure in white toque and black mustache, bearing a vast silver platter of flaming baked Alaska. It was just like Millie — and, I understand, just like her chef — to exhume baked Alaska from the distant past and make something special out of it.

It was splendid. When we had all finished the last perfect slurp, she summoned Marcel from the kitchen. He was a well-paid employee of many years, perhaps the only person Millie consistently treated with respect. Although he had to have known from all the empty bowls and plates coming back to his kitchen that his dinner was a great success, he managed to wear a slightly worried look as he waited for Millie's verdict.

"Marcel," she said loudly enough for all to hear, "the entire dinner was brilliant. You have surpassed yourself — as usual."

Sincere applause from all three tables. Marcel produced three bows, one to each table, and a happy smile. He would have had to be singularly ungrateful, only half an hour later, to knock her off. Although with chefs you never know.

When Marcel had departed in triumph, Leonard Marsden rose to his feet from his seat at Millie's right and tapped his champagne flute with his dessert spoon. It's usually difficult to get celebrities to stop talking, but they all knew that Marsden's subject would be themselves. Harris Lawford finished a last angry sentence to Jill Klein about AIDS, and then the room was silent.

Marsden was a tall shaggy man who looked sixty-five but was more than a decade older. He had bristly gray-brown hair and was not the least bit British, in spite of the guardsman's mustache. He was already a bright, brash young editor way back when Bennett Cerf ran Random House, and Alfred Knopf ran Knopf, and Simon and Schuster ran Simon & Schuster, back in the days before the money men and the Germans took over. A rare WASP in a predominantly Jewish industry, he had founded his own publishing house with the support of a handful of optimistic investors who had grown rich in prestige though not in money. He christened it Okapi, over the protests of his investors, because, he explained, the okapi was an elegant antelope and a familiar word in crossword puzzles.

His was the perfect publishing house for Mildred Silk. Okapi's reputation for excellence and intellectual heft suited her. She knew that at Okapi she would never have to compete with a Danielle Steele or a Judith Krantz. In turn, Okapi could not have survived as a business based solely on excellence and critical admiration. It needed to sell books, and Millie's books sold forever, hard cover and trade paperback. They were a good match.

Leonard Marsden let the silence stand for a few moments before he said, "This is a wonderful year for me and for my publishing house." He had a strong baritone voice, rich in the self-confidence that comes from years of holding authority. He looked fondly down at Millie. "After a wait of five years — five years of some impatience, I must say — we are again publishing a book by our brilliant hostess. I'm proud to say that this is Millie's eighth consecutive book to bear the Okapi imprint." Since no one applauded, he did, and then others joined in. He looked around the three tables. "As I think you all know by now," he said with a smile, "this book is called *Celebrity Watch*, and it is very much about you people in this room."

A ripple of nervous laughter from everybody except me. I was the only one present who was certain not to be included.

"Quite a few other people are in the book," Marsden said, still smiling, "too many to fit into this dining room. If Millie invited all the Vineyard celebrities who are in the book, she would have to give a clambake on her beach."

Another ripple of laughter into which Millie injected, "I despise clambakes."

"A mere figure of speech," Marsden said, waving her off, not afraid of her. "Even Bill and Hillary Clinton will be in the book, although many Vineyard Republicans do not consider them celebrities."

This was far-fetched. Although the Island's celebrity buildup started before the Clintons first came here, the recurrent Presidential summer vacations, trailing brigades of press and TV cameras and Secret Service, have done more than anything else to overpublicize the Island. Many of us — Republicans, Democrats and anarchists alike — fear that the Clintons will make this their permanent summer home.

"Princess Diana will also be in the book," Marsden said, "and I think all of us can agree about her celebrity status."

Marsden should not have mentioned Diana. During her single one-week visit to the Vineyard in the summer of 1994, Millie had tried desperately to give a dinner party in her honor but had been turned down because the Princess wanted "a very private vacation" with her host and hostess. After pulling every string, every thread, Millie did get to meet Diana briefly, but that was all. What rankled Millie especially was that the Princess played ladies' doubles on the private tennis court at Kay Graham's Lambert's Cove estate. One of the four ladies, a friend of mine, told me that Diana was "a nice player and a lot of good fun." Surely a much friendlier judgment than Diana would receive in Millie's book.

"I would like to drink a toast," Marsden said, "but I seem to have an empty glass." I felt sure he had used that ploy before to gain some friendly amusement and extra attention. He picked up Millie's flute and tipped her champagne into his own flute. "Since the toast is for you, you won't be needing this." He raised his glass. "A champagne kiss to our hostess, to my favorite writer and to the success of her brilliant new book."

Scattered hear-hears around the room, many of them patently insincere. I could imagine everyone thinking, *What awful things does she say about me?*

Marsden sat down. Millie did not get up to respond. She reached for his flute and said, "Lenny, I'm going to need this after all," and she poured some champagne back into her glass. Raising it, she looked slowly from table to table, almost person to person. It was a look of pleasure, self-satisfaction and malice.

"Here's to all of you," she said. "All of you who made this book possible. I have enjoyed studying you, some of you for years, some of you only recently. And as Mr. Marsden says, I have also been studying your many counterparts who aren't here tonight. Yes, including Bill and Hillary, who have been here twice for dinner. I have loved writing about you. I think you may well be the best subject I have ever had in my long and not-too-shabby career as a writer. I am afraid, however, that I have enjoyed writing this book a great deal more than you will enjoy reading it. But anyway, here's to you."

I was the only one who raised high my glass and drank along with her. She saw me do it and nodded. "That's right, Jason," she spoke across the room, "you're not in my book — for obvious reasons."

What followed when we got up from the table was an elaborate, well-established tradition at Millie's dinners. Even before we had first entered the dining room, the antique liqueur glasses and the enormous brandy *ballons* were lined up on the buffet in front of the bottles of Cointreau, Grand Marnier, Chartreuse, Armagnac, Calvados and Sambuca, along with several fine brandies, both French and Spanish. Since we were all expected to help ourselves, a good bit of confusion took place. Discussion, indecision and recommendations from Millie were all part of the ritual. Millie, her own glass poured, masterminded and encouraged the melee.

Later the police went round and round and round on this scene, interrogating each of us repeatedly, trying to discover who had stood next to whom, who had seen what, who had heard who said what. They never learned anything important. Only the murderer knew what happened.

Finally settled in the living room with our drinks, and with the maids pouring coffee, Millie still had a lighted cigarette in her hand and had just taken a slug of her favorite liqueur, green Chartreuse. She always chose it, as she had so often said, and as she said again tonight, "because it goes with my eyes." A typical Millie lie — and her last. Her eyes were, at best, hazel.

Suddenly she gasped, dropped the cigarette and put both hands to her throat. I thought her cigarette smoke must have gone down the wrong way. But then a wild, beseeching look in her eyes struck all those nearest to her. She was choking, suffocating.

Although I was only a few steps away, the Heimlich maneuver never occurred to me. The guest who thought of it was not the defense attorney Jill Klein, who knew so much about death and physical violence. Nor was it Elena Bronze, who had once played a particularly memorable bare-breasted scene involving the Heimlich. Millie's attempted savior was her fellow author Everett Munk. In spite of his bulk he sprang forward, hauled her to her feet, wrapped his thick arms around her chest and squeezed violently, half a dozen times.

Too late. She was already dead. Naturally, all but one of us thought she had had a fatal heart attack or a stroke.

My fictional detective heroes always tried to determine who was the greatest beneficiary of the victim's death. The greatest immediate beneficiary of Millie's death was Lulu Waring, hostess and star of *Celeb/Celeb*. Because she was a dinner guest, she got a mammoth jump on all the rest of the media. The medical examiner later set the time of the death at 9:30, give or take a few minutes. While others were trying to revive Millie and to phone the hospital and the Emergency Medical Service, Lulu was talking to CBS from the phone in Millie's office. The famous cooing little voice was now strident. She was demanding an instant ENB — an eyewitness news bulletin. "Break into whatever's running," she shouted into the phone. And then, to underline the urgency of her request, "Right now, you stupid fuck."

So the world learned about the death of Mildred Silk through a voice-over report from the very scene only a few minutes after it happened. Bob Hergesheimer, absent on assignment, had missed out to Lulu, a major professional rival. If Hergie had been at the dinner instead of me, the struggle for telephone access would have been something to see. They were both great reporters with matching egos.

But Lulu Waring was in such a desperate hurry to report her exclusive that she was out of the room and missed the best part.

Jane Millhouse, the hefty black opera star, was down on her

knees beside the body, slapping the dead cheeks and crying "Millie! Millie!" Straight out of the last scene of *Tosca*, which I had seen her perform. She could just as well have been crying "Mario! Mario!" I caught myself waiting for her to screech *"Morto! Morto!"* I thought she was better when the resuscitation was addressed to her dead lover than to her dead hostess, but she was still damn good, considering this was real life, on short notice and with no rehearsal.

But suddenly Jane Millhouse stopped the slapping and wrinkled her big nose. She leaned closer and sniffed, then made a face. She looked up at our circle. "There's a funny smell," she said. More nose-wrinkling. "A very funny smell."

Everett Munk's ditsy wife Nancy was first to react. Drawing on some confused but obviously exciting memory, she asked, "Could it be — ? Is it — ? Is it like bitter pecans?"

At least three people including me had read mysteries and spy thrillers. "Bitter almonds," we corrected her in unison.

Nobody present had ever smelled either bitter almonds or bitter pecans. I suppose we could have called in Chef Marcel for an expert opinion, but instead we called the police.

Sure enough, as it would turn out. Cyanide.

Here Come the Cops

$\mathcal{O}$N JULY 1998 in the town of Oak Bluffs a drug-related stabbing took place. It was the first murder on the Vineyard in twenty years, so the Island police have had no practice. Each of the six towns has its own police force and its own police chief, and they are all experts on summer traffic jams, burglaries, drugs, drunk driving, winter vandalism and moped accidents. Murder, however, is not in their province.

The Vineyard Haven police, whose station was only five minutes away by siren, were first to arrive. It looked like every cop in town had come, including those off duty.

Nobody yet knew for sure that Millie had been murdered, but whatever had happened to her at this star-spangled dinner party, it was sure to be a lot more fun to investigate than the trashing of a summer home by high school kids on a February night when there was nothing else to do. Even the chief had come. I'd known Chief Angus for years, a big, burly, friendly man, considerably tougher than he looked and somewhat smarter. He said, "Hiya, Jason," to me and then told us all not to touch anything.

Jill Klein said, "I already told them that."

"Who are you, ma'am?"

"I'm an attorney," she said stiffly, quite disappointed not to be recognized.

Indeed she had told us. As soon as the smell of "bitter pecans" was mentioned, she took charge. Her natural air of dominance was familiar to all of us who had watched her confront a jury on *Court TV*. The straight black hair swept severely back and tightly pinned, the strong nose, the snapping black eyes, the no-nonsense voice. She could have made herself look much softer, more attractive, she didn't have to be so ferocious, but her style was to command, not cajole. She ordered us to back away from Millie's body and to touch nothing. She ordered the maids to leave every plate, every coffee cup, every piece of silver, every glass (including the liqueur glass that had droppped from Millie's dying hand) just exactly where it was. I wondered if she was deliberately controlling the crime scene so that, later, she would be prepared to defend one of us in a courtroom.

Chief Angus thanked Jill Klein for her good sense, then the police herded us out of the dining room, leaving one officer to stand guard over the body and whatever evidence might be lying around loose. We were all in the living room — a sizable crowd of guests, cops, maids and one chef — when three members of the state police arrived from Oak Bluffs. Two were in uniform. The other one, in a red polo shirt and blue jeans, was clearly the boss. Chief Angus said, "Hello, Kenny, glad you're here. She's in the next room." The three state troopers headed for the dining room, plain-clothes Kenny leading the way.

One of the rules is that the state police must be called in whenever there's a death, even if it's just from a traffic accident. With anything as serious as a murder, they are in command. Chief Angus was relieved to turn over the responsibility on this one. The state troopers were back with us in five minutes. They all looked stern. One of them was talking in a low voice into a cell phone.

Kenny walked straight up to the chief. "Has anybody touched the body?"

"I don't know, we just got here."

"Help me keep everybody here. I'm sending over to Bourne for the Crime Scene Unit and the pathologist."

"But that's a whole couple of hours at least."

"Not by helicopter. I'm in a real hurry on this one." He turned to the room and raised his voice. "Ladies and gentlemen!" When they quieted, he said, "I'm Sergeant Kenneth Waters. I'm the state detective trooper on the Vineyard. Did any of you touch Miss Silk's body?"

After a pause Everett Munk put up his hand. "I did. She was choking, so I tried the Heimlich."

"She was still alive?"

"I don't know."

"Anybody else?"

Jane Millhouse said in her bright black soprano, "Yes, when she was lying on the floor, I tried to revive her. I slapped her cheeks. That's when I smelled…" Her voice trailed off.

"Yes," Sergeant Waters said. "It's still strong. And her fingernails are blue."

For an experienced mystery reader like me, that clinched cyanide poisoning.

"Anybody else touch her?"

"I may have," said an older man with fuzzy white hair, rimless glasses and a pink, cherubic face. "When it was obvious she was dead, I thought I should say a small prayer for her. I knelt down beside her, bowed my head and closed my eyes."

"Well," Waters said, "did you touch her or not?"

The cherub shook his head. "I may have. I'm not sure."

This may have been the first time in his life that Dr. Sunbeam was not sure of something. His real name wasn't Dr. Sunbeam, of course. According to his first insanely popular self-help book, he was Matthew Smeck, but the title of his first book — one hundred and forty-two weeks on the best-seller list before becoming a paperback perennial — was *Your Life Can Be a Sunbeam*. Smeck had been trained as a minister, then took a correspondence course in psychotherapy. As he later explained, he thought the combination of ministry and psychotherapy might help people solve their personal problems. When he found this to be true, he wrote a book "so that I could help even more people."

If Mildred Silk had been the darling of the critics, Matthew Smeck was their anathema. If there is anything literary critics can't stand, it is successful pap. In its Sunday Book Review section the self-righteous *New York Times* lists self-help bestsellers separately from "real" bestsellers. Critics try to avoid reviewing such books altogether, but when a book like *Your Life Can Be a Sunbeam* sells week after week and then month after month, notice finally has to be taken, usually in the form of a scathing, dismissive review that deplores the collapse of intellectual standards and foresees the downfall of the Republic. One such reviewer hooted at Matthew Smeck as "Dr. Sunbeam." Smeck, who admitted he hadn't much liked his real name, rejected the insult and adopted Dr. Sunbeam as his *nom de plume*. He also used it as his *nom de television* and *nom de lecture*. His second runaway bestseller, *The Bright Side Is the Right Side*, was published under that name. The local book-signing parties at our two leading bookstores, the Bunch of Grapes in Vineyard Haven and Bickerton & Ripley in Edgartown, were so jammed that the lines stretched out onto the Main Street sidewalks, blocking all pedestrian traffic and causing a good deal of hard feeling and a few scuffles with some nonreading tourists, of whom we have a good many. It was a hot summer evening at the Bunch of Grapes, and owner Ann Nelson had to supply a record fourteen punch bowls of lemonade along with four grapefruit-sized cheese balls, covered with crushed pecans and made according to her own secret recipe. Following these successes, the happy author built a pink-domed palace on the Vineyard, a "Life Center" paid for and owned by the tax-free Sunbeam Foundation and enjoyed tax-free by Dr. Sunbeam himself. Millie Silk had once characterized him as "an adorable charlatan, utterly devoid of principle."

Sergeant Waters decided the question of whether or not Dr. Sunbeam had touched Millie's body during the ecstasy of prayer could wait until later. "Chief," he said, "would your men help us get all these names and addresses? And phone numbers. And off-Island phone numbers." He had an afterthought. "Also where everybody was sitting."

"That'll take forever, Kenny. We can't hold these people that long."

"Excuse me, Sergeant," I said. "There were place cards for everybody at all three tables. They should still be there."

He looked at me for a moment, marking me down as somebody who might be sensible. "Good," he said, "that'll save time. Jake," he told one of his uniformed troopers, "get a diagram of the seating. Leave the cards where they are. Now, chief —"

A voice interrupted. "I'm sorry, I have to leave." This was the HumDinger software king Chick Bird. Young, confident, he was standing next to his spectacular "assistant" Harriet Gunn, who had accompanied him on his cross-country jet flight, leaving his wife behind in Silicon Valley. He probably wasn't eager to have his name, address and phone number taken down along with his assistant's name, address and phone number. Perhaps he thought the overlap would be too much for his wife. An inexperienced young man's concern, in my opinion. Wives of extremely rich men tend to be tolerant of misbehavior.

Another voice. "I am leaving, right now."

A third voice. "I have to use the phone. Immediately." This last was Lulu Waring, desperate to update her earlier news bulletin.

Other guests joined in, but none of the voices was mine. I had no intention of leaving a ripe crime scene when the investigation was just beginning. However, it was way past ten, what we call "Vineyard midnight," and everybody here except me and the maids felt they were far too important to be detained any longer.

"Sergeant," Jill Klein said, "you know you have no right to hold us. You don't have a homicide without an autopsy. Or at an absolute minimum, the opinion of the medical examiner. You can't hold us without a charge. Who are you going to charge with what?"

Kenny Waters, unlike Chief Angus, recognized the speaker. His answer was polite but not obsequious. "I'm not going to charge anybody with anything, Miss Klein. All we want is basic information. Who everybody is and how to get in touch with them later." He paused. "If that turns out to be necessary."

The way he said that last part, Jill Klein and all the rest of us knew it was going to be necessary.

"So I hope you will want to help us."

Some did, some didn't. Even with the help of the Vineyard Haven police force, there were more people to interview than there were cops. So Sergeant Waters divided us into small groups and said that all those who had a special need to leave should give their information first. The cops got out notebooks and pens and pencils. I was in no hurry. I volunteered to go last and then did my best to snoop without looking too nosy.

It turned out that practically every guest had some urgent reason to be interviewed first — or not to be interviewed at all. Or not to give an unlisted phone number. People who have unlisted numbers hate to surrender them. Sergeant Waters had a lot of placating and smoothing to do. He explained in the nicest way that if it turned out that a crime had been committed, as seemed likely, he could get a grand jury subpoena for every phone number tomorrow morning. He would fax the sub-poena to the phone company, and the phone company would immediately fax back the unlisted numbers. "Since we can get your number anyway, why not make things a little easier for everybody?"

Jiggs Cooley, the homely, curly-headed sitcom star of *Jigg-time*, still wouldn't give out his precious unlisted number — not on the Vineyard, not in New York, not in California. Now that *Seinfeld* and *Cheers* were both gone, *Jiggtime* was the nation's number one comedy sitcom, so of course, as he explained to the cops, Jiggs Cooley had to protect himself from both fans and press. But to show his willingness to cooperate, he volunteered his agent's phone number, both office and home.

"There's always somebody," one of the state troopers complained under his breath.

Drifting around, I managed to overhear and memorize half a dozen unlisted numbers. This isn't as difficult as you might think. Island phone numbers start with 693 or 627 or 645, so I only had four digits per celebrity to worry about. I also have an extremely good memory, which infuriates my father for reasons that I am about to explain.

When the cops finally got to me, most of the guests had been released. I told them more than they may have wanted to hear.

* * *

I am a summer person, but one of long standing. Lifelong standing. I first came here when in my mother's womb, and I liked the Island so much that I came back the following year when I was three months old. I haven't missed a summer since. I've always stayed in the same place, my grandmother's house on a waterfront bluff between Vineyard Haven and West Chop, no more than a twenty-minute walk from Millie's. It's my parents' house now, but before she died my grandmother set up a trust for me and my younger sister, against my father's strenuous advice. He argued that giving young people too much money too soon took away all sense of ambition and civic obligation. My grandmother said, "Nonsense. Money is meant to be enjoyed." I was her favorite. She was the only member of my family who ever held that preference. I in turn adored her, and I agreed with her about money — but I am afraid I have justified my father's concern.

I must explain my position, as I have often explained it, uselessly, to my father. My grandmother had a collection of ancient 78 records, including several by a vaudeville comedy team calling themselves "Two Black Crows." Today they would be politically incorrect in the most monstrous way, but I thought they were both funny and wise. On one of the records the straight man asks the comedian why he doesn't get a job, why he doesn't go to work. The answer comes back, "Well, I would work, if I could see any pleasure in it." He is speaking for me. Thanks to my grandmother I have the option of working only if I see any pleasure in it. Mostly I don't.

Millie had introduced me to Marsden as "an occasional writer." Just so. The only subjects I really enjoyed in school and college were English lit. and writing, so those were the only ones I bothered with. My memory got me through my other courses with minimum passing grades. The gentleman's C eluded me. I usually settled for C-minus. My father, whose memory is inferior to mine, used to rail against my failure to "put more effort into it." It was an attitude I could understand but not endorse.

After college, my enjoyment of English lit. and writing carried over into the real world, as it's supposed to do, but only to a certain point. I'll be more specific. I'm not an expert on anything, so I write about odds and ends that interest me. I don't like doing research, so I avoid anything that would force me to go to the library. I often review books, usually for one of the Vineyard newspapers, where I don't get paid but where my free work is welcome. Over a dozen years I have had three op-ed pieces in the *New York Times* and four in the *Boston Globe*, all of them timely comments about targets of opportunity. The most provocative, judged by number of letters received, was my *Globe* piece about the Clintons' first visit to the Vineyard, "There Goes the Neighborhood." I wrote a piece for *Opera News* about Pietro Mascagni, not because I am an expert on music but because I wondered how it felt to write one masterpiece, *Cavalleria Rusticana*, at an early age and then spend the rest of a long life writing endless music without ever again ringing the bell. I have published short pieces in *Sports Illustrated* because I am a sports hound, although my own competitive experience has been limited to tennis and such fringe pastimes as softball and touch football. I have received rejection slips from various publications but don't collect them. Currently I am "at work," if that is the proper term, on two novels, one set in New York City and one set on the Vineyard. I have completed a hundred or so pages of each and may some day finish one or both. Or I may not. I am indeed, as Millie told Leonard Marsden, an occasional writer, but I am not a compulsive occasional writer.

Whenever I have to fill out a form and come to OCCUPA-TION, I don't put down "Writer." I put down "Living." Living is something I do with real pleasure and, I believe, with considerable skill, except in the instance of marrying Doris. That two-year lapse in judgment taught me that one can have a great deal of pleasure with women without marrying them.

While I am at it, I am six feet tall, thirty-four years old, with light brown hair, halfway between brown and blond, light blue eyes, and no scars or other distinguishing features. Unless you want to count what several women have described as "an interesting smile." I have no idea what that means, but it seems to be a compliment.

I no longer stay in my parents' house when I am on the Vineyard. I stay in their guest house — originally my grandmother's guest house. The view isn't as good but I have my own phone, my own kitchen, my own bar, two bedrooms and my own guests. This works out better for everybody, because I get on my father's nerves when we are under the same roof. My sister Diane, on the other hand, always stays with our parents in the main house, along with her industrious husband and their three children. Diane is industrious too, given to all sorts of good works requiring much time and energy. I applaud but do not emulate. My father and mother approve of Diane and her whole family, but their earnestness is too solemn for my taste. Even their children, my young nephew and two nieces, are already solemn. However, Diane serves a useful purpose. She is the buffer zone, the messenger, the translator, the peacemaker between me and my parents. Thanks to her, my father and I can get through several months at a time without direct communication.

I gave the police both my own phone number and my parents' number. I told them to feel free to call my parents. I knew it would cheer up my father to know I was a suspect in a celebrity murder case. Since he has always predicted that I will come to no good end, I try to encourage him.

Actually I was not a suspect in the murder of Mildred Silk, although at this stage the police naturally thought I was. I said nothing to dissuade them. Eventually they would learn that I was invited to the dinner far too late to plan such an act, and although I disliked Millie, I had no motive to get rid of her beyond the general welfare. This is not one of those mystery stories like Agatha Christie's *Murder of Roger Ackroyd*, where the narrator did it, or like Scott Turow's *Presumed Innocent*, where the narrator should have done it. Trust me, I didn't kill Millie. I am innocent of Millie's death, although not heartbroken.

By my count there were twenty suspects. Since Millie had treated her chef better than she treated anybody else, and had praised him just before she was killed, I eliminated him. If one of the maids had done it, I wouldn't bother to tell this story. And I ruled out suicide because, with a new book coming out that was guaranteed to upset all her closest friends, Millie would not have dreamed of missing the show. Besides, she had far too high an opinion of herself to deprive us of her presence. Her secretary Miss Quinn, who probably had ample reason to hate Millie, wasn't even there. So it was just us chickens — the guests. I intended to stay in the chicken coop as long as possible so that I could learn what was going on. Once the police discovered my innocence, they were sure to lose interest in me. But maybe I could find some other way to stay in the act.

By the time the police had finished interviewing me, the helicopter contingent of state police had arrived from the mainland. I had hoped to watch the Crime Scene Unit at work, taking photographs and dusting for prints and all that, but they wouldn't let me in the dining room. They wouldn't even let me peek through the door. I had also hoped to see the pathologist in action, doing whatever he had to do with Millie's body, but that was not allowed either. I did hang around long enough to see them take Millie's body away. They rolled her out of her house on a gurney with a covering blanket strapped over her. The blanket was mottled gray, the three wide straps were dirty white. Millie would have been offended by her last enrobement.

By that time two still photographers and two reporters from the newspapers and one TV cameraman were lined up along the driveway to witness Millie's exit. Since Lulu Waring was standing next to the TV man and cooing into a microphone, he had to be hers. I wondered where she had found him this late at night and how she had managed to get him to the scene in time to film it. Gumption, no doubt. Journalism is nine-tenths enterprise and one-tenth luck.

* * *

Next morning Millie's death and our dinner party were all over TV, radio and the newspapers. Cyanide poisoning had been confirmed by the pathologist shortly after midnight, and there were identifiable traces in Millie's Chartreuse glass. Suicide and murder were the stated possibilities, with no suggestion from anybody that it might have been an accident. Cyanide accidents are rare.

One of the police had leaked the guest list, so there I was, Jason Arnold, right up among the Island's very biggest celebrities. In fact, when the guests were listed alphabetically, lo, my name led all the rest, just like Abou Ben Adhem in Leigh Hunt's poem. The *Gazette* and the *Martha's Vineyard Times* and the *New York Times* and the *Boston Globe*, and local radio and TV, and network radio and TV all telephoned me for comment. Since I have "call-waiting," I was able to catch all the calls. I was generously cooperative. Now that I was in the big time, I stayed by the phone, not wanting to miss any opportunities to be quoted. Some publication would surely want me to write a piece when they got around to thinking about it.

The particular interest of the *Los Angeles Times* reporter was Chick Bird, the software king from nearby Silicon Valley. He dismissed my beautiful Elena Bronze — rather unkindly, I thought — as "kind of old hat," but young Bird was current news. The reporter knew everything about Bird in California

35

but nothing about Bird at the Vineyard, other than that he had bought "a big house."

"It's much more than just a big house," I corrected him. I explained that it was the old Waverly Farm with a magnificent view over Edgartown Great Pond. During the last two centuries, family descendants kept adding to the original farmhouse section by section in a totally haphazard way. It has so many different rooflines of different heights that it's laughingly known as the House of Eight Gables, going Hawthorne one better. I had to explain that jest to the reporter, who had not heard of either Hawthorne or *The House of the Seven Gables*. Bird was visiting here with his architect, going over plans to modernize it. I said, "We're all very nervous about what he's going to do."

The reporter was thrilled to learn that Chick Bird had been sitting on Millie's immediate left at dinner, a table with only six people. "You think Lord Byron did it?" he asked, just to see what I might say. If I had said yes, he couldn't have printed it anyway because of libel, so I said, "Well, he had one of the two best seats for opportunity." "Great!" he said. I also described Chick's hand-embroidered suede shirt, and I could hear the keyboard clicking away. I threw in the fact that Chick's so-called assistant, Harriet Gunn, was a knockout — in fact, a HumDinger like Chick's software. The reporter was extremely grateful for everything, and I told him, as I had told all the others, to call back if he had any further questions. I was having a real good day.

The phone rang again fifteen seconds after I hung up. Who would it be this time?

Washington Post? Des Moines Register and Tribune?

"Hello."

"Is this Jason Arnold?"

"Yes it is."

"The suspect in the Mildred Silk murder?"

None of my previous callers had put it that way. Any reporter hoping for a good quote from me would hardly say that. But I was pleased, since a suspect is just what I was, at least for the nonce. "Yes indeed," I said cheerfully. "How can I help you?"

"Would you be willing to take a lie detector test about your actions last night?"

It took a few seconds to sink in. Then I realized. "Dirk!"

"How you doing, Jason?"

"Just fine. It's fun to be a suspect again after all these years."

"I thought that's how you'd feel. You know, Jason, most people really don't like being suspects. And most people don't get to be murder suspects even once, much less twice."

"Born under a lucky star."

"Where'd you get the cyanide?"

"That's a good question. If the cops ever ask me, what should I say?"

"Actually it's not a very good question."

"If it was arsenic, I'd tell them my father has a gardening shed. That's where they get all their arsenic in British murder mysteries. Why isn't it a good question about where I got the cyanide?"

"Because the answer is most anywhere," Dirk Schultz said. "It's used in all sorts of things — metal work, pigments, gold mining. You can find it in every hospital lab or medical school lab, or even a good university chemical lab."

"You know, cyanide is what they snuck in to Hermann Goering so he could commit suicide just a couple of hours before he was supposed to be hanged."

"It's also what they gave spies in World War II so they could kill themselves before being tortured and telling all their secrets. You remember, the cyanide capsule hidden under a false tooth cap?"

"Right. Everybody had one. I wonder what they did with all those capsules after the war. Maybe I bought my cyanide at an Army-Navy surplus store."

"Sure. Or from the CIA catalogue. Anyway it's not impossible to get. Who do you think did it? Got any suspicions?"

"Lots. I suppose you read that Millie had a new book coming out about Island celebrities. Just before she was killed, she told her guests that they were all in her book and they were going to hate what she said about them."

"Sounds like fun. All my years, I never had a homicide with a lot of famous people in it."

"It is fun. You'd love it."

"Actually, Jason, that's why I called you. Why don't you invite me up for a visit?"

"What for?"

"I don't know. I keep reading the Vineyard's such a great summer place. I'd kind of like to see it. Maybe I could clear your name. I could be your private detective."

"I don't need one. I'm innocent."

"That's what they all say."

"I can't afford you." We were both just playing around, or at least I was, but then it struck me that if Dirk was here, he could talk to all the other cops and detectives, and I'd learn a lot of things they would never tell me. "What do you charge?"

"Not much. How about a bedroom in your house? And breakfast, of course. And an occasional drink, of course."

"Are you serious? It really would be fun. And besides, we could probably solve it together. My brains, your legwork. I'd be Nero Wolfe, you could be my Archie Goodwin."

"That's funny. I was thinking of you as Archie. Listen, Jason. Serious for a minute, okay? I've never been to the Vineyard. And I got to admit I miss not being on a case any more. This sounds like a good one. How about it? I'd bring my own car so you wouldn't have to drive me around."

"Hang on a minute," I said. "I'll get the ferry schedule. You'll need a car reservation. But don't try to come tomorrow, there's too much weekend traffic."

* * *

By late that afternoon the State Police Barracks in Oak Bluffs was crammed with imported detectives, including a bigshot from Boston named Captain Andrew Mulvey.

They showed him on TV, a squat, redheaded Irish dynamo who was taking charge of the Mildred Silk investigation. He took charge at once. No more than two hours after he landed on the Vineyard, I got a phone call from Sergeant Kenny Waters.

"Captain Mulvey would like to see you back at Miss Silk's house at five o'clock. Can you make it?"

"What about?"

"I can't say, sir. Do you need a ride?"

"No, I'll be there." Although I didn't want to miss any late calls from the press, I couldn't resist the chance to meet Captain Mulvey and maybe even be interrogated by him. But why was I being singled out? Perhaps they were wondering why Millie had invited me?

Her house and lawn were now bordered by yellow police crime tape, as well as by members of the press and some tourist rubberneckers. There was even one of the Island's pink-white-and-blue tour buses, with summer visitors peering through the windows. In case the yellow tape was not deterrent enough, a uniformed cop stood at the entrance walk. I had to give my name and show my driver's license with its photographic ID before they let me through.

I was five minutes early when I walked in the front door and

39

found Sergeant Waters waiting for me. He was in the same red shirt and blue jeans as last night, but he looked a lot more tired. Maybe he never got to bed, but he had found time to shave.

"Hello, Mr. Arnold," he said. "The others will be right along."

"What others?"

"Some of the others from last night. Captain Mulvey will explain when everybody gets here. If you'll wait in Miss Silk's office."

Three others arrived soon after me. Millie's publisher Leonard Marsden and the novelist Everett Munk, both in casual sports shirts, and, to my delight, Elena Bronze. Today she was wearing a slightly more revealing loose white cotton sweater and pink slacks. Her short, gray-blond hair was so casually perfect that it must have been done today. She gave me a smile, which I suppose she gave everybody, but it was a nice human smile, not a movie star dazzle.

We had just finished establishing that none of us knew why we were here, or that any of the others had been invited, when Sergeant Waters reappeared.

"Captain Mulvey would like to talk to you on the deck. If you'd please come with me."

We followed him down the hallway and through the sliding glass doors to the scene of last night's cocktail hour. A sunny, pleasant late afternoon, just like yesterday. Everything on the deck was where it had been — Millie's swing, the benches and even the fully equipped bar, this time with a uniformed state policeman standing guard behind it. The main difference was that the casual deck chairs had been arranged in a neat circle with a white wicker table in the center. A large black tape recorder sat in the middle of the table. Sergeant Waters invited us to be seated and, to my surprise, took drink orders. Were they hoping to loosen us up for whatever was about to happen? Or was this just the way people got treated in a celebrity murder case? We all accepted. Vodka on the rocks for Marsden and me, bourbon "with a very small splash" for Munk, Dewars on the rocks for Elena Bronze. A quartet of serious drinkers.

Immediately after the last drink had been passed by the policeman-bartender, Captain Mulvey barged through the doorway. Short, chunky, very athletic, very strong, wide shoulders. He looked like a pro football lineman, about a foot short. His hair was even redder than it had appeared on television, and his eyes were a cold, cold icy blue.

His voice, however, was warm, vigorous, Irish-accented, as he introduced himself and shook hands all around. He did not order a drink, but he looked like a man who would order one the minute he was off duty. When we were all seated, including Sergeant Waters, he said, "I asked you here because I want your help. Sergeant, turn on the tape."

Kenny Waters reached forward and pressed the record switch. The little red light went on. Mulvey could just as easily have pressed that switch himself, but if you are a captain, you tell the sergeant to do it.

"I asked you here because Sergeant Waters told me that during last night's proceedings, each of you seemed to have a good memory. Also, unlike some of the others, each of you was willing to cooperate. Now I intend to find out if he was right." This statement was followed by a wide Irish smile that never came close to reaching the icy blue eyes.

I wondered why Jill Klein, who had more experience in crime than the rest of us put together, was not here. Maybe she refused to come, although that seemed unlikely. Maybe Mulvey did not want to deal with such a dominant, antagonistic witness.

"First off," he said, "I'd like to know if anybody saw or heard anything that made you think Miss Silk might commit suicide.

Anything at all. Mr. Marsden, you were sitting next to her and you knew her best, so we'll start with you."

Marsden shook his head. "I would say no. No indication whatsoever. As far as I knew, she was in good health, given her age. I suppose she could have had cancer or something like that, but I think she would have told me. Maybe she wouldn't. I've been thinking about it all day. One could make the case that with this book, her professional career was at an end. Her work was finished. She certainly had no plans for another book, and that might have depressed her. Writers are strange people, as I'm sure Mr. Munk would agree. But I have no evidence of any such depression. It's merely a possibility. But I guess that means suicide is also a possibility."

I stepped right in. "Captain," I said, "it's a complete impossibility. Last night she was excited about her book. I wasn't at her table, but every word she said to the group showed she was looking forward to publication. She was in high spirits the whole evening." I thought about what I might have said, if it hadn't been for the rule, *de mortuis nil nisi bonum*. Then I went ahead and said it anyway. "Millie Silk was a malicious woman — just naturally malicious. And last night she was thoroughly enjoying the chance to be malicious in public. She was very much herself."

"Anybody else agree with that?" Mulvey asked, looking around the circle.

"I agree completely," Elena Bronze said. "I wasn't at her table either, but I had a talk with her here on the deck before dinner. We didn't know each other very well — maybe once or twice at each other's house and maybe a few cocktail parties at other people's houses. But last night she was deliberately unpleasant to me. And she liked being unpleasant. A real sparkle in her eyes and a nasty kind of smile."

"What did she say to you?"

Quite a long pause before Elena answered, "I'd rather not say."

Mulvey jumped on her, voice crackling. "Miss Bronze. We're in a murder investigation. We need to know everything we can learn about what happened last night. What did she say?"

"Captain," Everett Munk said, "if it's a murder investigation, why are you asking us about suicide?"

"It's still a possibility," Mulvey said shortly. "Miss Bronze?"

Munk's interruption had given her a moment to think. "It was a personal remark. A nasty remark about my body and my age and my professional career. It had nothing to do with what happened. I only mentioned it as further evidence that Mr. Arnold is right. As he says, she was in high spirits, and she was malicious all evening long. She was not about to kill herself."

Everett Munk held up his hand. For a novelist he was burly and rather threatening, much closer to the Hemingway mold than the Saul Bellow mold. Around sixty now, some gray in his black hair, he still exuded athletic strength. "I knew Millie a lot better than these two," he said, waving a large bony hand at Elena and me. "Marsden maybe knew her better professionally, but I think I knew her better personally. We spent a lot of time together here on the Vineyard. A lot of time. Forget about suicide, that's not Millie. Even if she'd had a fatal cancer, or a terrible depression, we'd have heard all about it, straight from her and with full details. Suicide is impossible. So let's move on to who killed her."

I had never heard that Millie claimed Everett Munk as one of her lovers, but he had just made it sound quite likely. He may well have been jealous of her financial success as a writer, but he was sticking up for her as a person.

"All right," Mulvey said. "Who killed her then? Any ideas?"

This created a long silence. The tape recorder picked up a thirty-second stretch of nobody saying anything.

"I'll put it another way then. You spent the whole evening here. Who said anything against her? Did anybody sound worried about her book?"

This silence was shorter. It lasted only until I said, "Everybody at the dinner had to be worried. Millie as much as said she was going to cut them all to ribbons. If they hadn't known before dinner, both Mr. Marsden and Millie told them so."

"Everybody agree about that?"

Both Marsden and Munk nodded, and Elena said, "Of course. I'm sure that's why she invited us."

"All right," Mulvey said. "You were all here on the deck for cocktails, and we have somebody here from each of the three tables. Who heard anything strange from any of the other guests?"

"How do you mean 'strange'?" Marsden asked.

Mulvey gave a small exasperated twist of his head. "Strange. Like threatening. Like alarmed. Like frightened. Or even just interesting. Mr. Arnold, you seem to enjoy speaking your mind. What did you hear?"

"Sorry," I said, and I was truly sorry. "I got here very late for cocktails and only had time to say hello to Millie, who was sitting on the swing, and to meet Mr. Marsden, who was sitting with her. Then we went in to dinner. Nothing was said at my table that's worth reporting. When Marsden and Millie were giving their toasts, I did see that a lot of people looked nervous, but nothing was said." I didn't mention that at my table the two most nervous-looking people were Senator Washburn and Elena Bronze.

"That sitcom fellow," Munk said. "'*Jiggtime*' or whatever it's called. He was two seats away from me, and I could see those toasts shocked him. He kept pulling at his chin — like this — and whispering 'Jesus! Jesus!' And Sunny — that's Dr. Sunbeam, a much nicer man than he is a writer — Sunny leaned over and said, 'Hush! Hush!'"

I thought the most surprising thing about this statement was that Munk could overcome his scruples about Dr. Sunbeam's treacly prose to say that he was a nice man. But if Jiggs Cooley had actually been surprised by what Marsden and Millie said, it was unlikely that he just happened to be carrying a cyanide capsule in his pocket.

Mulvey extracted a few minor reports from both Leonard Marsden and Elena Bronze, but they did not seem to impress him any more than they impressed me. Finally he thanked us for coming and promised to be in touch. "Anybody have anything to add?"

Since I had been left out of this whole last part, I felt I should say something, so I did. "Captain, I've been thinking about this a lot. Absolutely anybody could have put that poison in Millie's drink. She poured her Chartreuse first, sort of leading the way, and then she put her glass down on the buffet while she told everybody else what to drink, what to try if you haven't tasted it before, pointing out different bottles. It took quite a lot of time, just as she meant it to. I've thought about that scene, and I know I could have poisoned her myself." I smiled blandly at my colleagues. "How about the rest of you?"

Again Elena was first to respond. "Yes, but I didn't."

"Yes, I could have," Marsden said.

"I suppose so," Munk said, more thoughtfully than the other two. "Millie always made a production out of her after-dinner drinks, and last night was standard. So I wasn't paying attention until suddenly —" He broke off. "And then she was dead."

I got the feeling from the blank looks on the faces of both

45

Captain Mulvey and Sergeant Rogers that they had already reached my conclusion. Anybody could have slipped her the poison.

Mulvey thanked us again and got to his feet. We all stood up to leave. "You still going to publish her book?" Mulvey asked Marsden.

For the first time this afternoon the editor looked surprised, even astonished. "Why of course!"

"Doesn't it matter that she's dead?"

"Of course it matters." Marsden gave a short bitter laugh. "Damn right it matters. She can't give interviews, she can't be on the *Today* show, she can't sign books, and she can't go on a book tour. Yes, it matters. But Captain, you obviously don't understand book publishing. Her death, especially if it really is murder, will sell thousands and thousands of books. Am I going to publish it? Absolutely. It's our most important book in years."

"How soon?"

"Millie and I had some more editing to do — minor things, clarifications, really not much more than copy-editing. She was a very clean writer. I'll have to do that without her now."

"Did she leave a will? Who's her literary executor?"

"You'd have to ask her lawyer about her will. I'm sure she left one."

"Yes, she did," Munk said.

"But I'm her literary executor — have been for years."

"I'd like to see the book," Mulvey said.

"Of course."

As we all walked back through the house, I stayed close to Elena Bronze. I'd been looking at her as often as I could without staring. Maybe if I stayed close, she would smile at me again. When we were near the front door, I heard myself ask her, "Can I give you a ride home?"

She must have heard that offer four thousand times, starting at age sixteen, but her answer was quietly polite. "Thanks," she said, and she did smile, "but I came in my own car."

That smile was too much. "Oh," I said. And then, rather foolishly for a grown man, "Oh, well then, how would you feel about giving me a ride?"

"What?" she said, coming to a full stop and turning to look straight at me from a distance of no more than eighteen inches. I guess she had not heard that so often.

The others had gone ahead. I don't blush, but I wondered if I was blushing.

"I'm sorry," I said. "I've admired you for years, and I was trying to spend a little more time with you."

She looked me over and thought me over. At least she hadn't made up her mind to dispose of me. "Where are you going?"

"Actually I live about two minutes down the road. But if you'll drive me to Edgartown with you, I can hitch back home." Or I could take a taxi, but hitching sounded more winning. Maybe it was.

Suddenly she laughed. It was a wiser and older laugh than I could have expected, a real lived-in kind of laugh. I suppose I should not have been surprised. She had been married twice and supposedly had had serious affairs from time to time, although with movie stars you never know how much is truth and how much is publicity. "Come on then, Jason, I'll give you a ride."

Her black BMW convertible with the tan top down was in Millie's graveled parking area. I held the door open for her, not believing this was happening, then got in the passenger seat.

She backed out, then drove around the West Chop loop and down Franklin Avenue toward Vineyard Haven on the way to Edgartown. Here I am driving down Vineyard Haven's main back street in an open convertible with a major movie star.

I wished I could have a videotape to show my father.

"I thought Hollywood people didn't drive their own cars."

"I'm not Hollywood people." She kept her eyes on the road. "Why were you at that dinner party? She said you weren't going to be in her book."

"I was a last-minute substitute. Bob Hergesheimer got called away on an assignment, and Millie asked me to fill in. Actually it was her secretary who asked."

"You didn't like Millie much, did you?"

"I didn't like her a lot. Really an awful woman. What did she say to you last night?"

A quick glance at me, then eyes back to the road. "If I wouldn't tell Captain Mulvey, do you expect me to tell you?"

"No, I suppose not."

A few seconds of silence. Then her jaw set. Maybe it was because I was not a cop. Maybe it was because she just wanted to tell somebody. "She asked me how many breast lifts I'd had. And how much longer I could get away with nude scenes in good lighting. Then she said, 'Isn't it about time you became a character actress?'"

"That's dear old Millie."

"I've always been a character actress." She was angry. "For thirty years. That really hurt — as though I hadn't been acting all this time."

She had won two Oscars, one for Best and one for Best Supporting. "I know," I said.

"No, Jason, you don't. I've been a good actress all along, and then somebody like Mildred Silk implies that it's nothing but showing off my breasts. And then she gets murdered and I'm all tangled up in this mess."

"I kind of enjoy it," I admitted. "I spent most of today talking to reporters."

"You wouldn't enjoy it if you had to do it all the time. I spent my day telling my publicist over and over that I wouldn't talk to anybody."

She took State Road to West Tisbury. It was getting close to sunset, already a pretty evening and going to be a clear, pretty night. When she turned onto the Edgartown Road, she asked, "Do you want to go all the way to Edgartown?"

That would be well out of her way since her house was far down on Edgartown Great Pond.

"Thanks. I'll just get off where you turn in." I swung around in my seat to face her. "Listen, I really appreciate this, Elena. It's a great pleasure just to sit next to you. A great pleasure."

She nodded, accepting my thanks. Then she looked at me for a moment, a look like a searchlight. After we had passed the airport, she said, "Would you like to see my terrible house?"

Even those of us who hadn't yet seen it knew by the grapevine that it was a totally inappropriate house for the Island, one more celebrity monument of glass and teak and steel.

"Sure I'd like to see it. Why is it so terrible?" As if I didn't know.

"I didn't pay enough attention to it. In fact I didn't pay any attention. I just bought the land and hired a good expensive architect. I was making a picture in the Australian Outback, so I left it to him. He just had no sense of the Vineyard. I guess I didn't either. Maybe it would be a good house in Palm Springs or Scottsdale, but not here."

I could not imagine building an expensive house without paying attention to what I was building. That's the difference between having money and having wealth. "I'd still like to see it," I said. That much more time to spend with her.

The long, long dirt road down to the pond was one of those private rural highways created and maintained by wealthy owners whose homes were tucked out of sight behind the trees. The normal private dirt road on the Vineyard is bumpy and narrow, with potholes that become mudholes after a rain. Usually there is no room to pass unless one car pulls off into the bushes. Elena's road was two and a half lanes wide with nary a bump or pothole. I knew this road served a dozen houses, each facing the water. I also knew that Elena's property was four-plus acres on a spit of land surrounded by pond water on three sides, and that it looked over the barrier beach to the ocean beyond. We all know the exact selling price of every piece of property in all six towns because it becomes public record. Hers cost $3.3 million — without the house. It would be much more today.

Even though I had heard horror stories about her house, I was shocked to drive up and confront it. Acres of glass separated by vertical bands of brushed steel.

"It's better inside," Elena said drily.

She left her car in the circular driveway, put the top up against the dew, and we walked in together through the imposing front door, a solid slab of dark teak with brass fittings. We were barely inside when a stocky bald-headed man appeared. He wore a white long-sleeved shirt and a black bow tie. The shirt might be a concession to Vineyard summer, but the bow tie said this butler was an import from California. Elena had a lot to learn about the Island look, in butlers as well as houses.

"Good evening, Miss Bronze," he said.

"Hello, Paul. This is Mr. Arnold, and he would like a vodka on the rocks, with no fruit. The usual for me, please. We'll be on the terrace."

No, no, Elena. Deck, not terrace.

The house was indeed better inside, although the antique New England furniture did not go with the glass walls. Nothing would have, except maybe Scandinavian blond wood. Over the mantelpiece was a dark landscape, a bleak winter field with stone walls. Obviously by Caleb Stone, the up-Island artist who could not be bothered with Millie Silk. That, at least, was the authentic Vineyard look.

Elena led the way through a sliding glass door to the "terrace," which certainly looked like a deck to me. A fancy deck, to be sure, with lampposts and a fence with a wavy-top rail that came to a stark point in the center, like the prow of a ship. The prow aimed at, and matched the shape of, the point of land that jutted into the pond. Some view. You can be on the Vineyard a lifetime and feel you know it intimately, and yet every year I visit new places that are different from anything I've seen before.

When the butler Paul brought my vodka and her Scotch, she said, "Thanks, Paul. I won't be needing you and Gloria."

A short bow of his bald head. "Can Gloria fix you anything, Miss Bronze?"

"No thank you. We can help ourselves."

We? Ourselves? Was I going to be invited to stay? I felt a small lurch in my stomach. I had the feeling that something splendid was going to happen.

"Here," she said, "let's watch the rest of the sunset." She swung two black wrought-iron chairs around to face the west. The sunset was pretty far gone, but streaks of pink and orange still floated in the pale sky. "This is my favorite time of day on the Vineyard."

"Mine too," I said. We sat down and sipped our drinks. "Do you live here alone?"

"In theory, but not really. I have six houseguests arriving tomorrow, and I'm giving two parties for them. A lot more guests and business associates scheduled. I hope the police leave me alone."

"I doubt it."

51

"So do I."

We had our drinks and watched the pink and orange fade from the sky. It was still light enough to see. She was surprisingly easy to talk with and laugh with, a wonderful warmth about her that was not acting. As I was nearing the end of my drink, it occurred to me that I would never again, never in all my life, enjoy a moment like this, alone with a famous and beautiful movie star who seemed to like me. Houseguests were arriving, there might be houseguests all summer. I might never see her again, except in the movies. This opportunity would not rise again. If I don't ask, it will never happen.

"Elena," I said. I cleared my throat. "Elena, I have a very special favor to ask."

"What's that?"

"Well, it's really quite special."

"So?" She cocked one eyebrow in what struck me as a friendly and even provocative way. *Go ahead and say it*, the look said, *whatever's on your mind*.

Come on, I told myself, *say it. The worst she can do is throw you out. It's not a crime to ask. Just say it.* "Would you please let me see the bronzinis?"

I guess the last thing I expected was a wicked laugh, but that's what I got. Her eyes danced with amusement. "Why?" she said. "Haven't you already seen them? Everybody else has."

Now I could laugh with her. I even knew she was going to do it. "Not in real life," I said. "Only in the movies."

She shook her head at me, still smiling. "Well, Jason, if it would mean that much to you."

She crossed her arms, grabbed the bottom of her loose white sweater and pulled it up over her head. Underneath was a strapless white bra so lacy and filmy that it could only have been designed for decoration, not support. Looking me straight in the eye, her lips slightly parted, she unclasped it and let it drop. She was still smiling at me, a nice wicked smile.

There they were.

Once upon a time in the Forties, there were probably a thousand American women who had legs as perfect as Betty Grable's. But nobody got to see them except friends and family, so they went unappreciated. *Full many a flower is born to blush unseen and waste its sweetness on the desert air.* Today there may be a thousand American women with breasts as perfect as Elena Bronze's, but I have not seen them. And I'll bet Betty Grable's legs didn't look this good when she was over fifty.

I kept on staring. At last I asked, "Could I touch one?"

"Jason," she said, "as an old friend you can touch two."

One thing led to another, but we did not require much leading.

As I would have guessed by then, ever since the moment of her wicked laugh, she was a warm, lively lover. After we had made love and while we were still undressed, we had clam chowder and English muffins in her kitchen. We sat naked across from each other at her kitchen counter, unembarrassed. Then we spent the night in her old-fashioned canopied bed — some talking, some sleeping, some lovemaking. She told me she had decided to go to bed with me from the way I said, driving here in her car, what a great pleasure it was to sit next to her. From my husky voice she knew we could have a lot more pleasure than that — as indeed we did.

Early the next day she drove me back to Vineyard Haven. She let me off at the foot of my driveway. She gave me an affectionate morning kiss and a wonderful goodbye smile.

I hoped very much that she had not killed Millie.

Writers for Sale

Six messages were waiting on my answering machine. Dirk Schultz was arriving on the four-thirty ferry, driving a black Toyota, and I'd better be on the dock to meet him. Three were from my editor friend Bert Stevens at the *Boston Globe*, saying I must call him as soon as I heard this, office or home, giving both numbers. It had to be an invitation to write about Millie's murder, but I was not sure the *Globe* was my best bet. Maybe if I waited, the *New Yorker* or *Vanity Fair* would call. They would ask Everett Munk first, of course, but he would refuse. The *Vineyard Gazette* had a question, but I knew it could wait since the paper wasn't closing until tomorrow. My sister Diane had called to say my parents were concerned about my "escapade," please call.

I called Bert at home and woke him up.

When he had adjusted, he asked, "Where were you all night?"

"Busy. What's up? As if I couldn't guess."

"Actually it's not what you think. Or not quite what you think. Do you realize there were three writers present at the Mildred Silk murder?"

"Sure. Everett Munk, Millie and Dr. Sunbeam."

"I wasn't including Millie, since she's no longer available for assignment. I was including you."

"Oh, well thanks."

"Right. We want all three of you to write a short piece about Mildred Silk. A nice piece, what she was like, why she was important. Just a tribute, from the scene of the crime, so to speak, but nothing grisly. We'll run them all on the same page."

The prospect of being included on the same page with as serious a writer as Everett Munk and as successful a writer as Dr. Sunbeam made the *Globe* much more attractive. "I guess if it's short, I can say something nice. Count me in. When do you want it?"

"Today, but there's a catch."

"You're not going to pay."

"Of course we'll pay. But we want all three of you."

"Fine with me."

There was a pause at Bert's end. I was sure he was lighting his first cigarette of the day. "The thing is, Jason, you're right there on the Vineyard, and you were all there together that night, and you know Munk and Sunbeam, and I don't. So do you think you can get them to do it?"

"Why me? You're the editor."

"I tried Munk, but he wouldn't even talk to me."

"He doesn't like to talk on the phone."

"So I gather. But he's the one we really want. You and Sunbeam are just part of the stunt."

"Thanks."

"Listen, it's your chance to be one of the big boys. Why not give it a try?"

* * *

The woman who answered the phone at the Sunbeam Life Center said, "Dr. Sunbeam is meditating. Could you call back in half an hour?"

Elena had delivered me home very early. Dr. Sunbeam was probably still asleep. I made coffee and shaved and drank coffee. I decided I wasn't tired after last night, just happy. I tried Sunbeam again. "This is Jason Arnold. Is Dr. Sunbeam through meditating?"

Apparently he was, because almost immediately a cheerful voice asked, "Is that you, Jason? Good morning!"

"Good morning, sir."

"Not sir, call me Sunny. How are you on this lovely day?"

I could imagine his fluffy white hair and cherub face beaming in the sunshine.

I explained the *Globe* proposition. "It won't be much money. And I should point out that we might be able to do better somewhere else."

A chuckle from Dr. Sunbeam. "Oh my dear boy, of course we can. You must think of the *Globe* as a teaser, a loss leader. They want short pieces for tomorrow? I'll dictate one as soon as we hang up. Once we appear in the *Globe*, the others will come right after us. Trust me, I know something about marketing."

"You mean you'll do it?"

"'Never miss a chance to be noted or quoted,' that's one of my Guidelines to Life. Besides, I'm thinking of writing a book about death. It's one of our biggest social problems, don't you think?" He laughed happily.

*   *   *

"Hell-o-o," came Nancy Munk's would-be sexy voice. Everettt never answered the phone himself for fear that some stranger would engage him in conversation about one of his novels. To be fair, Nancy did have a sexy voice, but I had just spent the night with Elena Bronze and had a new standard for sexy voices.

"Hello, Nancy. It's Jason Arnold."

"Who?"

Early in the morning for Nancy. She would be sharper by noontime, though not much.

"Jason Arnold. You remember, we sat next to each other at Millie's when you and Senator Washburn were schmoozing."

"Ooh. Don't say that to Everett."

"I wouldn't dream of it. Could I speak to him?"

"He's supposed to be writing."

"Tell him it's about Millie. It's important." More important to me than to Everett.

"Have they found out who did it?"

"Yes, they think it was you."

A pause. Then, "You're kidding."

"Yes, I'm kidding. Will you ask Everett?"

I waited so long that I thought Nancy might have gone off to look for him and then forgotten what she was supposed to ask him. But at last she came back and said, "He says if it's important, and it's about Millie, you better come over."

For an esteemed author, Everett Munk lived modestly. He had a ramshackle old shingled house on Lagoon Pond, between Vineyard Haven and Oak Bluffs. He didn't have to live there, and Nancy didn't want to live there, but it had been his family's house. Nancy, a fairly recent wife, was allowed to hire a cleaning woman and a cook and a combination gardener-handyman, but Everett insisted that none of these could live in his private home. I had a feeling that Nancy's pleasure in being married to a distinguished writer would not last long.

Through random social encounters over many years, I knew Everett better than I did the other guests at Millie's dinner. He was not a friend, but he was more than an acquaintance, and I admired his books more than I had ever told him. He was a true Yankee, steeped in the area and its people and their carefully concealed passions, which he uncovered with great skill in his novels. He would have been more popular if he had been less austere.

I knocked on the frame of the screen door, waited, knocked again.

Everett came to the door himself and opened it. "Come on in."

"I apologize for interrupting your writing."

"It wasn't going anywhere this morning. Or yesterday either."

I'm six feet tall, but Everett towered over me, several inches taller, much heavier, altogether more imposing. Big and shaggy, with a rumpled yellow shirt open at the collar and baggy khaki slacks, he reminded me of Thomas Wolfe — the original one, not the white-suit waif.

"Want some coffee?" He was holding a navy blue mug in his big hand.

I felt too guilty to accept his hospitality, so I said no thanks.

"Made it myself, fresh ground beans this morning. You sure?"

"Then I'll change my mind." Writers as a class are tremendously proud of their small mechanical skills, perhaps because they have so few.

I followed him to the kitchen, a severe Yankee kitchen with no frills, and he poured me a matching navy blue mug from a twenty-cup pot. I then followed him out to a flagstone patio with an iron table and four no-nonsense iron chairs that proved less uncomfortable than they looked.

"Anything new on the investigation?" he asked as soon as we were seated.

"You mean since last evening?" I didn't know what he might be expecting.

He took a big swig of coffee. "I don't listen to the news until evening. You hear anything?"

I shook my head.

"What did you make of that session with Captain Mulvey?" This was the chattiest I had ever known Everett to be. I couldn't bring up the *Globe* until he was finished. "Mostly that they don't know much. They were desperate enough to ask us for leads."

He nodded. Another swig. "I don't like that Marsden."

"Why not? I thought he seemed all right — for an editor."

"Ha!" Everett said. "Exactly. 'For an editor.' He acted like he owned Millie."

I thought this was an exaggeration but did not say so. Everett sounded jealous, and I wondered again how much there had been between him and Millie. "Well, he's been her editor for eight books."

"Millie never needed much editing. All she needed was a publisher."

"He was that too."

"How do you like my coffee?"

"Delicious."

He almost smiled. "Nancy said you had something important to discuss."

When I described the *Globe* proposal, it sounded silly. Everett Munk? On the same page with Dr. Sunbeam and Jason Arnold? But he heard me out.

Then he said, "Sounds kind of shabby."

"Yes, I guess it does, a little. It has only one redeeming social value. It would be good for my reputation."

His shaggy eyebrows went up. "Why? You've written for the *Globe* before, haven't you? You wrote that funny piece about the Clintons coming to the Vineyard."

I was flattered he remembered, because that was way back during the first presidential invasion. "Yes, I've been in the

59

Globe. But not on the same page with you. That's the important difference."

Two swigs of coffee this time while he thought that over. Finally he said, "Every writer has to make his own way."

I attempted to laugh that off. "That's what I was trying to do."

He stood up "Want some more coffee? I do."

"Sure. Thank you. Very good coffee."

When he came back with our two full mugs, he said, "Reason I haven't been able to write, I keep thinking about Millie. You didn't like her, did you?"

"I'm afraid not. But she was a wonderful writer."

"Maybe if I write about her," Everett said, "I'll get her out of my system so I can go back to my book. When do they want it?"

"Today, I'm afraid."

"Good. Get it over with."

* * *

With all the coffee inside me, both my own and Everett's, I was jazzed up to write.

I finished off my Millie piece in an hour. Even if she was dead, I couldn't bring myself to say nice things about her that weren't true, but I did say what a wonderful storyteller she was, both in fiction and nonfiction (without mentioning that it was hard to tell the difference). I said that on the very last night of her life she was excited and eloquent and confident about her forthcoming book (without mentioning that she had terrorized her guests). I faxed it to Bert, who couldn't believe that I had not only captured both Everett Munk and Dr. Sunbeam but was delivering my copy ahead of time. He said he liked my piece, and he was thrilled about Munk and Sunbeam. I saw no reason to explain that it had been their own inclination, not my persuasion.

* * *

The celebrities at Millie's dinner come to the Vineyard by plane, but almost everybody else comes on the ferry. What's the point of an island if you don't have to cross a body of water to get to it? Our body of water is not extensive. The ferry can make it across Vineyard Sound from Woods Hole to Vineyard Haven in forty-five minutes, a little shorter than a flight from New York, a little longer than a flight from Boston. To me it has always been important to get on a boat to reach the Vineyard. Most of us feel that way. Every once in a while there is talk about building a causeway, but the idea is always squelched. A causeway would make the Vineyard as accessible as Hyannis, with the same horrible results. Development on the Vineyard is bad enough as it is, without adding wall-to-wall shopping malls.

I drove down to Vineyard Haven and parked in the A & P lot, then walked to the ferry dock. Our ferries are dependably on time. The *Martha's Vineyard* lumbered into the ferry slip, and her exit doors swung wide. One by one the cars began to drive off. A harsh fact we have learned to accept is that no matter in what order you drive on to the ferry, your car will be among the last to be allowed off. My wife Doris used to rail against the whimsical exit procedures employed by the ferry staff. "We'll be the last row to get off," she always predicted, and she blamed me because it was my Island, not hers. It was one of four or five dozen problems with our marriage.

I stood just to the side of the exiting cars, close enough to spot Dirk through the windshield. Several black Toyotas came by without him, but there he was at last.

I jumped forward waving. He saw me and stopped. Within fifteen seconds I had opened the door, hopped in and closed the door, but by that time the two drivers behind Dirk were already banging angrily on their horns.

"This ferry business is a zoo," Dirk said, as we drove ahead and the horns stopped. "I drive all the way from New York and get on the ferry, ready to relax, and they won't they let me buy a drink until after the boat leaves the dock. What's that about?"

"I don't know, but it's the rule. Welcome to the Vineyard."

"I'm reserving judgment."

I directed him to the A & P lot where I picked up my car, and we set off in tandem for my house, me first, Dirk following. We had gone exactly half a block when I lost him at Five Corners. This is an infamous intersection of five roads without a stoplight. It's not too bad in the off season, but in summer you have to be alert to seize any scant opportunity that is offered, especially when there is heavy traffic from an arriving ferry. We only had to make the right turn, a relatively simple maneuver, but Dirk failed to follow my lead quickly enough and got blocked. If I went ahead, he would never find me, and I could not go back to him. Hoping no cops were watching ("Murder Suspect Disrupts Traffic at Five Corners"), I pulled two wheels off the road and onto the sidewalk so that cars could squeeze past me. There was another chorus of horn honking, along with a few shouted imprecations. Summer traffic in the towns does not lend itself to deviations.

Finally Dirk's Toyota made the turn and came up behind me. I returned to the road and led him to the corner of Main Street, where we had to negotiate a less challenging turn into one-lane, one-way traffic, with a competing line of cars trying to make the same turn from the left. Once you have done this, the rest is easy, a question of patience as you creep through Main Street, interrupted only by cars aggressively entering from side streets and by other cars backing out of diagonal parking spaces into the main flow. Then we were through town and on the open road to my house. I waved my hand out the window to indicate to Dirk that all was well. To my surprise, I got a hard blast of his horn. He must have been tired by the long drive from New York.

My parents' house is on the high bluff that looks down on Vineyard Haven harbor. The guest house, my house, is close to the main road at the bottom end of the lot but is screened from the road by spruce trees. More spruce trees screen my house and its small deck from any car driving past to reach my parents' house. If my parents or my sister Diane really want to see what I am up to, they have to turn in my separate driveway to find out. By mutual understanding, this is never done. I went first into my two-car parking area. Dirk's Toyota drew in after me, but he was out of his car first. His sharp-featured face — sharp nose, lean pointed jaw — was full of anger. His short-cut gray hair was bristling with indignation.

"What the fuck kind of place is this?"

"You don't like my house? You haven't even been inside."

"Not your house, I'm talking about traffic control. Doesn't anybody here know how to manage traffic?" Although he told me he had always practiced patience on his homicide cases as a matter of policy, he was not a naturally patient man. "That goddamn crazy intersection doesn't have a stoplight."

"We don't believe in stoplights," I explained. "There's only one on the whole Island, over a drawbridge, and it's always green."

"How come these people drive the way they do? Aren't there any rules?" He was furious.

"Come on," I said. "Bring your bag and let's have a drink."

He calmed down halfway through his second Scotch and soda. Through the drinks and through the sunset, which you can't see from my house, I filled him in on what had been happening, except that I left out all the good parts about Elena. I told him about the night of the murder, everything I could remember. I told him about yesterday's conference with the detectives. I told him about the *Globe* pieces that were scheduled to run tomorrow. He asked how many of the guests were still on the Island. I said I didn't know, but a lot of them were on vacation here this month, and others flew back and forth for weekends or for important parties.

"So I can talk to them?"

"Sure, if they're willing. I doubt they'll want to."

"I'm kind of used to that."

Dirk was full of questions about the police on the case. I told him about Captain Mulvey and Detective Ken Waters of the state police and about Chief Angus of the Vineyard Haven police. I said Chief Angus was the easiest to deal with but would know the least, that Waters would know a lot and seemed responsive, and that Mulvey would know the most, had the most authority but would be the least responsive.

"I'll work on Mulvey," Dirk said. "I've spent a million hours with Irish cops. If I can't get anywhere with him, then I'll switch to Waters. I think I'll leave the local chief to you. Is he the one in charge of your traffic?"

By the time we finished our drinks, it was too dark to eat outside. I'm a very decent bachelor cook when necessary, really quite handy in the kitchen, but I find ways to avoid it. Vineyard restaurants are not one of my ways. If you have lived in New York or Boston, the Island restaurants are strangely disappointing for such a popular, high-level resort. The usual excuses are that the season, even including the increasingly popular shoulder months, isn't long enough to support outstanding restaurants, and that since four of the six towns are dry, their restaurants can't make the customary profit from cocktails and wine and therefore can't afford the best chefs and the best food. But there are A-plus fish markets, A-plus produce stores and A-plus bakeries, so if you know where to shop, you can eat well without having to cook.

We ate on my round wooden dining table in the kitchen. It seats four maximum, but I rarely have more than one guest. We had cold, boiled two-pound lobsters, precooked by John's Fish Market, corn from Morning Glory Farm, blueberry pie from the Scottish Bakehouse and two bottles of sauvignon blanc from Our Market. The only cooking I did was to boil the corn water, then take the corn out at the right moment. An A-plus dinner, Dirk agreed.

We went back outside into a starry night with pale moonlight to finish off the second bottle of wine. I left the deck light off because of mosquitoes, but we could still just see each other. Neither of us was in peak form, perhaps, but we were cheerful and reasonably alert. When I had poured the last of the bottle into our glasses, Dirk said something interesting.

"Chances are," he said, "that Miss Silk's murder had nothing to do with her book."

I had been referring to her all evening long as Millie, but out of habit in hundreds of homicide cases, Dirk always spoke of the deceased in formal terms.

"You've had too many drinks. Everybody at the dinner except me was in the book and about to be trashed. She said so. So did Marsden. It's got to be why she was killed."

"Not necessarily. What's the murderer's motive? Does he think that killing Miss Silk will stop the book from being published?"

"Maybe. Probably."

"But you said Marsden was definite. He told Mulvey it's going to be published."

"Well, the murderer didn't know that. Most of those people don't know much about publishing. Only Munk and Dr. Sunbeam and Marsden know the business. The rest of them don't know anything about books."

"So you're guessing that somebody who didn't know anything about books was dumb enough to think that killing the author would kill the book? Stop it from being published? Well, it's true, people are dumber than you think, especially when they're pissed off about something. But you're probably wrong. When people don't like something in a book, they don't kill, they sue. People don't usually kill people because of something somebody said about them. Except Italians, of course."

"I still think it's the book. Look, I just thought of another possibility. Somebody was so mad about what Millie Silk was going to say in the book that he killed her in anger. Not to stop the book from being published. Just to get even, just to pay her back." As I said this, I must admit that the thought of Elena Bronze crossed my mind.

"I thought you said nobody's read the book."

"I don't think anybody has. Except Marsden and Millie's secretary, who typed it up."

"Jason, you're not thinking clearly. If nobody read the book, how could somebody be angry enough about what he didn't read to kill her?"

"I don't know. Maybe just a possibility."

"Or maybe not. How did she write?"

"What do you mean, how did she write?"

"What do you mean, what do I mean? How did she write? Word processor? Typewriter? Quill pen?"

"Oh. She was very old-fashioned. It was one of the many things she boasted about. She wrote by pen, not quill but ball-point, Mont Blanc ballpoint on lined white paper. Mostly she wrote up here and sent it down to her secretary in New York who typed it up and sent it back to Millie for corrections or rewrite or whatever. The secretary had to send everything back to Millie, no files, no copies. Then when Millie had done fixes, it went back to Miss Quinn for retyping. Again, all copies to Millie."

"Sounds slow."

"Five years since her last book."

"That's a lot of paper going back and forth over a long period of time. Maybe somebody got a chance to read it. Or read some of it. Maybe the secretary talked about it. Lots of possibilities that it wasn't a total secret. Anyway, when Mulvey's team reads the manuscript, we'll know what she wrote about everybody. I still say somebody probably had a reason to kill her that had nothing to do with what was or wasn't in her book. That's what we have to think about. Any ideas? It could have been somebody who wasn't even in the book. Like you."

"Oh God, Detective Schultz, you wizard, you've caught me. I confess."

Dirk laughed. "The only trouble with you as the murderer is that you didn't get invited until just before the party. I don't think you're smart enough to get hold of a cyanide pill in that period of time. Not on this Island, with all the traffic."

"The way I did it, I'd been carrying the pill around in my pocket for months, just waiting for an opportunity that finally came."

"Hm. That's possible for the real murderer, too. Anyway, somebody had to bring the pill to the party with, as we say, murder intent." He yawned. "Is there any more wine?"

"Not any that's cold."

"Just as well, I guess. What say we go to bed?"

* * *

The *Times* and the *Globe* are delivered every morning. Normally I start with the *Times*, but this morning the *Globe* seemed like the paper of choice.

Everett Munk's piece started like this: "Many people are brave, at least some of the time. Mildred Silk was more than

67

brave, she was fearless, and she was fearless all of the time." He went on to explain that truth is often painful to hear or to read, but that that never stopped Millie from speaking out, regardless of cost, regardless of pain. I thought it was a fine tribute, even though I had never thought truth was one of Millie's strong points, either in fiction or nonfiction. Everett didn't say that others had to bear the cost and the pain, not Millie herself.

Dr. Sunbeam began by saying, "We can draw many useful and inspiring lessons from the life and death of Mildred Silk," and then proceeded to draw them.

Jason Arnold's piece was not in the paper.

I looked all the way through every section twice before I called Bert Stevens.

At his home number I got his answering machine but left no message. When I called him at the office, his phone was busy. The second time I got him.

"I was just going to call you," he said.

"Where's my piece?"

"That's what I was going to call you about."

"I thought you liked it."

"I did, I did. So did the boss. But you saw the big story about the fire in Southie? And the financial scandal in the mayor's office? You just got squeezed out, Jason. There wasn't enough room for everything. I'm real sorry, but it happens all the time. We'll pay you for the piece anyway. Extra payment, actually, because you helped get Munk and Sunbeam."

We have all been told that it is a mistake to be critical of the press, so I restrained myself. "Fuck you," I said, and hung up.

Terribly Special Specials

$\mathcal{A}$FTER HANGING UP on my former friend Bert, I went to the other bedroom to see if the conversation had awakened Dirk. It hadn't. His bed was made and he was nowhere in the house. His car was still in the parking area, so he must have gone for an early morning walk, maybe to look at the beach.

I made coffee enough for two, put out bagels for breakfast and drank some juice. The phone rang.

"Is this Jason Arnold?"

"Yes."

"Oh, I'm so glad I caught you. This is Molly Dodge in Miss Waring's office. Miss Lulu Waring at *Celeb/Celeb*, you know?" Her voice was friendly, close to gushing. She sounded young. "I apologize for calling so early, but Miss Waring said everybody gets up early at the Vineyard, so I should call you before you went off swimming or sailing or whatever you do up there." She added a merry little laugh.

I was not in a laughing mood after the *Globe* business, so I waited to hear what this was about. It was not difficult to guess. Chirpy, chunky Lulu had already got a lot of mileage out of being the only journalist present at the murder and the first to report Millie's death. No doubt this was more of the same.

"Miss Waring hopes you'll be willing to help her on this very special program she's doing. It's terribly special."

"Okay, put her on."

Molly Dodge did not even pause. "Oh, Miss Waring's not available just now, so she asked me to talk to you."

I was sure "not available" meant the same thing as Dr. Sunbeam's "meditating." Lulu was home asleep. Since I was not friendly to the media this morning, I said, "Well, when she's available, tell her to give me a call. When I'm not swimming or sailing."

"Oh dear. She really did want me to talk to you in her place, just till she has a chance to talk to you herself."

I.e., when she gets to the office. "I'm sorry," I said, "if Lulu has a favor to ask, I'd rather she asked me herself."

"Oh dear. Well, I'm sure she'll call you as soon as she can. She wants you to help her on this big special she's doing."

"All right, have her call."

Molly Dodge's voice turned less young and less gushing. She was suddenly a competitive professional. "Promise me something," she said. "This is important. Promise me you won't sign up with anybody else until she has a chance to talk to you."

That caught my attention. Were people going to bid for my services? What services might those be? "Okay," I said. Then I thought I shouldn't sound too generous. "But only until noon. After that I might sign up with somebody else."

"Will you be at this number until then?" All business now, no charm at all.

"If I'm not, you can leave a message."

"But suppose it's noon and I haven't reached you?"

This must be quite serious. It might even be fun — whatever it was. "If necessary, I'll call you at noon before signing with anyone else."

She gave me her direct extension to dial, asked me to read it back to her, reminded me of my promise and said goodbye with regret.

A full hour later Dirk walked in. I had given him instructions on how to dress for a Vineyard summer day. Casual slacks, either khaki or cotton, with blue jeans an option if you are thin enough, which Dirk certainly was. Open-neck shirt, either short sleeve or long sleeve, but no tie before evening except at a funeral or a wedding, and even then a tie was optional up-Island. No jacket before evening unless you are invited to lunch at certain homes on West Chop or Starbuck Point, which you won't be. If you feel cold, wear a sweater rather than a jacket. Loafers or sneakers. Shoes are okay only if they are really beat up and unpolished. This morning Dirk had followed my fashion guidelines, exercising the blue jeans option, but had added a khaki baseball cap, suitably shabby. He looked excited, eyes bright.

"Where have you been?"

He took off his cap and dropped it on the kitchen table on top of the *Boston Globe*. He noticed the paper. "How'd your piece come out?"

"It didn't. They didn't use it."

"That's too bad." He did not sound either interested or concerned. He was interested in whatever he had been doing this morning. "How's the coffee situation? What's for breakfast?"

"Lots of coffee. Help yourself. You're on your own for breakfast, but I recommend the bagels."

"Bagels? Vineyard bagels?"

"Certainly not. I bring bagels from New York and freeze them. That's a Zabar's bagel there on the counter."

Mollified, Dirk sliced the bagel and put both halves in the toaster oven. He poured a mug of coffee.

"If you tell me where you've been," I said, "I'll tell you what happened here while you were gone."

"I walked up to Miss Silk's house. It's much richer than you told me."

71

"She had a lot of money. Or at least her husband did, and then she did."

"Some of that furniture is worth buckets. Like the buffet where the drinks were."

"You peeked in?"

Dirk smiled. When he was working, his smile had a wolflike quality. "I never could learn anything by looking through windows. So I went in."

"You just walked in? It's unlocked? A murder scene is unlocked?"

"Oh no, it was locked. But I used to work vice, where you need to know how to get into places. I kept my tools." He took a ring of small metal picks from his pocket and jangled them at me. "They hadn't even bothered to turn on the alarm system. I know they're through with it as a crime scene, but if I had this case, I'd want to know if any of those guests tried to get back in. Somebody coming back to look for something or pick up something."

"Since you're not licensed anymore, you're lucky nobody saw you breaking in."

"Listen Jason, I spent twenty-seven years working by the book, keeping my nose clean so no defense lawyer could catch me off base. Now I don't have to. Anyway it was early enough so nobody else was around. Besides, that's why I wore a cap. People never notice people in caps. They think if you're wearing a cap, you must belong there. It's different if you wear dark glasses. People notice you if you wear dark glasses, they think you're trying to hide."

"I'll try to remember, next time I'm breaking and entering. So what did you learn? Have you solved it?"

He looked at me for a moment, taking my question more seriously than I meant it. "I always like to see where it happened," he said finally. The toaster oven gave a ding. Dirk took out his bagel and buttered both halves. "I stood there in front of that buffet, trying to figure out how it must have been with all of you twenty people milling around. Talking, pouring bottles, handing bottles back and forth. Elbows, arms, hands, voices. All the killer had to do was be careful not to drop his poison in the wrong glass. It would have helped if the killer knew what Miss Silk drank, and knew about this after-dinner drink ritual of hers, but even that wasn't essential. All the killer had to do was be ready at the right moment."

"Everybody knew Millie drank Chartreuse. And about the circus act she put on over the liqueurs. Even if you'd never been there for dinner, you could have read about it. She gave out interviews the way John D. Rockefeller gave out dimes."

"Yeah. Anyway, lots of killers are cowards. This one wasn't. This one had nerve."

"I could have told you that the night of the murder. Five minutes after I knew it was murder, I knew somebody had a lot of nerve."

Dirk smiled again, this time not his working smile. He was enjoying his bagel and coffee. "Jason," he said, "you're a frustrated detective."

"No, I'm a frustrated murderer. I've been busy too. I got a call this morning from one of the suspects. Or at least from a lackey of one of the suspects."

I told him about Lulu Waring and the prospect of my being involved in some way in some kind of special program.

Dirk heard me out. Then he said, "Sounds like they really want you. They might be willing to pay you to do something. Why don't you see if you can get me paid too? I'm probably the only experienced homicide detective who's on the scene and free to talk about this case."

"Sure. Because you're not involved and don't know anything."

"Listen Jason, I spent a long career not talking to the press when I did know something. Now that I don't know anything, it's the perfect time to talk. If I get paid."

He was on his second half bagel and his second mug of coffee when the phone rang again. Probably Molly Dodge, or maybe even Lulu Waring herself. But it wasn't.

"Jason? It's Mary Hergesheimer."

I put my hand over the mouthpiece and told Dirk, "It's another suspect, but not a very good one."

He took his bagel and mug into my bedroom and picked up the extension. He did it so quietly that I couldn't hear a thing.

I hadn't seen Mary, my nice dowdy dinner partner at Millie's, since the night of the murder.

"I suppose you've already heard from Lulu," Mary said.

"Sort of. Her assistant called me a little while ago. But I haven't talked to Lulu herself."

"Oh good. Then you're still a possibility?"

"Absolutely." Although I had no idea what I was a possibility for.

"Bob would have called you himself, but there are so many people to call that we had to divide up the list, and I got you."

"That's nice," I said, and I meant it. I liked both the Hergesheimers, but talking to Hergie himself was like talking to a pressure cooker — always under full steam. Mary took things easier.

"As you can imagine," Mary said, "Lulu's miles ahead of Bob on this one. After all, Bob wasn't even there. So we're running like mad to catch up. You have to help."

"Well, I promised Lulu —"

Mary busted right in, pretty steamed herself. "You said you hadn't talked to Lulu."

"I haven't. But I promised her assistant I wouldn't sign up with anybody else before talking to her."

There was a pause. Then Mary said sadly, "Lulu already has Millie's house."

74

Great Vineyard properties sell fast, but Millie's will hadn't even been made public. I couldn't believe Lulu had bought Millie's house only three days after her death. Besides, Lulu already had a nifty house in Edgartown. "She bought Millie's place?"

"No, no, of course not. She just rented it for her special. From Millie's lawyer. If Bob hadn't been off on that stupid story in Brazil, I know he would have thought of it before she did."

This was the first I had heard about why Bob Hergesheimer had been called away on assignment and had to miss Millie's dinner. I tried to think what story in Brazil could possibly have been interesting enough for a last-minute assignment.

"Mary, since I haven't talked to Lulu, I don't really know what this is all about, except that Lulu is doing some kind of special show."

"Bob is too. We both are. Lulu has an hour, or at least that's what she's telling everybody. How much time Bob gets depends on what he can put together."

It took another fifteen minutes for Mary to explain. Lulu Waring — operating straight from Millie's house, from Millie's deck, from Millie's dining room, from Millie's buffet — was planning to interview the entire cast of the fatal night, every guest and employee she could get her hands on. She was even trying to corner the police on duty that night, although Bob Hergesheimer had already learned that the police were under wraps, on dire warning from Captain Mulvey himself that they would be dismissed if they discussed the case with the press.

Because of Lulu's insider position, Mary said Bob's special would have to take a broader look. It would deal with the Vineyard, with the invasion of celebrities, with Mildred Silk as both celebrity author and celebrity figure, plus whoever and whatever he could steal away from Lulu. Both were calling in every chit they had, and I was one such chit. Lots of people would probably appear on both shows, that couldn't be helped. Bob's show was still "just shaping up," Mary said, but he wanted me both as a Millie dinner guest and as a longtime Vineyarder.

"Lifelong Vineyarder," I corrected her. "Every year of my life."

"Even better," Mary said.

"I still have to talk to Lulu."

"Why?"

"Because I promised I would."

"But you've played tennis with Bob!"

That was true, but only a couple of times when he needed a doubles partner. "And I've played bridge with Lulu." Also true, but only once.

While we were arguing about my conflicting loyalties, Dirk hurried in and handed me a scrawled note. It read: "Tell her hire me. Super murder expert."

I didn't have to think that over for long. The prospect of getting Dirk a big slice of network money was too juicy to resist.

"Mary, I still have to talk with Lulu, but I've just had an idea. A great, great idea. It will add a whole new dimension to Bob's show. And it's something Lulu won't have. An exclusive for you."

Dirk went back to the extension to listen to my sales pitch and to Mary's reaction.

She never knew what hit her. By the time we hung up, she had virtually guaranteed that her husband would hire, on an exclusive basis and at a hefty consultant fee, this fabulous retired detective, a man who was free to talk on camera, a man who was very bright, very articulate, a man who had personally solved many murders, a man who had already visited the Millie murder scene, a man who had already formed fascinating opinions about the crime scene and about the killer's character, a man who would be worth every dollar of the many dollars he would naturally expect to be paid. While I did not promise it, I perhaps led Mary to think that this incredible homicide detective might even solve the crime — maybe even live, on camera.

When Mary and I said goodbye, Dirk came back into the kitchen, grinning and clapping his hands. "What a performance, Jason! I always knew I was that good, but nobody ever said so."

He sounded as pleased by the recognition as by the money.

"As your agent, I get ten percent."

"I won't even argue. How much do you think I might get?"

"I'll ask for ten or maybe twenty, and with a bonus clause for the number of minutes you're actually on camera."

"Get them to pay for voice-over minutes too. When they're using my voice but not my picture. Listen Jason, we're going to make a lot out of these specials, and not just money. I'll do the Hergesheimer show, and you do the Lulu Waring show. That way we'll both be watching and talking to all the suspects."

"Maybe the murderer won't come."

Dirk shook his head emphatically. "Don't worry, this killer will come. One, to refuse would raise suspicion. Two, celebrities love this kind of thing, to be interviewed on a TV special. Three, this killer wouldn't miss it for the world — another chance to show the same nerve and guts. He'll be there — or she'll be there. You and I will have plenty of chances to ask questions and poke around and compare notes. It's a whole different way to tackle a homicide. Tell you what, I'll be your agent for Lulu Waring."

"Unfortunately she can't pay me. All the networks have a rule about not paying news sources."

"Think big," Dirk said. He waved his hand. "You have to think big in this world. You're not just a news source. You should be a consultant, like me."

* * *

Lulu didn't jump at the idea. When she finally phoned in at ten minutes before my noon deadline — a daring display of brinksmanship — she was all charm until I mentioned my hope for a consultant role. Then she told me how upset her producer already was about the terrible cost of the show. "He's so worried because we can't shoot anything here in the New York studio, not even the intro. We practically have to create a whole new studio up there in Millie's house, and he couldn't believe how much rent we had to pay Millie's estate to get exclusive use. And then we'll have to fly everything in, all the people, all the lights, all the cameras, all those dreadful sound engineers."

Her producer may have been worried, but I could tell she wasn't. She was looking forward to all the problems of shooting a one-hour special at the Vineyard, regardless of cost and difficulty. Of course she had done snippets on the Vineyard before, during every Clinton presidential vacation, but this would be her first major Island story.

I didn't know Lulu Waring very well, but like everybody else who met her, she made me feel like an old friend. With her chuckle and her Georgia drawl and her down-home folksiness, she was everybody's pal. It was part of what made her such a good interviewer, along with her intelligence and her concealed instinct for the jugular. With a warm friendly smile she could ask the toughest questions.

"So Jason, I do want you on my show, but I don't honestly think I can afford a consultant. I don't really think I need one."

"Yes you do," I said. "I know the Vineyard better than any other guest at Millie's dinner. You and all your people are going to need a lot of advice on where to find things around here and how to get things done. Don't forget, we're in midseason."

"Maybe we can work something out," Lulu said. She wasn't exactly hurrying, but I sensed that was all the time she could spare for this matter. "I'll talk to my producer and we'll see. But I can count on you for my special?"

"Hergie wants me on his special too."

"Well honey, maybe we can figure out a little consulting. I just need you to say yes to my show. A real definite old-fashioned yes, okay? It's going to be terribly special."

"Okay. Yes."

"Good. Bye-bye then."

* * *

At his request, Dirk and I spent the rest of the day driving around the Island looking at houses. Not sightseeing. The only places he wanted to see were the homes of Millie's dinner guests. When I asked what was the point, he said, "You can tell a lot about people from where they pick to live and what kind of house they live in."

I was skeptical, but it was a sunny, breezy day, and I like showing off the Island to new visitors. I wished I had Elena Bronze's BMW convertible for the tour. In fact, I wished I had Elena herself for the tour, but I was under no illusions. She and I had not started an Affair. What we had was an Incident, a delightful happy Incident for both of us, which I would surely remember longer than she would. We had said goodbye with splendid feelings about each other but with no expectation of renewal. Just the same, with the TV specials about to take place, I would see her again. Anything can happen and sometimes does. Maybe when I showed Dirk her house, I would see her.

I had spent some time thinking about Dirk's theory that Millie's murder might have nothing to do with her book. I didn't agree, but I had gone over in my mind the things Millie had done to her various guests that might have led one of them to get even.

Indeed, I knew a few things and had heard a few things that might have aroused a spirit of revenge or, in one case, a spirit of enterprise. I would tell Dirk what I knew or suspected, but Captain Mulvey and his detectives were in a better position to pursue those threads. I still thought it was the book.

I explained to Dirk as we drove off in my Mustang that the Island is divided into six townships. The three big towns are all down-Island — Vineyard Haven, Edgartown, Oak Bluffs — and the three small ones are up-Island — West Tisbury, Chilmark, Gay Head. However, no serious celebrity would be caught dead in either Oak Bluffs or Gay Head. Oak Bluffs is too honky-tonky, and Gay Head is too complicated by the Wampanoag Indians, who own various tribal lands and wish they owned many more. But there was one celebrity exception in both Oak Bluffs and Gay Head. Dr. Sunbeam built his Life Center palace on Sengekentocket Pond in Oak Bluffs because he wanted — and wheedled — fantastic tax breaks. His tax-free home was part of his nonprofit (but very profitable) Foundation. And Jackie Kennedy Onassis had owned more than four hundred acres of gorgeous land in Gay Head, the most gorgeous and secluded home on the Island. But she and her lawyers had to keep fighting off the Indians about sacred burial grounds and tribal rights of way and tribal this and tribal that. At times she must have felt like Custer.

"We'll start with the Vineyard Haven suspects, since that's where we are. You've already seen my house. You've already seen Millie's house, and that's where Leonard Marsden always stayed whenever he visited. Now that he's her literary executor, he'll probably still stay there. She had an office full of file cabinets he'll have to go through."

"Just what does a literary executor do?"

"One of two things. Either he burns all the juicy diaries and letters, pissing off the biographers and critics, or else, like Mary Hemingway, he publishes all the stuff Ernest didn't think deserved to be published. In Millie's case Marsden has to publish her last book and then decide what to do with everything else. The papers themselves, after he's checked through them, will surely go to Wellesley, where Millie had been sending all her completed manuscripts. That's probably in Millie's will. Three to one says Marsden decides to publish an anthology of her best stuff. And then maybe a collectors' matched set of all her books."

Close to town I turned in Hatch Road with its big stately houses lined up along the edge of the harbor. I pointed out the grandest. "That's the Cones' house, Sam and Bebe. He's the tabloid press lord that everybody despises, so Bebe, who doesn't want to be despised, insisted on a very respectable house in a very respectable neighborhood. Also she's bigtime in real estate, so she wanted a big house in a big town, sort of as a showcase. She sells a lot of celebrity properties."

"This looks like some suburb in Westchester," Dirk said.

"No, it's not my idea of the Island. Not Sam Cone's idea either, he practically never comes here because they fight all the time. His presence at Millie's that night was an exception. Maybe he was here to discuss the divorce they're supposed to be getting, only rumor says she's asking too much. Millie's book will tell us all about it, I expect. You told me to think about reasons outside the book why somebody would want to kill Millie. Okay, here's one. Here's two, in fact. She put Sam and Bebe next to each other at dinner, something no other host or hostess has done in ten years. It made one of them furious enough to kill her."

"Jason, try to get a hold on your imagination."

We drove to Everett Munk's old family home on Lagoon Pond.

"I could live in that one," Dirk said. "Even though it looks like it might need a lot of repairs."

"Most of the old ones do. Lots of wet weather here, and there's moisture from the ocean and the ponds, even when the weather's good. So you get lots of leaky roofs and rotting shingles. But shingles always feel right on the Vineyard. Another motive for you. My guess is that Everett Munk had a serious affair with Millie. Maybe it was still going on. So you can have Nancy Munk as a jealous wife, trying to preserve her marriage and her livelihood."

"You believe that?"

"No. So how about Nancy Munk was having an affair with Millie, and Everett killed Millie to preserve his marriage?"

"You can't be serious."

"No, I can't. Just trying to help your theory."

Since we were already partway to Oak Bluffs, I took him the rest of the way so that he could see why celebrities don't live there. Fairly obvious. I took him on the beach road to Edgartown so he could see where they filmed many scenes in *Jaws*. More relevantly, he could see Dr. Sunbeam's Life Center, a stately pleasure dome, pinkish in color with lots of glass. It towers over Sengekentocket Pond, much to the dismay of a Pond association called Friends of Sengekentocket.

"People come here for counseling and therapy and spiritual uplift," I explained. "It's quite expensive, especially if you have private sessions with Sunbeam himself. Some people stay for a whole month. Rates are lower from November through March, just like everything else on the Vineyard."

There were no other suspect homes until we reached Edgartown, our super-quaint town of old white clapboard houses with black or very dark green shutters, all nestled so close to each other that there's hardly any grass to be seen in the whole downtown area. Edgartown is a serious celebrity center, although no longer the most serious. I showed him Lulu Waring's 1786 whaling captain's house on North Summer Street, right smack in town but with a harbor view out her back door. Like all the other old houses, the date of Lulu's was posted just above the door in black numerals.

"Here's a motive for you," I said. "One that has nothing to do with the book. Lulu was the only journalist at Millie's dinner, so she got the scoop of her life when she reported the murder a few minutes after it happened. Now she has a super TV special lined up, right from the scene of the crime, another terrific scoop. All she had to do was drop a pill in Millie's Chartreuse."

Dirk thought it over. "Unlikely," he finally said, "but possible. Journalists will do anything to get a story."

Quite near Lulu's house is the Scrimshaw Inn, run by a fierce old lady named Eloise Abernathy. This is where all the rich visitors stay and eat if they don't yet own homes. Chick Bird, the California computer software king, had reluctantly given the police this address — reluctant because it was the same address as his luscious assistant, Harriet Gunn. The Scrimshaw probably sees a lot of that sort of thing. I promised Dirk we would later see the house and property Chick Bird had bought and was trying to figure out how to modernize.

Then we drove out Planting Field Way to the house Rufus Mainbocher rented every summer. This is a newer area, well out of downtown, so he got to see a lot of grass as well as water. I knew only a few things about Rufus Mainbocher, originally a French name but now Americanized to "Mane-bokker." He was a widower in his late fifties. An acknowledged genius, he was so rich in the stock market that he could have bought Edgartown if he had wanted it, but he did not believe in owning real estate because, he said, "you can't trust it." He had houses and apartments all over the world but strictly as rentals. He not only owned his own investment company but also ran the exclusive Mainbocher Fund, with a minimum entry level of ten million dollars. A small, mousy man, balding, fiercely intelligent and blandly unpretentious, he had been one of the six at Millie's head table. I told Dirk I had no idea what his secret scandal might be.

"If you're that rich," Dirk said, "there's bound to be something."

Out the other side of Edgartown, a long, wide macadam band called Katama Road runs down to the great public surfing beach on the south shore. On the left-hand side of this road, hidden from snooping eyes by trees and by distance, great houses have recently been built facing Katama Bay. In Edgartown "recent" is anything since 1900, but some of these houses are so recent as to be considered new. One of these belongs to Jill Klein, the defense lawyer. Legal fees for great defense lawyers are apparently large enough to support a house on Katama Bay, although her place was modest by Katama standards. Modest in size but striking: stark white stucco with burnt-orange window frames and a shiny black slate roof. She could never have got away with this look in central Edgartown. Because there were three cars in the circular bluestone driveway, I could not take Dirk around to the front of the house as I would have if the driveway had been empty. You have not really seen a waterfront house unless you see it on the waterside, with its deck, balconies, floodlights, boat dock, sundial and outdoor sculpture.

"Pretty severe house," Dirk said.

"Yes, so is she."

"I know, I've watched her on *Court TV.*"

"She was pretty officious the night of the murder. Telling all of us what to do and what not to do until the cops got there.

Millie, by the way, talked a lot about Jill Klein's jury-tampering case."

"The Hector Lyman business?"

"Right."

"What did Miss Silk say?"

"She just took it for granted that Klein did it."

"Jason, I told you, people don't kill people because of what somebody says. What's that land over there?" He was looking past the house and across the bay.

"That's Chappaquiddick. It's an island, and everybody who lives there thinks it's the greatest, most beautiful part of the Vineyard. No celebrities, though."

"Why not?"

"Too inconvenient. No supermarkets, no restaurants, no liquor stores. You can only get back and forth to Edgartown by a little three-car ferry, and during busy times the cars are lined up waiting on both ends. Celebrities don't like waiting. They don't care much for inconvenience, either."

Back on Katama Road, I pulled over to the side. "For the next part," I told Dirk, "you're going to need a map." I unfolded my road map of the Island and handed it to him. "Where we're going next is the new Promised Land."

The long straight south shore of the Vineyard contains a string of ponds that were formed ten thousand years ago by the retreating glacier. Over the centuries the ocean has dumped enough sand ashore to create barrier beaches that enclose the ponds. These are not the neat, smooth circles that most people think of when they say pond. The retreating glacier left many long fingers of water jutting far into the land. Every piece of land between the fingers has a superb view, not only of the nearby pond waters, lapping at your front door, but of the distant ocean, with its big waves banging on the sands of the barrier beach. Elena Bronze's was a perfect example of a big-money pond house.

I've never tried to count all the Vineyard ponds. There are three large ones — Edgartown Great Pond, Tisbury Great Pond and Chilmark Pond — but each of these contains a number of coves and inlets. Then there are other ponds that are completely separate from the big ones. Even after all my summers here, there are many I have yet to see, but whether or not I've seen them, I like the names. Big Homer's Pond. Job's Neck Pond. Crackatuxet Cove. Turkeyland Cove. Uncle Seth's Pond. Oyster Pond. Wacha Pond. Deep Bottom Cove. Slough Cove. Thumb Cove.

The broad flatlands around the edges of the ponds were once used for farming and grazing. In the olden days the only people who lived way out on these hard-to-reach ponds and coves were farmers and fishermen. Some of the farms were gigantic — properties of several hundred acres owned by a single family. But in those days the only roads were narrow dirt tracks that turned to mudholes after every rain. No electricity, just kerosene lanterns. Since the ponds were brackish, you needed wells for water. In short, this was not celebrity country.

But now it is. The farmers discovered they could make a heap more money by selling their land to rich people than by grazing sheep. And the rich people discovered that they could bring in electricity and hot water and heat and good roads if they had enough money to pay for them. They did. Now the ponds are the place to be. The Clintons always stayed at the pond home of a wealthy Boston real estate developer who happens to be a Democrat.

Half a dozen of Millie's last dinner guests have homes out on the ponds, but only Bob and Mary Hergesheimer have lived there for any length of time. When Hergie became a major television news figure a decade ago, they moved out of the house they had rented every summer in Vineyard Haven and bought an old farmhouse on Edgartown Great Pond. It wasn't just because of Hergie's new money, Mary said. Vineyard Haven was getting much too crowded for the kind of privacy they wanted. They didn't do what most rich people do when they buy an old Vineyard farmhouse. They didn't bulldoze it and start over from the ground up. That kind of house is called a tear-down. As in, "We bought an awful old tear-down just because the view was so great." The Hergesheimers added all the standard improvements — a modern kitchen with a Garland stove, a new wing, central air-conditioning, instant forced-air heating, picture windows overlooking the pond, an excavated wine cellar, a guest house. But they managed to preserve that old farmhouse look. Even the guest house looked like a smaller old farmhouse.

Studying the Hergesheimer spread, Dirk said, "Already I like him better than I like him on TV."

"This is the right way to do it," I said. "Now we'll drive over to look at the wrong way."

Jiggs Cooley, the post-Seinfeld sitcom star of *Jiggtime*, had bought a perfectly good, fairly new, quite expensive house which was definitely not a tear-down. That didn't stop him from tearing it down and building a California hacienda, surrounding a swimming pool and a glassed-in patio with palm trees. The patio was glassed in so that the palm trees could be kept cozy warm through the Vineyard winter. The roof was brilliant red Mexican tile.

"Why did he come here to build this?"

"That's what all his neighbors say."

When I showed him Elena Bronze's house, with its glass and brushed steel and teak (but unfortunately with no Elena in sight), Dirk said, "I would never have guessed it from her movies. That's the house of a real ice-cold woman."

I thought about what to say and then didn't say it. "She says she doesn't like it either," was what I wound up with.

"Then why did she buy it?"

"She didn't, she built it. Actually her architect built it while she was away in Australia."

Dirk shook his head, not believing that story. Repeating it out loud, I wasn't sure I believed it either.

"Funny," he said. "Sometimes the sexiest looking women are the coldest."

I thought about that too. "Well, on to the next," I said.

Danny Rothman, the pudgy cable company entrepreneur, had built a trophy house in Oyster-Wacha for his trophy wife Wendy. The house probably cost more than the wife, but it didn't look as good as she did.

Bitsy Betsy Pope was out in this area too, but not by choice. When she came to the Island right after the first Clinton invasion, she tried to buy a house in a high-priced enclave on the north shore of the Island, with a splendid view across Vineyard Sound to the Elizabeth Islands. But the association that controlled the enclave refused to let her in, not for financial reasons — Bitsy could have paid cash for three or four houses — but because of her personal reputation. Too many parties, too much loud music, too many live-in boyfriends, too many orgies. She spoke of suing but, on advice of counsel that she could not win, she decided not to. Instead, she bought a big place on Edgartown Great Pond when the couple who built it got divorced.

Dirk and I dropped by to look. A large gray shingled house, properly weathered and slightly dilapidated, and an even larger fake barn, painted barn red but otherwise unrelated to cows, horses, hay lofts, hay rakes, tractors or any other accouterments of farming. The original owners had just wanted "a barn," so they built one. Bitsy Betsy had converted it to a soundproof recording studio and party center. Way out here she could have as many orgies as she liked without disturbing any neighbors. Half a dozen cars, a Jeep and a pickup truck were parked haphazardly around the barn. Too early for an orgy, maybe she was recording. In spite of the vehicles, the whole scene had a sad emptiness. Perhaps I only imagined that, remembering what young Bitsy used to be.

"I still like her music," I told Dirk.

"Who doesn't?"

We drove on.

Chilmark has the highest hills on the Island. This isn't saying much because the two highest are just over three hundred feet. The soprano Jane Millhouse had chosen to build her home on a Chilmark hill overlooking Chilmark Pond and the ocean beyond. It's surprising how much difference a little elevation makes, especially if you have been looking at sea-level houses for the past few hours. The Millhouse view was sensational, a long stretch of the south shore with the island of Nomans Land clearly visible to the left of the Gay Head peninsula. The house was a bit dramatic for Chilmark, but then so was its owner. Dirk and I got out of my car to admire both the view and the swooping dark wooden beams and rafters that framed the building. Up this high the breeze was a real wind. Because there were no cars in the driveway and no sign of life, I assumed nobody was home and that we were free to walk around. That proved not to be the case.

A sliding glass door opened, and onto the deck came the diva herself. She was wrapped in a full-length white terrycloth robe, stark white against her deep black skin. She was an angry frigate under full sail. Her great bosom and hips filled the robe, her long black hair streamed behind her in the wind, unfettered by any ribbon or band. Her large brown eyes were snapping and flashing. It was quite an entrance, even for a great soprano who was used to making terrific entrances onto the Metropolitan Opera stage.

She stopped at the end of the deck. She towered over us, huge, close to six feet tall and two hundred pounds. She glared down. I was sure she did not recognize me from our one meeting at Millie's. I felt quite small.

"Just what do you think you're doing here?"

Over the years I've been asked that question many times when caught snooping a Vineyard house, thinking nobody was home. The unwritten Vineyard rule used to be that it was all right to house-snoop after Labor Day — even to peer in people's windows — because everybody had closed his house and gone back to Boston or Cleveland. But snooping during the summer was considered bad manners, so you better have a story ready if you get caught. Now, of course, so many retired people stay on through October, even through Christmas, and so many more people live here year-round that the only safe snooping period is February when everybody who can afford to escape from the Island does so.

I always have a story ready. If some irritated homeowner catches me on his turf, I say, "Can you please help me? I'm lost and I'm looking for —" Then I produce a plausible name, preferably the name of somebody who actually lives in that very neighborhood. If I can't think of a neighborhood name, I make up somebody "who is renting a house somewhere around here." This is less convincing but better than having to apologize for trespassing, which makes the homeowner even more angry. Ha! So you admit it!

Jane Millhouse was so formidable that my mind went blank. I tried to think of a Chilmark name.

"Miss Millhouse," a confident voice said, "I'm investigating the Mildred Silk homicide in Mr. Arnold's behalf."

She lost not an ounce of her presence. "And who are you? And who is Arnold?"

I rose to the second question. "I'm Jason Arnold. I was a guest at Millie's dinner party."

"I'm Lieutenant Dirk Schultz. Homicide Division. NYPD." Dirk paused several seconds before adding, in an equally firm voice, "Retired."

"Oh yeah, I remember you," she said to me, no longer in her diva voice, just plain Jane Millhouse. "You're the one told the cops about the place cards." She laughed. Her laugh was as big as the moon. "That probably saved us all a couple hours answering who sat where." She turned to Dirk. "What're you about? I got cops coming out my ears over this. Why do I need another one?"

"I'm sure you don't," Dirk said. "But Mr. Arnold has hired me to clear his name, so I'm talking to everybody who might be able to help."

Dirk said that so smoothly that I almost believed it. I guess if you had been a detective as long as Dirk was, you learn how to say things.

"So you just showed up here without asking?"

Dirk shrugged. "Sorry, Miss Millhouse, we didn't have your unlisted phone number."

This also sounded true but wasn't. While the cops were interviewing the guests on the night of the murder, getting their phone numbers and then reading them back to make sure they were right, I picked up several unlisted phone numbers, including Jane Millhouse's. I had written them down and given them to Dirk for future use.

"I don't know anything I haven't already told five or six times." She was still standing at the end of her deck, looking down on us, her hands now resting on the railing, still an imperious figure but no longer threatening.

"I understand you were the first person to touch the victim after she died."

"What's that supposed to mean?"

"And you slapped her cheeks, I understand."

"Sure. Trying to make her come to. I thought she'd fainted."

"And you were the first to notice the odor of cyanide poisoning?"

The diva stood tall. "It's time for both of you to go," she announced.

"I'm sorry we bothered you," I said.

"Buzz off."

"Of course." Dirk and I headed for my car.

Then I thought, I'll probably never have another chance to say this person to person. I turned around. "Miss Millhouse, I saw you last winter in *Tosca*. I thought you were better than anyone since Maria Callas."

I meant this as a supreme compliment. I never saw Callas, of course — I've only heard her records.

Opera stars are like other celebrities. "Callas was a long, long time ago," Jane Millhouse said.

Our last stop of this long day was out of sequence, but I had done it on purpose because I wanted Dirk to see the old Waverly place in the late afternoon light. So back we went to Edgartown Great Pond. We drove down an endless dirt road between scrub oaks just tall enough to hide our view of anything. The new owner, Chick Bird, had not yet converted it into a proper celebrity highway.

"This — is — awful," Dirk said. His voice altered pitch as we bounced over the bumps and ruts. "One of — Miss Silk's — guests lives — down here?"

"Not yet. But — going to. Hang on, it'll — get better."

Up ahead stood the slatted, crossbar gate that used to keep the Waverly sheep from leaving the farm. Even with the sheep gone, it was still locked. I parked my Mustang in the turnaround area beside the gate.

"We have to walk from here," I explained.

"How far?"

"Not far."

We climbed over the gate and headed down the road. Soon the walls of scrub oak ended, and we walked out onto wide open grassland — the great brown-gold sandplain, now almost yellow in the late sunlight, stretching far down to the waters of the pond. Rising from the middle of the sandplain, like some ancient pagan temple, was the Waverly family's unique and preposterous House of Eight Gables.

"Good Lord!" Dirk said. "Who thought that up?"

"Nobody. It just happened piece by piece, decade by decade."

For close to two centuries the Waverlys had farmed and grazed this beautiful wide land we were standing on. They had started with a simple, straightforward one-room house, but as the family grew and as the farm prospered, they added to the house. Later they added to the farm as well, buying up land from their neighbors and continuing to prosper. Piece by piece they added to their land, and piece by piece they added to their house. They never had a house plan. Whenever they needed more space — another bedroom, a pantry, a bigger dining room for the expanding family — they just knocked a doorway through a wall and tacked on the new room. The whole house was built through the decades by Waverly hands, with no architect and no professional carpenters or plumbers or masons. And especially no professional roofers. Each new room got its own roof at its own pitch and its own height. The final result that Dirk and I were now looking at, and that Chick Bird now owned, was a haphazard mishmash, a bizarre tribute to the energy and vigor and determination and growth of the Waverly clan, as well as to their total indifference to style and uniformity. And yet it was marvelous. There was nothing like it on the Island — or perhaps anywhere.

When the sheep business died out, and when the Waverly clan itself died out or petered out or moved away, or simply lost whatever magical drive it once had, the remaining members decided that the time had come to get rich by selling out. As soon as the farm and the old house went on the market, there was speculation about a developer buying the huge property and breaking it up into house lots. There was also speculation about it becoming a golf course. Conservationists talked about trying to preserve some of the great sandplain. There was even talk about turning the house into a museum, although no one could figure out what that museum might contain.

Before any of this could happen, Chick Bird bought the entire property for cash at the Waverlys' full asking price. As he told the newspapers, the land was large enough and flat enough for him to build his own landing strip. He would not have to use the overcrowded Edgartown Airport when he jetted in from California.

When I explained all this to Dirk, he asked, "What's he going to do with that house?"

"That's what we're all worrying about. He's got two or three architects figuring out how to modernize it."

"Huh," Dirk said. "Good luck."

Dr. Pepper Hits the Spot

YES, YES, I know it's Pepsi-Cola, not Dr. Pepper.

> *Pepsi-Cola hits the spot,*
> *Twelve full ounces, that's a lot,*
> *Twice as much for a nickel too,*
> *Pepsi-Cola is the drink for you.*
> *Nickel, nickel, nickel, nickel,*
> *Trickle, trickle, trickle, trickle.*

You can tell how ancient that singing commercial is by the use of the word nickel, an antique American coin that no longer buys anything except five pennies, which don't buy anything at all. That Pepsi commercial was, as Jane Millhouse said about Maria Callas, a long, long time ago. And yet it is still sung on the Vineyard every year at the home of Henry Chaffee, an Edgartown summer person known for his total recall of old singing commercials. We all sing the commercials together at dinner parties, to mixed reviews.

Nevertheless Dr. Pepper is appropriate for this story because Lulu Waring sponsored it. She even liked it and drank it. Although she did not actually appear in the Dr. Pepper commercials on her show, she was cute and skillful about dropping in friendly mentions of the product, and she cheerfully and shamelessly served it to all her interview guests on *Celeb/Celeb*.

Not many of them actually drank it, but Lulu did. She probably did more to promote Dr. Pepper through her casual comments than the expensive commercials did. She even attended Dr. Pepper ad sales conventions and swigged a few with the boys — first the Dr. Pepper, later the bourbon.

Considering how much she did for Dr. Pepper, I think it's unfair that Dr. Pepper did Lulu in. Not Dr. Pepper's fault, of course. That was just the vehicle.

* * *

I am not used to working hard at the Vineyard — or anywhere else, actually — so I was surprised and annoyed by how much work I had to do to earn my consultant fee for Lulu's special. The guests on the show — mostly Millie's dinner guests — had their own Island homes, or at least places to stay. But Lulu's TV production crew had to be parked somewhere, and she had no intention of parking her underlings — such as those "dreadful sound engineers" — in her own Edgartown house, even though it could easily have held half a dozen. The Island has many hotels, inns and bed-and-breakfasts, but most of them get booked early in the summer season. If the Clintons had been vacationing, my search for rooms would have been hopeless. When the Clintons invaded, the White House press corps and the Secret Service gobbled every available spot on the Island. But even without the Clintons I had to scramble for space. On top of the housing problem, every new TV crew member had to be met at the airport or the ferry, either by me or by somebody else.

The first to arrive was Lulu's executive assistant Molly Dodge, the gushy one who had tried to sign me up for the special. Since Lulu said she would be "my right-hand man," I decided for political reasons that I better pick her up myself at the airport. "Short and blond," Lulu said, "you can't miss her."

Lulu Waring comes to and from the Vineyard on other people's jets, so she rarely has to meet anybody at the airport. She has no idea how many short blond women get off every flight from New York. And yet as I watched the passengers walk down the exit ladder and cross the tarmac, many of them short and blond, I quickly picked out the one I wanted to be Molly Dodge.

She was no more than five feet two, if that, with a lively, sprightly figure. About thirty, probably. Her bright blond hair was loose and hung just short of her shoulders. She wore trim black slacks and a bright pink shirt. She carried a floppy leather shoulder bag, and she looked ready to take charge of anything that came her way.

As she walked through the entry gate in the chain-link fence, I said, "Are you Molly Dodge?"

She stopped and looked up at me. Dancing brown eyes. Round pink cheeks to go with her shirt, and a small but determined chin. "Right. So you're Jason Arnold." Not a question but a statement.

"Right."

"You're better looking than you sounded on the phone."

"So are you."

"Really? Everybody says I sound good on the phone."

"A little too gushy, I thought."

That provoked a cute quick smile. "I was just trying to persuade you."

We picked up her tweedy Hartmann suitcase from the row of luggage lined up on the tarmac, and I carried it out to my car.

"You been with Lulu long?"

"Three years. That's pretty long for her show. She wears them out."

"She tells me you're going to be my right-hand man," I said.

"That's funny," she said. Again the cute bright smile. "That's just what she told me about you."

Obviously we were going to get along.

I delivered Molly Dodge to Millie's house, now the designated headquarters of Lulu's terribly special special. The entire show would be shot here, so Lulu wanted Molly in full-time residence. I took Molly and her suitcase to one of the second floor guest bedrooms.

"Nice room," she said. "And I get to see the water."

"It's the second nicest," I said. "Leonard Marsden has the best. His is down at the other end of the hall." Marsden stayed here when he came up to work on Millie's papers. Today he was flying up from New York to take a major part in Lulu's show.

"You have the run of the house," I told Molly, "except for Millie's office."

"That's what you think. Wait till the production crew gets here. They'll take up every inch of open space."

Tomorrow afternoon two twenty-five foot trucks from New York would arrive on the ferry, loaded with all the equipment for the show and the technicians to handle it. I had been told to line up twenty beds for the TV team to sleep in during the five or six days they would be on the Island. Also rental cars so they could all get to and from the storm center at Millie's house. Also special parking permits from the Vineyard Haven Selectmen's Office to park those big trucks and all those cars in this very private residential area. The Town was thrilled to have a big TV show shot right here, and pleased about all the extra money the TV people would spend here, so the permits were a cinch. Millie's neighbors were very upset about this noisy invasion of their sanctuary, but they were helpless to stop it. Everybody else considered it a great coup for the Island.

I handed Molly the printout of technical activities and scheduling, the whole mysterious production plan that Lulu's New York office had faxed to me. She read through it quickly and said it looked fine.

"Good," I said, "because that's now your responsibility."

"Oh? What's yours?"

"I'm the housing authority. And the transportation authority. Also the social secretary. What are you doing for dinner tonight?"

"What do you suggest?"

"I suggest dinner with me."

"Great. Your expense account or mine?"

Since she had never been to the Vineyard before, I thought it would be more fun for her if we ate out her first night. Dirk was buying a few beers for the state police over in Oak Bluffs, planning to pick up some inside information, so I would not have to subject Molly to a *ménage à trois*. I took her to Le Grenier in Vineyard Haven, where Dirk said he might join us later.

My rule of thumb in New York is never to eat in a second-floor restaurant, but many big city rules don't apply at the Vineyard. Le Grenier is upstairs via a narrow, steep staircase, but once you make the climb, it's a spacious two-room, hundred-seat restaurant. The tablecloths have pale pink flowers on a light blue-gray background, the chairs are open-back white plastic. The lighting consists of those strings of tiny Christmas tree lights running all along the overhead ceiling beams. The primary decorative note is hundreds of wine corks lined up on the top of every window frame and every picture frame of the French posters. Wine corks, wine corks everywhere, but not a drop to drink. All the Vineyard towns are dry except Oak Bluffs and Edgartown, so you cannot buy a drink at Le Grenier but have to bring your own bottle. Enough customers had brought enough wine bottles to Le Grenier over enough years to provide all those decorative corks.

I had told Molly not to get too dressed up, and she hadn't. An open-neck yellow polo shirt with short sleeves. A dark brown ribbon in her hair and three dark wooden bangles on her bare

99

right arm. I gave the waitress both the red wine and the white wine to open. Two more corks for the décor.

Molly checked out the crowded restaurant and the other customers with a few quick glances, discovering nothing and nobody very interesting, then gave her attention to me.

She leaned forward across the table, brown eyes eager. "Who do you think did it?" she asked.

"Did what?"

"Murdered Mildred Silk. You were right there, you must have some idea. Or at least a guess."

"Maybe I did it."

"Huh. Lulu says you're the only dinner guest who won't be attacked in the book. Mildred Silk said so herself."

"Maybe I did it because I was left out. Hell hath no fury like a celebrity scorned."

"Come on, who do you really think it was?"

"I think it was Lulu."

A merry laugh. "Wouldn't that be fun! They could arrest her right in the middle of her own show."

"Don't you like her?"

"Don't be silly. I love Lulu, or I wouldn't still be in this job. But just the same, it would be exciting if they arrested her right on the show. I don't think there's ever been a live arrest for murder on TV."

I was really going to like Molly. She shared my happy lust for murder.

"Well, it's probably not Lulu. But my friend Dirk is convinced that the murderer will be on Lulu's show."

I had told her who Dirk was and why he was staying with me. Now I told her about his conviction that the murderer would, in effect, return to the scene of the crime in order to appear in the show. When I explained Dirk's reasoning, she said, "That calls for a lot of arrogance."

"Sure, but isn't that what all celebrities have?"

"Sometimes it's all they have," Molly agreed. "But if he's right, that means anybody who doesn't come on the show isn't the murderer."

"Yes, if Dirk is right. But if he's wrong, it won't mean anything."

We picked out our dinners. She ordered oysters Rockefeller and scallops *à la russe*, which I told her was a Grenier specialty, along with swordfish *à la russe* and shrimp *à la russe*. All that means is a spicy pink sauce. I chose clam chowder and sweetbreads — support your local fishermen, and don't be afraid of cholesterol.

When the oysters landed in front of Molly, she stared down at them, plainly taken aback. "Could that be grilled cheese on top of the spinach?"

"Good guess. Things are a little eccentric here. You're not in New Orleans."

"So I see."

"Cheer up," I said. "The oysters will be good."

We drank a lot of wine with our dinner, with our murder talk and with our cappuccinos, so there wasn't much left when Dirk showed up. I saw him standing at the entrance, the small trim figure in khaki slacks and a loose sportshirt with the tail hanging out, the detective uniform for off-duty beer drinking. "There's Dirk," I told Molly. I held up my hand and waved him over.

After introducing them, I got the waitress to bring another chair. "You want any dinner?" I asked.

He shook his head. "I'm full of peanuts and pretzels and potato chips. I'd like some of your wine though."

The bottle of white had vanished with the oysters and the chowder and the scallops, but I poured him the last of the red. "Did you learn anything?"

I saw him shoot a little sideways glance at Molly, as if thinking how much to say and then deciding it didn't matter. He knew who she was and how much she already knew. He looked back at me and nodded a couple of times. His eyes were very bright, that look he had when he had learned something interesting.

"Marsden won't let them read Miss Silk's book," he said.

"What do you mean? I heard him tell Captain Mulvey he'd show him the book. Right there on Millie's deck. Right there, the day after the murder."

"Yeah, Mulvey remembers that too. And so does Kenny Waters."

"They're state police," I explained to Molly. "Mulvey's in charge of the investigation."

"Well," Dirk said, "Marsden's changed his mind."

"Why?"

Dirk took a long, mouth-rolling swallow of his wine. I couldn't tell whether he was thinking about the wine or about the case. Finally he said, "Marsden claims it's too valuable. He says he's got five magazines interested in first serial rights. *Time*, *Newsweek*, *New Yorker*, *People*, *Vanity Fair*. He says that means big, big bucks."

I had often heard stories about two magazines bidding against each other for the right to publish excerpts from a forthcoming book. On a book that had big national news value, like the memoirs of a major government figure, usually it was *Time* versus *Newsweek*. And I had read about the famous long-ago bidding war between *Life* and *Look* for rights to William Manchester's inside account of the Kennedy assassination. First serial publication of an important book was supposed to be great for a magazine, not only for its newsstand circulation but also for all the press and TV publicity surrounding each excerpt, with the magazine prominently mentioned and quoted in every story. Understandable why two rival magazines would be desperate to get their hands on such a property. But five magazines all bidding for the same book? That could be a whopping auction.

"Why can't he show the book to the police and still sell the first serial rights?"

"That's what Mulvey says. But Marsden says that once the police get their hands on anything, all the juicy stuff leaks out to the press." He smiled and turned to Molly. "I've known that to happen."

"So then the value drops," Molly said. "Lulu will report every leaked tidbit on her show, and so will everybody else. All for free. So then first serial isn't worth nearly so much."

Dirk looked at her with approval. "Right, that's what Marsden says. He also says Okapi is a small publishing house, and something like this is very big stuff for them. He has to protect it."

"But it's a murder investigation," I said. "Millie's book must be full of clues. It's bound to be."

"Yeah, maybe," Dirk said. "Probably. But to find out they'll have to go through district attorneys, both Massachusetts and New York, and subpoenas and hearings and all that courtroom stuff." He drained his glass and picked up the wine bottle, now empty. "I'm tired of all these soft drinks. You suppose there's any Scotch at your house, Jason?"

"Highly probable." I signaled for the check.

"This island," Dirk said to Molly, shaking his head. "You practically have to mount a safari to get a drink."

* * *

The sheer amount of physical and electronic paraphernalia needed to create a one-hour network television show is more than I could ever have imagined, or ever wanted to. Molly said it was much easier in a studio because everything was already built in. "It's only when you get out here in the boondocks that it turns messy." Fortunately I neither had to understand it nor use it. All I had to do was avoid tripping over cables or knocking over light stands. The TV people walked through the forest of equipment without hesitation, not even looking down at the floor to avoid entanglement. And it was not just the technicians, who had installed all this junk and knew where it was, but even Molly Dodge and then Lulu Waring herself.

I had thought the director, a bushy-haired, busy-busy man of fifty named Fritz, was in charge of the show — until Lulu appeared. She walked in that morning, plump and cheerful, dressed in one of those loose, blue hip-length smocks that all French workmen wear. Molly and I listened to the director take her through the arrangements. She already had a rough script for the show, so it could not have been much of a surprise. First this scene in this room, then this one in that room, all perfectly sensible and chronological. Lulu stood there in her smock with a tall frosted glass of Dr. Pepper in hand. The glass was emblazoned with a red LULU. She sipped away as she heard him go through the whole list. Then she told him what changes she wanted. Her familiar Georgia drawl slipped away as she gave orders. Clearly Fritz was not in charge.

"I don't want to do my wrap in Millie's office. I want to save the office for me to interview Marsden about her book, now here is where she wrote it, blah-blah. I want you to set me up in the living room. That way I can say, right off the top, this is where Mildred Silk was killed, and I was sitting right here in this very chair. I saw it happen, she dropped dead right over there in front of me. Then I'll tell how I ran to the phone and broke the news to the world over CBS. Think the network will like that plug? Every time we come back to that set, they'll remember that I saw the murder from that chair. Now Fritz, in the dining room segment, the buffet with all the glasses and bottles will be perfect. The other guests and I can stand there and talk about how somebody dropped in the poison. I can ask each one what they were doing at the time. But I don't want those three round tables set up the way they were the night of the dinner. And I don't want the guests to sit where they were sitting that night. Too many empty seats. It'll just remind the audience that we couldn't get everybody to come back for my show. That's why we want them in casual clothes for the show, not all dressed up the way they were for Millie's dinner. We want them to look real Vineyard, and it'll help hide the fact that a whole bunch of people are missing. So scrap that overall dinner scene. I'll do interviews about what happened at dinner."

"But Lulu, we have to show the dining room the way it was. These were famous dinners. And this is now the most famous dinner of them all. Everybody will want to see what the room looked like."

Lulu shook her head. "Use a still picture from one of her other dinners. The *Gazette* has lots of them. Molly, get one. The best would be the first time the Clintons came to dinner because I was there. Pick one where I can point myself out. If the *Gazette* doesn't have a good one showing me and the Clintons, that White House photographer must have one. Anyway, I want a still picture with my voice-over."

"But Lulu —"

"The deck segment is going to be the hardest. We have to tape it and tape it and tape it, and then edit the holy dickens out of it. But we want the bar set up just the way it was, the same bartender, and we'll have all the guests with their drinks in their hands and talking about whatever, blah-blah-blah. I'll be walking from group to group, explaining who they all are. The Steadicam is lined up?"

"Of course. But Alex still hopes we won't need it."

(I whispered to Molly, "Who's Alex?" She whispered back, "The producer, the money man.")

Lulu's eyes narrowed. "We agreed we weren't going to cut costs on this."

"Alex said he just wanted to remind us that it's fifteen hundred dollars a day for the Steadicam operator, plus his assistant, plus the rental cost of the camera, plus the transportation cost."

"Okay, we stand reminded. Do you see any other way for a camera to follow me around the deck from group to group and to the bar and to the swing?"

"Of course not. We'd have to do a separate take in each spot, then shift to another spot for another take."

"All herky-jerky, right? That's not following me around the deck, is it?"

"Of course not. It spoils the flow."

"So we need the Steadicam."

I learned from Molly that the Steadicam is a camera with a built-in gyroscope that holds the image smooth and steady, even though the operator is walking around, following his character from place to place. A very expensive piece of equipment with an expensive operator who knows how to use it. So expensive that you can't afford to own it, you just rent it the rare times you need it.

Lulu was moving on. "Now I like your idea that for part of the scene I sit on the swing with Marsden and say this is where Millie and Marsden sat during cocktails. Maybe it's better without Marsden, just me, we'll shoot it both ways. The cocktail hour on the deck is just a walkup to the dinner, but it's got to feel right. And look right. It sets the stage for everything else. So it's the first segment to do, once all the guests are on the Island. Molly?" She turned to where Molly and I were standing and listening to her shape her show. "When's that going to be?"

"Marsden gets in this afternoon. Then Chick Bird is the last one. He's flying in from California tonight."

"ETA?"

"Seven o'clock."

"And he's not bringing the bimbo?"

"That's what he said. He said she's too busy at the office."

"Too bad." With a chuckle Lulu turned back to the director. "You'd have liked her, Fritz. You'd have used her up front in every shot." Lulu looked at her watch and drained the last of her Dr. Pepper. Now that work was done, the familiar drawl crept back into her voice. "I have this awful old lunch in Edgartown, so I have to run. Molly, let's get everybody here at ten-thirty tomorrow morning for blocking and run-through. Then we'll have to give them lunch, so better fix that too. Just sandwiches, nothing fancy, but really good sandwiches. Make sure you get a smoked turkey for Millhouse. And I want a tuna salad on white. Then we'll tape after lunch. With the Steadicam. Jason honey, you be sure you get that bartender here."

She did not allow for the possibility that the bartender or any of the guests might have to be somewhere else. Since they had all promised to appear on her program, they must now by God show up. As Molly told me, Lulu Waring expected everything to happen just the way she wanted it to happen — and usually, thanks to a lot of thrashing around by other folks, it did.

Lulu was determined to get Captain Mulvey to say something about the case on camera, but I didn't see how he could. After all, he personally had issued the proscription against any police officer discussing any aspect of the Silk case with any member of the press. Molly bet me five dollars, even money, that Lulu would get him to talk on camera. After we shook on it, she said, "Wait till Lulu cuddles up and begs him. No Irish cop is going to miss a chance to talk to Lulu on national TV."

What happened next between Molly and me was an accident. We were standing out in the entrance hall. The only explanation I can offer, which actually strikes me as a pretty good one, is that she was fun and quick and lively and pretty, and we were both caught up in the same exciting project. Murder is, after all, a sexy subject.

When we had settled on our bet about Captain Mulvey, she said, "Okay, time to go to work. I know I can get all those people, but where am I going to get all those damn sandwiches?"

"From Jaime."

"What's that?"

"It's not a that, it's a who. Jaime Hamlin, she's the Island's master caterer."

"She does sandwiches?"

"She does everything. Of course she does sandwiches. Pastrami, ham, corned beef, roast beef, egg salad, smoked salmon, even watercress. Even smoked turkey, I suppose. What's with the smoked turkey?"

"Lulu had Millhouse on her show, and she said a smoked turkey sandwich was her favorite snack. Smoked turkey on whole wheat. Bleck. But it sure did a lot for the smoked turkey business, which I don't think was going anywhere before that.."

"Well, Jaime can do a bleck sandwich on request. She can also do Lulu a tuna salad on white, although personally I recommend the pastrami on rye."

"But you said nobody has time to do anything during the summer. This is sandwiches for thirty people, counting crew. Can she do all that in time for tomorrow?"

"She's a friend of mine," I said. "But your producer will have to pay top-dollar sandwich prices for a rush order."

She looked up at me, those bright brown eyes, with real admiration and pleasure and relief. It was a look well worth receiving and remembering. "Jason," she said, "you're terrific."

"So are you." Suddenly I had to touch her. I just wanted to touch her. I put my hands on her shoulders and squeezed. "So are you," I repeated.

The look in her eyes changed. And then that cute quick grin. "Jason," she said, "I hope you're making a pass at me."

"Actually I wasn't. But I will."

I slid my hands down. We were still standing there in the entrance hall with various TV technicians moving around in adjacent rooms. We looked at each other, quick friends and, we both knew, about to be quick lovers. So then we kissed.

Our arms were still around each other and our bodies pressed against each other with considerable animation when one of the technicians barged through the entrance hall, some large black piece of equipment slung over his shoulder, and snarled, "Listen, you're blocking the way."

We both laughed, but neither of us lost what we were feeling.

"You told me I have the run of the house," she said. "Right? So let's go upstairs."

We climbed the stairs to her bedroom and made love, just like that, right then and there, in Millie's second nicest guest room with a view of the water. Afterward she said, and I could feel her lips moving against my neck, "That was very nice."

"I thought so too. Very much so."

"Listen," her lips still moving against my neck, "I don't do this with just everybody."

"No," I lied, "neither do I."

We lay happy and silent for maybe ten seconds.

Then, without any transition, she jumped up out of bed. "My God," she said, "I have to call all those people! And you have to call about the sandwiches!"

"Molly, that's not very romantic."

I loved the laughing way she said, "Some other time. Let's get on the phone."

Dirk and Molly and I agreed that Lulu had a much better lineup than Bob Hergesheimer had been able to attract for his competing special. And indeed, why not? Lulu had Millie's house for her set, and she would re-create the fatal evening as an eyewitness participant. If a celebrity had been important enough to be invited to that dinner in the first place, then it was still more important to appear on national television, person to person with Lulu Waring.

Even so, Lulu lost ten people from Millie's original dinner. Dirk and I went over the dropouts to see what we could make of them. Rufus Mainbocher, the Wall Street superstar, was vacationing at his rented castle in Scotland and sent his regrets. Sam Cone, the tabloid press lord, had already spent one weekend on the Vineyard with his wife and had no intention of enduring a second. (On the other hand his wife Bebe, the Vineyard Haven real estate queen, was deliriously happy to accept.) The Rothmans, cable company Danny, and his trophy wife Wendy couldn't come because Danny had just been charged by the FCC with franchise fraud and was too busy being deposed.

"That could be legitimate," I told Dirk. "Under your theory, even if he was the killer and wanted to come, he could be tied up by the lawyers."

"No," Dirk said, "if he wanted to come, he could get his lawyers to postpone. He just doesn't want the bad publicity of being on television when he's under a fraud charge. If he was the killer, that wouldn't matter because he'd want to be here. Forget him, he's innocent."

"That's too bad. He's such an awful person."

We also lost the bimbo Harriet Gunn, Chick Bird's smashing assistant. My dinner partner Mary Hergesheimer could hardly be expected to come when she was working on her husband's rival TV special. Harris Lawford, the gay rights activist, had demanded the right to say something on the show in support of lesbian marriages. When Lulu refused, he refused. We also lost Senator Max Washburn, who was leading a Congressional tour on an in-depth investigation of teenage brothels in Thailand. And finally, of course, we had lost Millie.

But Lulu still had a good lineup. Some newspapers would later print our names in alphabetical order as guests on the *Celeb/Celeb* special that ended in disaster. Alphabetical suits me fine, so here they are, with added comments from me.

Jason Arnold (me, the only non-celeb)

Chick Bird (bimbo-less, by jet from California to promote his software)

Elena Bronze (sometime friend to Jason Arnold, owner of the fabled bronzinis)

Bebe Cone (hoping to sneak in a real estate plug)

Jiggs Cooley (sit-com star of *Jiggtime*, all publicity helps)

Jill Klein (showcase opportunity for a great defense lawyer to discuss murder)

Leonard Marsden (publisher of eight Millie books, with this one the biggest)

Jane Millhouse (the most massive presence, even when not singing)

Everett Munk (novelist, maybe closest of all to Millie?) and ditsy wife Nancy

Betsy Pope (sadly faded songbird)

Dr. Sunbeam (a.k.a. Matthew Smeck, friend and advisor to the world)

Lulu Waring (hostess and star)

Also present was bartender Jack Crimmins. Dirk wanted to come, but he would be off earning his consultant fee by taping his lifetime thoughts on homicide for Bob Hergesheimer's special.

That night, the night before the gathering of the guests, Millie's house was occupied by Leonard Marsden and by TV technicians rigging last-minute sound and light effects. My house was occupied by Dirk. So Molly and I took a blanket down to Millie's beach and made love under the stars, with the ocean wavelets murmuring against the sand. It was a warm, clear night. We agreed this was much more romantic than jumping out of bed to phone for sandwiches. But even with a blanket, beach love is always sandy.

* * *

Surrounded by ocean, the Vineyard seldom has to endure hot days, even in midsummer, but we drew one for the first taping. I was glad that casual summer dress had been decreed. We had been told to look "real Vineyard-informal, but nice informal." I would not have wanted to wear jacket and tie in this heat. Our bartender would be busy today, pouring more soft drinks than hard liquor.

I wondered about seeing Elena Bronze again. I hadn't seen her since she dropped me off at my driveway with a goodbye morning kiss. I had not called her because I had the feeling she had meant it to be just one delightful night, not the beginning of anything. This morning I wondered, was I right or wrong? Either way, how would she act? Would she pretend nothing had happened? Pretend not to notice me? I decided to leave it to her. But whatever the nature of our meeting, I hoped it would not take place in front of Molly. At the moment Molly was safe inside with Lulu and Director Fritz, going over last-minute details.

Dirk had impressed on me the importance of watching and

listening closely, since he couldn't be there himself. I was to report to him in full, though he would not expect me to report verbatim the way Archie Goodwin reported to Nero Wolfe. I was out on the deck half an hour ahead of time, eyes and ears open, ready for work. The bar table had been set up yesterday, then meticulously moved an inch forward, then two inches backward, then one inch to the left, by the chief cameraman, who checked each placement through his viewfinder. If it took this much time to site an inanimate object, I feared the worst when it came to placing live people.

The bartender, Jack Crimmins, was in the kitchen collecting bottles from the refrigerator and ice from the freezer. Two fixed cameras were in place at two corners of the deck. A couple of sound and lighting technicians were arguing with each other. Light stands with their trailing wires were planted everywhere around the edges of the deck, although I had been told not all of them would be needed if the day was bright. The day was indeed bright, as well as hot.

At parties I play a game with myself, deciding who will be the first guest to arrive. Since Lulu's show was a party of sorts, I played my game. I decided that the first to arrive for the ten-thirty gathering would be Leonard Marsden. He was staying right upstairs, he had a big solo role as the spokesman for Millie's book, and he had a daily job as head of Okapi Press and would therefore be accustomed to showing up for work on time. I decided the last to arrive would be the entertainers — Elena Bronze, Jiggs Cooley, Jane Millhouse, and especially Betsy Pope — because in that world they show up late, if at all. According to my wisdom, stars are never on time.

Ha! My wisdom did not account for the siren call of television. For an entertainer — in movies, sit-com, opera or pop music — there is apparently an irresistible compulsion to be on camera. And it follows as the night does the day that it's best to show up on time and not miss one second of opportunity.

Jiggs Cooley came first, looking more cheerful than any murder suspect should look, perhaps because he would be in his element today. His orange madras sports shirt would surely catch the camera's eye. But so would the pale blue billowing silk kaftan sported by Jane Millhouse, as the great black dreadnought came steaming onto the deck. And then Elena, more quietly but no less effectively dressed. Her beige slacks fitted her legs and hips like Saran wrap. A loose white shirt concealed what was underneath, although every moviegoer above the age of Parental Guidance knew what was there. Especially me. I had tousled her short gray-blond hair. Her lively gray-blue eyes had looked into mine from a distance of inches.

As soon as she saw me, she walked straight up with a friendly but mocking smile.

"Most men call," she said. "Am I getting old?"

This time I know I blushed because my face felt hotter than the heat of the day. Usually I can think of something to say to a woman that is not the truth. I could have said I didn't know her phone number, but I did. I just told her the truth. "I didn't think you would want me to," I said.

She looked at me for a moment, eyes softening, then touched my face lightly with her fingertips. "That's really very modest, Jason. And quite sweet. Just the same, give me a call and we can watch another sunset together."

I had to clear my throat. "I'd love to."

"That's better," she said, laughing.

The others arrived soon after. Everybody was in light, cool clothes. In recent years Betsy Pope had had few invitations to appear on TV, so she wasn't going to miss this reminder of what her life used to be. Very dark, very large sunglasses covered a large part of her lost face. A long, loose white billowy shirt concealed the heavy shoulders and hips, and a high turned-up collar concealed the thick neck. Black, close-fitting tights emphasized her graceful racehorse legs, the last remnant of yesterday. Dr. Sunbeam ("Call me Sunny") was the only person in shorts, his pink Bermudas more or less matching his cherubic cheeks.

The last to arrive was, of course, my pick to arrive first. As soon as Lulu and the director came out to get things started, Leonard Marsden finally appeared, tall and shaggy, with his brown-gray hair and his guardsman's mustache. I figured out what must have happened. Working upstairs in Millie's nicest guest room, he had a clear view of the deck and saw no reason to come down until the show was ready to start.

Lulu gave us a short, charming speech of thanks and welcome. She apologized for the hot day, said the bar was already open, and promised "a delicious lunch from the best caterer on the Island." Fritz gave a short speech asking everybody to be patient and to listen carefully to all instructions. And for this deck scene, he said, please don't look at the camera. "Just talk to each other, look at each other, just like a real cocktail party."

It was nothing like a real cocktail party. The next two-and-a-half hours were ghastly and boring. The working TV people kept experimenting with different arrangements, different groupings, different placements within groupings. Some of us stood, some of us sat on Millie's deck furniture. Each change, each experiment, was accompanied by variations in lighting and sound and camera angle. They put different colored sheets of gelatin over lights to change the quality of the light, each gel attached to the light by old-fashioned paper clips. When they didn't like one color gel, they tried another. They tried having different people walk up to the bar to get a drink from Jack Crimmins, then walk back to their group. Then walk back to a different group. Then a different person walking up to the bar. Then, why not try two people walking up to the bar together.

To a layman it was absurd. To the TV people, including Lulu, it was bull's blood. Their patience and determination about getting it just right was monumental. So was their indifference to us. Although they were polite about their requests, we were just pegs to be moved and moved and moved until they were satisfied. And none of it was even being taped, none of it was for real. The Steadicam had yet to make its appearance. It was all rehearsal, a "prep" for the real thing.

With all the heat, with all the standing around in the sun, we gave Jack Crimmins a busy morning at the bar. He had a big run on his pitchers of iced tea, but also calls for Perrier, Diet-Coke, ice-cold beer and, as we reached noon, white-wine spritzers. The TV people did not drink while working, except for Lulu herself, who was running through Dr. Peppers at a great rate, sending her tall glass marked with the red LULU back to the bar for refills. Everybody was hot and thirsty.

The only redeeming social value of the morning was that I got to talk to the other guests during the many groupings and regroupings. In the course of the morning I wound up standing or sitting next to each of them. I learned some things worth passing on to Dirk.

LEONARD MARSDEN: "Yes, I remember you. You're the 'occasional writer.' Millie said you might be pretty good if you worked at it. . . . No, as Millie said, you're not in her book. . . . Yes, the interest in first serial is tremendous. The book clubs, too. And that's without anybody reading it. It's a brilliant book, perhaps her finest. . . . No, I will not show it to the police. They are such bastards."

JILL KLEIN: "I would love to defend this case, whoever did it. Millie was such a total bitch. Whoever did it had a perfect reason to kill her. If they ever catch the killer, I want this case. And if I get it, no jury will convict."

DR. SUNBEAM: "Why didn't you write your piece for the *Globe*?... Oh my dear boy, what a shame! My piece went over very well, I must say. Lots of letters and phone calls already. My publisher is very excited about my writing a book about death, looked at from the positive side. I've already started collecting anecdotes, they're the secret of my books. Please tell me if you think of any good ones. Any recent deaths in your own family?... No, I'm not absolutely set on a title, but how do you like *The Sweet Breath of Death*?"

BETSY POPE: "I don't think I've met you before, but you have an interesting smile.... Oh? You were at the dinner?... Listen, I'm having a barn party tomorrow night. Why don't you come?"

CHICK BIRD: "I like flying back and forth. It gives me time to solve problems away from the office. I get my best ideas for the business while I'm flying.... I'm afraid that old house is hopeless. Too bad ... Sure, I admit it's special, but three architects have failed to solve the problem.... No, I'm going to bulldoze it, I have no choice.... Is that what you call it? A tear-down?... Listen, buster, it's my property, I can do whatever I want."

BEBE CONE: "Oh definitely. This is the best house and land that will come on the market all this year. Of course I never thought it would be available so soon. Poor dear Millie, don't you think?... Yes, I've already talked to her lawyer about representing the property. He says he can't act until her will is made public, but I'm sure I have the inside track.... Yes, I've already promised Lenny Marsden that his work on her papers won't be disturbed. I can show the house without showing the office."

EVERETT MUNK: "I feel damn awkward about this. It's cashing

in on Millie's death, but I couldn't say no to Lulu. I couldn't say no to Bob and Mary Hergesheimer either. They're all old Vineyard friends. . . . Yes, you're probably right. Millie would have enjoyed all the attention. Just the same. . . ."

NANCY MUNK: "Isn't this fun? I've never been on television before. Except just once, when Everett got an honorary degree, but you could just barely see me and I didn't get to say anything."

JIGGS COOLEY: "This is nothing compared to some of what we have to go through for *Jiggtime*. This is practically a breeze — a pretty hot breeze, though. . . . I almost never say no to an appearance like this. My publicist wants me to say yes all the time, and I think he's right. I'm still building my character and my show. I'm going to be bigger than Seinfeld ever was, and when I get there, you won't catch me quitting. . . . No, I have no idea what Millie wrote about me. Lies, I'm sure. My producer and my lawyer say we can always sue her estate for libel. More publicity."

ELENA BRONZE: "I read her book of essays over the weekend. *Hearts and Flowers*. That woman was just as nasty in print as she was in person. . . . Yes, movie stars sometimes read books." (Private, not reported to Dirk: "I'm glad you like the way the slacks fit. They help make me keep my weight steady. If I gain a pound, I can't get into them, and if I lose a pound, they sag around my ass. . . . Why, Jason, what a sweet compliment.")

JANE MILLHOUSE: "Jesus, I'm starving. When is lunch?"

* * *

The diva had asked a good question. We were all hot and tired and ready to take a break from this long boring rehearsal. The TV people at last seemed satisfied with all their arrangements and were themselves ready to stop, rest, eat and drink.

Now I want to be as careful as possible about this sequence. The police went over it again and again with everybody, and I went over it with Dirk. As you might expect, with all the guests and all the television people, considerable disagreement arose about who was where and who did and said what. But I had been making a serious effort all morning to watch and remember. I have a good memory, and this is how I saw it happen.

Jaime Hamlin's catered sandwiches emerged from the house on big oval platters and were placed on one of Millie's wrought iron deck tables. One of the platters was carried by Molly, the first time she had been out on deck this entire morning. We winked and smiled. Two of Jaime's catering people brought out plates, silverware, napkins, mayonnaise, mustard, ketchup. All the TV people, except Lulu and Fritz, had a separate lunch-and-drink area at the far end of the deck. Two of the crew carried out a heavy ice-filled washtub of beer, soft drinks and wine, followed by the crew's separate platters of sandwiches. We guests were moving toward the bar table and the food table for refills and to get our lunch.

As Jaime's sponsor, I had a proprietary interest in this being a successful lunch, so I took a close look at the sandwiches. I knew that Jaime would have covered all the platters to keep them fresh, then uncovered them in the kitchen only when it was time to serve. Each sandwich carried its own little paper flag on a toothpick, announcing what it was. I checked to make sure there was a tuna salad on white for Lulu and a smoked turkey on whole wheat for Jane Millhouse. Yes, there they were, along with pastrami, roast beef and everything else.

So here is the picture. The TV people are down at their end. The guests are milling around the bar and the sandwich table, but no one has yet started to eat. Lulu and Fritz are behind us, discussing some final bit of production business. According to what Fritz said later, they were only deciding what time the

Steadicam operator would begin his work. Since no one else heard that conversation, we have only Fritz's word.

But then I personally heard Lulu say, and I guarantee that this is verbatim, "Okay, fine. That's good. Now where did I leave my Dr. P.?"

How would you like those to be your last words? Not much, I'll bet. But none of us gets a chance to edit our last words.

The glass inscribed with the red LULU rested on a small, square deck table a few feet behind me. About half full, ice cubes still floating. It had been in and out of her hand all morning, and now it went into her hand for the last time.

She took a last huge cold swallow, almost emptying the glass. Within seconds, a look of terrible, terrible surprise. A gasp, hands to throat, eyes bulging. Dr. Pepper hits the spot.

* * *

This time nobody had any difficulty guessing what had happened to Lulu Waring.

This time none of us thought it might be a stroke or a heart attack.

Although it marked the end of Lulu's special, it did not mark the end of the day's excitement. The cops were summoned. During the ensuing interminable period when they were all over us, trying to interview thirty people about what had happened, Jane Millhouse, presumably still starving, ate her smoked turkey sandwich on whole wheat.

Well, she ate part of it.

Halfway through the first half, she shrieked, then gasped, then staggered across the deck toward the railing, clutching her throat. Then, like her Tosca at the Castel Sant' Angelo, her vast black body, shrouded in pale blue silk, toppled over the parapet.

O! What a fall was there, my countrymen! Her huge body

began to roll down and across the lawn in the direction of the beach. For one horrible moment it appeared that she would go right over the edge, all the way down the slope onto the sand. But she fetched up against a lilac bush at the very brink of the slope. The bush trembled under the onslaught, but the roots held. Her body came to a stop.

Bitsy Betsy Pope, whose voice had survived all the other depredations, began to scream — and scream and scream. Still a marvelous voice.

Millie's Will

$\mathcal{D}$IRK WAS RAVING. I had never seen him so angry.

"You missed it," he said. "You missed it twice."

He was so angry he couldn't sit still. He jumped up and started pacing around my living room, banging his right fist into his open left hand. The room is so small that his pacing had very little scope. Only three or four steps before he came to the wall and had to turn back. "I spend twenty-seven years, twenty-seven whole fucking years working in homicide, and I never saw one happen. Not one! Not even an attempt! And today you stand there and watch two of them take place right before your eyes, and you don't see a thing."

"Neither did anybody else."

"Don't make excuses. You blew it."

I knew what really angered him. It was not my failure but the fact that he hadn't been there. "Listen, Dirk, you're lucky you weren't there. You wouldn't have seen it either, and then you'd look like a complete horse's ass. The great detective fails to spot a murder. In fact, the great detective fails to spot two murders."

"Of course I'd have spotted it — them."

"No you wouldn't. Lulu's glass of Dr. Pepper was just standing there for who knows how long. Forever. Everybody walked past it. Everybody had a chance to drop something in. Same with that sandwich. Everybody had a crack at the sandwich platter while the cops were asking questions and taking pictures and all that. Everything was confused. There was time enough to poison half a dozen sandwiches without getting caught."

"I'd have caught whoever it was. Anyway, I sure wouldn't miss it twice."

"You know, Dirk, actually I've witnessed three murders, counting Millie. Maybe that's a record."

"Don't try to be funny about it."

"I don't feel funny about it. I liked Lulu a lot. I was looking forward to being on her show. And I admired Jane Millhouse. I saw her at the Met every chance I got. I listen to her records. She had a great voice."

* * *

The Lulu special was canceled, of course. They never even got to use the Steadicam. I wondered if the producer would still have to pay for it. Even if he didn't, the cost of everything else — the rental of Millie's house, the transportation, the salaries, the hotel rooms, the car rentals, the per diems, even Jaime Hamlin's catered sandwiches — was stupendous. And not one single foot of tape to show for it. Molly Dodge had been in tears, crying about her boss and about the show. She kept saying, "What a waste! What a waste!"

I reminded Dirk that when Millie was killed, the most immediate beneficiary had been Lulu Waring, who had first reported the news to the outside world, a super scoop. And this time the most immediate beneficiary was another television figure, Bob Hergesheimer, who now had the field to himself for his own special. How's that for a motive? And a subsidiary beneficiary, I reminded Dirk, was none other than Hergesheimer's expert homicide consultant, Dirk Schultz, who would now get more air time and therefore a higher fee. Dirk agreed that would be beneficial, one advantage of being retired.

"Another advantage," Dirk said, "is that I won't have to go through all that shit that Mulvey and the state police now have to do. They're going to have to eliminate all the other possibilities."

"Like what?"

"Like, did somebody in the TV crew have a motive to kill Miss Waring? Bound to be somebody who hated her. And after all, every one of them, including your friend Molly, had an opportunity. Got to check it out. Or like, did somebody else, maybe somebody who wasn't even there, have a motive to kill Miss Millhouse? If so, how did the killer slip the poison into the turkey sandwich before the caterer delivered them? Were the sandwiches ever out of the caterers' sight, unattended, before they were brought out on deck? Got to check it out. Or like, were Miss Waring and Miss Millhouse killed by two different people? Or like, did Miss Millhouse kill Miss Waring and then commit suicide? Like, did they both commit suicide? If I was still a detective on the force, I'd have to look into every possibility, just in case."

Betsy Pope came up with still another possibility that Dirk hadn't mentioned. On the radio, and repeated in all the morning papers, she announced that somebody, some mad male chauvinist, was deliberately and systematically killing famous women on the Vineyard. "Like me! Look at the list!" she cried in her radio interview, with an unmistakable note of hysteria. "Mildred Silk, Lulu Waring, Jane Millhouse. All famous. Don't tell me that's coincidence. I could be next! I'm getting out of here. I'm getting way the hell out of here, and I'm not coming back until they catch him."

It was a moment in the spotlight that Bitsy Betsy had not enjoyed in quite some time.

Bob Hergesheimer, who had thought she was going to appear on his special, was mistaken. Without even a phone call of apology Betsy left the Island on the first plane she could catch and fled all the way back to California.

Apparently her theory had validity for at least one of Millie's other guests. Bebe Cone, real estate queen and ardent publicity seeker, canceled her promise to Hergie. "I won't take that chance," she told Mary Hergesheimer. "I can sell houses without the risk of getting killed."

Mary was usually diplomatic, but she thought her husband's special was unraveling. "Even if Betsy Pope is right," she told Bebe angrily, "you'd be perfectly safe since you're not famous."

Bebe was furious and swore never to speak to Mary again, an oath that would surely be rescinded if the Hergesheimers ever decided to sell their house.

Dirk dismissed Betsy's theory. "Miss Waring was killed for one obvious reason, to stop her show."

"Of course."

"Only a layman would say 'Of course.'" Then Dirk had the decency to smile. "Only a layman, or a very experienced detective."

"What about Jane Millhouse?"

"What you should ask is, 'Why Jane Millhouse?'"

"Okay, why Jane Millhouse? What does a very experienced detective say about her?"

"I don't know. But at least I don't have to explore the possibility that she killed Miss Waring and then killed herself. Or the possibility that two different people killed them, with both killers just happening to use cyanide. Or the possibility that these two murders are not connected with Miss Silk's murder. Like Betsy Pope, I don't believe in coincidence. It's obvious. One size fits all. It all comes out of Miss Silk's book."

"You said the night you got here that Millie's murder probably had nothing to do with her book."

Dirk shrugged. "A preliminary hypothesis, based on experience. It's no longer valid."

"I never thought it was."

"Listen, Jason, you have to consider these things while the windows are still wide open. If you close up your mind too fast, you start missing things. Important things that don't fit your theory get lost. I don't really know about Miss Millhouse. But I do know that somehow today grows right out of Miss Silk's book. Somebody is trying very hard to keep that book from being published. If I were Mr. Marsden, I'd sure think about hiring a bodyguard."

"Or better yet, a food-taster. Like those old Roman emperors. 'Hey there, Marcus, check out this smoked turkey sandwich, will you, before I eat my lunch. That's right, take a good bite. Whoops! Hey now, that's a shame, Marcus. Okay, Julius, you're promoted. You're my new taster.'"

"Jason, we have to get hold of that book."

"You want me to steal it from the Okapi Press offices? It's probably locked up."

"It's definitely locked up. Marsden has it in a safe somewhere, maybe even a bank vault. No, what I mean is the Massachusetts D.A. has to get it by court order, if he can. Then you and I will get to see it."

"Why is he going to let us see it?"

"He won't, but there are ways."

*　*　*

Millie's house was once again an official crime scene — locked up tight, yellow crime scene tape, crime scene fingerprinters and photographers, guards on duty so nobody could get in. The

126

TV people had to leave all their equipment in place until the police investigators and lab technicians were finished with it. Both Leonard Marsden and Molly Dodge, the only inhabitants of the house, were forced to move out. Marsden flew back to New York, but Molly had to stay on the Vineyard to oversee the dismantling of Lulu's last show. I could have put her in any of the hotel rooms vacated by the TV crew.

Instead, I took her into my house. I usually don't have two guests at once, so it was a little crowded, but she was crushed about Lulu. I didn't want her to have to be alone.

She stayed in my bed, which comforted both of us.

The day after the double murder, the Last Will and Testament of Mildred Silk was finally made public. It raised as big a fuss as Millie intended.

Millie had had the lifetime use of all the income from husband Harry's mammoth estate. But at Millie's death, all that went into the Harry Harkness Foundation to encourage the propagation and improvement of suburban shopping malls, where he had made his fortune. He had even made provision for the creation of a Harry Harkness Museum at the site of his first mall outside Boston. The homes Millie had lived in, both the New York townhouse and the Vineyard beachfront property, were to be sold for the benefit of the Foundation. I felt sure that Bebe Cone, eager to handle the Vineyard sale, was already on the phone to Millie's lawyer and the Foundation's director, promising great things.

Millie's own estate was not commensurate with her lifestyle. Her personal belongings — the jewelry, the furs, the art, especially the jewelry — were indeed significant but not quite museum quality. The income from her writing had also been significant but not stupendous, even though two of her stories had sold to the movies. What made the tabloid front pages and the lead story in *People* magazine were her "Very Personal Bequests." These were in a different league from her merely "Personal Bequests" to her secretary, to her chef, to her housekeeper and other odds and ends.

The VPBs, as they were instantly known, were divided into two groups. Since Millie's explanatory statements were brief, I quote them in their entirety.

"I hereby bequeath one thousand dollars each to the following people who have given me personal pleasure."

"I hereby bequeath one hundred dollars each to the following people who have attempted to give me personal pleasure."

The first group contained nineteen names. The second group contained twenty-seven names, including a President of the United States. For a total tab against her estate of just over twenty thousand dollars, Millie got a tremendous ride for a relatively modest amount of money. I could imagine her making up the two lists, puffing away on her cigarette, a delicious smile of malice as she wrote down each name. In case anybody was too dumb to understand what she meant, all the names in both groups were male, with the solitary exception of Jane Millhouse, who made the first list.

Millhouse was not the only member of our little murder club to receive a VPB. Everett Munk, confirming my suspicion, was on the thousand-dollar list. So was Leonard Marsden, which seemed only natural, considering that they had worked closely together on eight books and must have had a fair amount of spare time to kill while waiting for galleys. Whether or not Marsden had legitimately earned his spot on the "A" list was, in my opinion, less certain. After all, he was Millie's literary executor. She would not have risked insulting such an important proprietor of her work by putting him on her hundred-dollar "B" list.

But the "B" list is where she put Jiggs Cooley. This surprised me because Cooley was supposed to be gay, even though he had never said so out loud. I wondered if he had actually "attempted to give pleasure" to Millie. Or had she just stuck his name on the list because he was young and famous, thereby "proving" to the world that even at sixty she was still devastatingly attractive? Or, knowing he was gay, was she just making one of her malicious little jokes?

And speaking of young and famous, what about President Kennedy's appearance on the list? Even if Millie had been whisked into the White House or into the Hyannisport compound in the last year of his life, she would have been only twenty-four and the author of only one published book. Would Jack Kennedy have even noticed her? Much less tried — and failed — to give her pleasure? Another of Millie's jokes?

And as long as Kennedy was on her list, why not Bill Clinton? He had spent ample time on the Vineyard in recent years and had twice been Millie's dinner guest. Wouldn't two Presidents on the "B" list be more fun than one? But perhaps she felt that after Monica and Paula, the inclusion of Clinton would be more sordid than amusing.

Millie's biographers would have a lovely time tracking down the forty-six names, trying to prove or disprove the validity of each one. That, too, was probably part of Millie's plan.

Jiggs Cooley was the first to make a large, public, strenuous denial. That night he and his statement were on every TV news show. "I can't understand it," he said. He looked so earnest, so lovable, so *Jiggtime*. "I never had any personal relations with Mildred Silk. Nothing, nothing, absolutely nothing. No kidding, no sex of any kind. I don't understand why she put that nonsense in her will." And then, suddenly smiling, suddenly cheerful, he quoted a familiar tagline from *Jiggtime*. "Listen, man, I never laid a glove on her."

Of course, now that he had denied it, nobody believed him. Even the people who thought he was gay were persuaded that he was guilty as charged.

Lyndon Johnson, while President, once explained to a reporter friend of mine why he would not deny a story the reporter was about to print, even though the story was unfair and inaccurate.

There was this young fellow back in Texas, President Johnson said. He was running for office for the first time. He was a good-looking young fellow, good manners, nice way of talking and all that. But he didn't know the first thing about politics, and he was up against a real popular incumbent. Now this young fellow, he had an old campaign manager who did know politics, and he told him, "Son, you're going to make only one speech in this campaign. Everywhere you go, everybody you talk to, you give them this one speech. You are going to say that your opponent, the incumbent, fucks hogs." Well, the young fellow gets all excited and kind of sweaty behind the ears and he says, "Is that really true?" And the old campaign manager says, "No, son, it isn't. But you just keep on saying it. And if we can get him to deny it just once, you will be elected."

Jiggs Cooley should have handled Millie's bequest the way Everett Munk and Leonard Marsden did. Everett, as usual, didn't answer his phone but left word that he had no comment. Leonard Marsden said, "I am always happy to get a thousand dollars from any source, for any reason."

* * *

A phone call from Jill Klein.

"I want to talk to you," she said, in her crisp, strong courtroom voice.

"Fine," I said. "What about?"

"I'd rather talk in person. How about the Edgartown Yacht Club?"

I have to admit I was impressed by my own significance. How many people get invited to the EYC by a famous defense attorney? "Fine," I said again.

"Free tonight?"

Wow! How many people get a short-notice invitation from a famous defense attorney? "Fine." I was beginning to sound monotonous.

"Would your detective friend be able to come?"

"I don't know, I'd have to ask him."

"Would you? Six-thirty, then, cocktails and dinner. By the way, I'm not a member, so would you make the reservation?"

"You're not a member?"

"Don't worry, I'll pay."

"You can't pay. No cash, no credit cards, no checks, it goes on the member's account."

She sounded exasperated by my failure to understand how the world turns. "I know that. I will reimburse you."

If I was to be the host of record, even though reimbursed, I thought I should assert my privileges. "I want to bring Lulu Waring's executive assistant. Her name is Molly Dodge."

"Yes, yes, I know her." A pause, thinking it over. "All right. Six-thirty. I trust you will be prompt."

Enough of this. "I trust you will be too."

You do not have to own a yacht to belong to the Edgartown Yacht Club. In fact, you don't have to own a sailboat or even a dinghy. The club has six hundred members but fewer than five hundred registered boats — yachts, racing sailboats or whatever. The three ranking officers — the Commodore, the Vice Commodore, the Rear Commodore — are indeed required to own or charter a boat, but not the rest of us. This is lucky for me, since I tend to throw up on any boat smaller or bouncier than the

Vineyard ferry. Since my parents are ardent sailors, I was automatically a family member and then, at age ten, a junior member and finally, at age twenty-five, a full member but, like the Ruler of the Queen's Navee, I never went to sea.

The Club does offer amenities to its landlubbers. The tennis courts are plentiful and excellent, there are dances and regatta parties and other whimsical festivities. But best of all the Club is a good place to eat and a great place to drink. The clubhouse and dining room and bar are smack on the water overlooking Edgartown Harbor. The floor is just a couple of feet above sea level. You can sit there, cocktail in hand, and watch hordes of pretty boats sailing hither and yon. I can watch boats without getting sick.

"Why do I have to wear a tie?" Dirk asked. "This is a vacation resort."

"Because it's the Club rule."

"I don't like dress codes. I gave up uniforms."

"If you don't wear a tie and jacket, they won't let you in. It's your best chance to talk to Jill Klein. Maybe your only chance."

"Fucking rules," Dirk said. He borrowed one of my ties.

Without complaining, Molly obeyed orders and wore a dressy dress, pastel blue with a big stand-up white collar. She looked wonderful, and I told her so.

"I don't feel much like a party," she said. Lulu haunted her.

Parking in downtown Edgartown on a summer evening is impossible. All of us old-timers have special, secret parking places. Mine is a two-car, private-home parking area belonging to a former girlfriend who has only one car. If I call ahead, I can use her other parking space, which is only a five-minute walk from the Club. I have managed to keep on good terms with all my former girlfriends except my former wife. Molly and I walked down the narrow brick Main Street sidewalk, Dirk right behind us. Every time somebody came the other way, we had to go into single file. Dressed up for the Yacht Club, I know I look elitist to the rest of the Main Street pedestrian traffic. They are all in slacks and T-shirts and shorts and halters and sneakers and sandals, dressed for a vacation summer evening.

The stores on this lower end of Main Street leading down to the water are small and ticky-tacky. The population explosion and the lack of parking space have destroyed the street's former charm. A few years ago if you needed to buy a special wedding present or Christmas present or birthday present, you came to an elegant lower Main Street shop called Tashtego, named after the Vineyard harpooner in *Moby-Dick*. It somehow always had just what you wanted. But Tashtego is gone, and in its place is a T-shirt emporium, which also has just what you want, provided you want a souvenir T-shirt with a socko message.

The old shingled clubhouse stands at the very bottom end of Main Street, jutting out into the harbor with water on three sides. I held the swinging gate open for Molly and Dirk. We passed through the entry office where two attractive young girls made sure we belonged there. This is where Dirk and I would have been expelled if we weren't wearing ties. Then on into the big main dining room with its polished wood floor and lofty dark-wood ceiling. Thursday is a buffet night, so the long table of cold food was set up in the middle of the floor, with the hot table and the dessert table off to the side.

At the reception desk I said hello and asked if Miss Klein was here.

"Not yet, Mr. Arnold."

It was six twenty-five, so she wasn't late yet, although I felt sure she would be. It's part of celebrityhood.

The maîtresse d' looked approvingly at Molly and indifferently at Dirk, then studied her big seating chart. "I'll take you to your table."

"I think we'll have drinks outside," I said.

A narrow wooden porch runs across the front of the dining room, just wide enough for a few small tables and chairs that place you right next to the water. This porch area is called "the string piece," although nobody knows why. One spot was still open. We took it and ordered drinks. A pleasant breezy evening with the late sunlight sparkling on the water.

The flagpole with the American flag and the Club flag rises from the string piece. Beside the flagpole, facing out to sea, squats a very small, stubby black cannon.

"What's that for?" Molly asked.

"That's to repel boarders who try to sneak into the Club by sea. Nonmembers, or members who aren't wearing ties."

"It's a sunset gun," Dirk guessed.

"Right. As you'll see, a ceremony goes with it."

We were halfway through our drinks when our waitress came out and said, "A Miss Klein asked me to tell you she's at your table."

We hadn't even said hello and Jill Klein was already trying to run the evening. "Fine," I said. "Would you tell her we're at this table?"

"Oh, she knows that," the waitress said. "I told her."

She was one of the fresh-faced young college girls and boys that the Club hires for the summer. They look snappy and attractive in their white shirts and black skirts and slacks and patterned ties, but they have to endure one major hardship. The Club does not allow tipping. So most of them, girls and boys alike, are first-timers who want to spend a summer on the Vineyard. The service gets better as they learn their jobs, but once they learn, then they are ready to move to a place where tipping happens.

"Miss Klein says it's too windy for her hair." There was a definite smile in the girl's voice, since this breeze was not a wind.

I looked at Molly, whose hair was barely moving in the light air. "Do you find this too windy?"

"It's practically a hurricane."

"So tell Miss Klein —"

But Dirk interrupted. "Listen, Jason, if I'm going to talk to her, let's not start by making her sore."

"You're right." I stood up. "Come on, bring your drinks, let's all be nice to our hostess."

Jill Klein was seated at a square table, three tables away from the Commodore's, which is the big round one in the corner right next to the flagpole. She had taken the chair with the best view of the harbor. Maybe she thought she deserved it because she was buying the dinner. Maybe she just thought she deserved it. Her straight black hair, pulled back severely and tightly pinned, would have stayed in place in anything less than a Force 7 gale. She wore a navy blazer with a small gold pin. No earrings. No makeup except pale lipstick. A plain white shawl hung over the back of her chair. The glass of white wine in front of her was untouched.

Every time I saw her I thought how much nicer she could look if she wanted to. With her good bones and black hair and snapping dark eyes, she could have looked quite marvelous in spite of her too-strong nose, a defect she could certainly have afforded to soften with minor surgery. But looking marvelous would have interfered with her professional stance: Jill Klein for the defense, don't fuck with me.

I introduced Lieutenant Dirk Schultz, retired. She already knew Molly from the show. Dirk and I sat down on either side of her, with Molly across.

Jill Klein was abrupt, no preliminary chit-chat. "I want to defend this case, no matter who it is." She looked straight at me. "That includes you," she said. "although I doubt that you are responsible."

My feelings were hurt. Even the police had not yet concluded that I was innocent. "Why not?"

135

"You're not in the book."

"You've read the book?" Dirk asked.

Before she could answer, from the Commodore's table came a clear call in a strong male voice. "Attention to colors!"

Chairs scraped back from tables throughout the dining room as we all got to our feet for the sunset ceremony. Molly and Dirk, not knowing what this was about, hesitated. Then they played it safe and stood up with the rest of us, the way people do in church when they aren't sure what's coming next but rise when the congregation rises.

After a few seconds of complete silence the sunset cannon went off with a loud enough bang to make Molly jump. Then we all remained silent and standing as two Club employees hauled down the American flag, gathered it and folded it.

The Commodore's voice called, "As you were." We all sat down.

On evenings when the Commodore is not at his table, the Vice or the Rear calls out the orders. When none of them is present, some former Commodore leaps into the breach, showing that he has not lost his touch, even though he is no longer in office. It is not a heavy burden, but much cherished.

"That's kind of nice," Molly said. "Do they do it every evening?"

"Every evening except Sunday."

"Quaint," Jill Klein said.

"So have you read the book?" Dirk repeated.

"No, not yet."

He jabbed a thumb in my direction. "Then how do you know he's not in it?"

Her cold courtroom look. "Mr. Schultz," she said in an icy, superior voice, "I was present at the dinner when Mildred Silk said that he was not in her book. I am a reliable witness. You weren't even there."

Dirk's look was as cold and tough as hers. "It's Lieutenant Schultz," he said in a blunt voice.

"Oh? I understood you were retired."

"So are Schwartzkopf and Colin Powell. They are still addressed as general."

Her laugh was scornful, humorless. "You put yourself in very lofty company — Lieutenant."

Ignoring the scorn, Dirk nodded shortly. "Good. That's settled. Why did you ask Mr. Arnold to bring me along tonight? In fact, why did you want to see Mr. Arnold?"

"Does anybody want to go to the buffet?" I asked. "Molly?"

Nobody showed any sign of moving. Molly didn't answer. She and Dirk were both looking at Jill Klein, waiting for her answer, so I supposed I should stick around and look interested too.

"He knows more of those guests at the murder dinner than I do. I hope he will mention my interest in defending the case whenever he talks to any of them. He talks a lot, so he might be helpful. As for you" — a deliberate pause before she said the word — "Lieutenant, I know you have been investigating these murders. Unofficially, of course, since you are no longer on the force. Supposedly investigating on behalf of Mr. Arnold, although I find that hard to believe. I thought you might have learned something. I thought you might have something you could tell me."

"Why?" Dirk asked. "Are you getting scared?"

"Certainly not," she snapped. "Don't be ridiculous."

Too quick and too strenuous a reaction. Maybe she really was scared. Maybe she shared Betsy Pope's theory about famous women being killed one after another. If so, she could be next in line.

"A lot of other people are nervous," Dirk said. "Two women have changed their minds about being on the Hergesheimer show."

"Both are twits."

"Are you going to be on it? Plenty of room for you. I can even arrange it."

"I make my own arrangements, thank you. Do you or don't you have anything to tell me about the investigation?"

Yes, she was definitely nervous.

"I can't report anything to you," Dirk said, "since I'm not working for you."

The animosity between them, once started, continued to grow.

"That means you don't know anything."

"I'm working on it," Dirk said coldly. "Incidentally, I wonder if you want to guess what Miss Silk says about you in her book."

"I have no idea."

"Maybe about jury tampering? In the Lyman case?"

She didn't answer immediately, but I could see no change in her expression. Then she said, "That is very close to slander."

"No it isn't," Dirk said cheerfully. He finished his drink and waggled his glass at me to indicate that I should do something about it. "It was all over the press at the time, so it's already completely public. And I didn't accuse you of jury tampering. I just asked if you thought that might be in Miss Silk's book. And I have witnesses about what I said." He waved at me and Molly. "Two more than you have." He smiled at her. "So what do you think, counselor? Is that what's in the book?"

Very likely, since it was right up Millie's alley. Hector Lyman had murdered his parents, then stabbed both his father and mother in the genitals, and ended by cutting off his father's penis. He was a nasty looking fellow, twice charged with attempted rape but not convicted. He was his parents' sole heir. Three psychiatrists found that he was sane and that he knew what he was doing. Although he had planned the crime three days ahead, including the purchase of a fourteen-inch Bowie knife, Jill Klein got him off with a hung jury. The jury voted eleven-to-one for conviction. The twelfth juror, a woman, thought Lyman was probably a victim of child abuse. She said that she herself had been a victim of child abuse and could recognize the signs. Most people thought she was a victim of money, but nothing was ever proved.

I had to give Jill Klein credit. There wasn't the slightest twitch in her expression. She studied Dirk for perhaps fifteen seconds. I would not want to be under such scrutiny.

Then she turned to me. "Send me the bill," she said. She stood up, took the white shawl from the back of her chair and left us. Long hard strides, out of the dining room, out of the Club.

In silence we watched her go. Then I said, "Gee, Dirk, I'm glad I didn't make her sore. That gave you a chance to talk to her."

"What a bitch," Molly said. "And if she defends Mildred Silk's killer, she'll be defending Lulu's killer."

"Not proved," Dirk said. "How about a round of drinks?"

I found our waitress. Since she was still learning her job, I reminded her which was our table, what we were drinking and what my name was so that she could charge it to my account, then led Molly and Dirk to the buffet.

The long cold-table down the center of the room is loaded with salads and rolls and sliced tomatoes and cheeses and cold pastas, but I advised Molly and Dirk to concentrate on two items. At one end of the table is a monster platter of filleted poached salmon, a great pink slab. It is popular and goes fast, but as soon as it's near the end, a fresh slab arrives from the kitchen. On a busy buffet night the membership will go through six slabs. There is a mayonnaise sauce and a pale green remoulade sauce. The other super item is the iced bowl of giant shrimp, tail shells still attached, with a spicy red seafood sauce in a nearby saucer.

Also popular, also goes fast, also immediately replenished with another bowl. My first course always consists of a generous slice of salmon with the green sauce, along with all the shrimp I can then crowd on the small round white plate. After all these years, as I pile on the shrimp, I still have to remind myself: Don't be vulgar, Jason. You can always come back for seconds.

Dirk said he didn't like cold fish. Molly said she was allergic to shrimp. I left them to explore all the other dishes that run down both sides of the long table and moved straight to the shrimp bowl.

It was suddenly an enchanted evening. There, across a crowded bowl of shrimp, my eyes met those of Elena Bronze. Mutual surprise. Mutual pleasure, mutual smiles. I try hard not to be dazzled by women, because it puts you at such a disadvantage, but I was dazzled. She wore black trousers with a lime-green sheath top, long-sleeved, not too snug for propriety but snug enough so that you could identify the fabled bronzinis if you knew where to look for them. A black pearl bracelet stood out against the lime green cloth. Her short gray-blond hair looked as though it had just been tousled — or was just about to be tousled — by a loving male hand. I kept both hands on my plate.

She was far quicker than I. "Jason!" she said. "I thought of you just now when the sunset gun went off."

Even as a joke, this was so flattering that I didn't know what to say. Normally I can think of something light and sexy, but I just kept on smiling and admiring.

"Well," Elena said, enjoying my confusion, "shall I make conversation? The Club is full of murder suspects tonight. Chick Bird is a guest of the Commodore. And I just saw that Klein woman leaving."

That unlocked my tongue. "I know. The table she just left

was mine." I explained that my detective friend Dirk Schultz had managed to upset her and drive her away.

"I'm impressed. I don't think she upsets easily."

We moved away from the shrimp bowl because other shrimp fiends were stacking up behind us.

"Would you like to take her place at our table?"

"That's sweet, Jason, but I'm a hostess myself tonight."

"More houseguests?"

"I'm afraid so. Four of them, New Yorkers this time. They're better than Californians." She gave me a friendly but quite specific smile. Her blue-gray eyes were smiling too. "They leave Sunday afternoon."

Molly was leaving for New York on Monday morning. "Are you busy Monday evening?"

Dirk appeared beside us, carrying his full plate of this and that. "Miss Bronze? I'm a detective, working for Mr. Arnold. Could I ask you some questions?"

"Here?" She was incredulous. "Now?" Elena turned to me. "Is this a joke?"

"I'm afraid not." I was annoyed at Dirk. "I'm really sorry, I didn't know he was going to ask you anything."

Elena told Dirk, "I've already talked to all the detectives I care to. I have to get back to my guests. Excuse me."

She stalked off without saying yes or no about Monday night, but Dirk had not improved my prospects.

"You didn't stick up for me," Dirk said.

"You didn't deserve it. That wasn't nice."

"Do you want me to solve this or don't you?"

"Why don't you go badger Chick Bird? He deserves to be badgered. He's going to tear down that great old Waverly house I showed you."

"Where is he?"

"At the Commodore's table, so you can't do it now."

When Dirk and I returned to our table, Molly was already seated. Our drinks were on the table, so our waitress was learning. Molly had been subdued most of the evening but not now.

I was dipping my first shrimp in red sauce when she said, "I have never in my life, never in my whole life, seen a grown man make such googly eyes at an aging movie star."

I could tell by the way she said it that she had thought up the sentence ahead of time, even polished it while she was waiting for me. I smiled at her. "That's the first time in my whole life that I've heard anybody use the word googly."

"Lulu used it all the time. She used it to describe the way you were looking." She let her jaw drop open and sideways in an idiotic expression. I hoped I hadn't looked like that to Elena.

"I can't help it if I'm a fan. Besides, she's not that old."

"Ha! Lulu used to call her 'Ole Miss Tits.'"

I couldn't help laughing. "I can't wait to tell Elena."

"You wouldn't dare."

"I promise. Next time I see her."

"When's that?"

Sometimes you can tell the truth straight out because you know it's the one thing that won't be believed. "As soon as you go back to New York."

"I'm going back too," Dirk said. "You're right, these are good shrimp."

"What you should have next is the clam chowder. It's too thick, too much flour, but it's great for flavor. Why are you going back? Are you sore about having to wear a tie?"

"Very funny."

"Are you giving up?"

"No, I'm going back to New York to find out some things. Like, why is Miss Millhouse on Miss Silk's thousand-dollar list? And like, did that have anything to do with why she was killed?"

"Do you think it did?"

He shook his head. "I don't know." He stood up. "I'm also going back to New York because that's where the book is. Come on, Molly, let's try the clam chowder."

Hot Property

ARMED WITH a stopwatch and a pad and pencil, Dirk sat on the end of my couch nearest the TV set. Along with the rest of the performers on Bob Hergesheimer's Vineyard special, he had been invited to watch the show in Hergie's big basement screening room. But since he was nervous about his first TV appearance, we watched in my living room.

At first, just Dirk and I. Molly said she couldn't bear to watch it because of Lulu, but Hergie was only thirty seconds into his introduction when she emerged from the bedroom and joined us on the couch.

Offstage, Hergie is demanding, competitive, energetic. His determination — on the golf course, tennis court, croquet field, backgammon table — can wear you out. And he talks a lot, rapid fire. But aim a camera at him and he turns wise, thoughtful, reassuring.

White-haired, with craggy lines in his rugged anchorman's face, he looked right into our eyes as he said, "Welcome to this ABC special presentation on Martha's Vineyard. I'm Bob Hergesheimer. We call our story 'Island in the Spotlight.'"

After explaining why the Vineyard was in the spotlight — the three recent murders, the celebrity invasion, the Presidential vacations, the tourist explosion, the skyrocketing property prices — Hergie told us what we were going to see and whom we were going to meet during the next hour. Fourth on his list of notables came "Our expert on murder, the distinguished New York City homicide detective Dirk Schultz."

I said "Yay!" and clapped. The camera gave us a close-up of Dirk, looking serious but not particularly distinguished. Dirk clicked his stopwatch, then clicked it again when his image disappeared.

"You shouldn't lick your lips," Molly said.

Dirk ignored her. "Only seven seconds," he said. He wrote the figure on his pad. "Can't get rich that way." His contract with Hergie specified that he would get a bonus payment for time on camera and a smaller bonus for voice-over time. Since he didn't trust ABC to do a fair accounting, he was clocking it himself.

Hergie wound up his introduction. "One further disclosure seems in order. I myself am a Vineyard homeowner and have been coming here for almost twenty years, a long time before the First Family and all the other recent arrivals. I trust that the advantages of personal knowledge and experience will compensate for any loss in journalistic objectivity."

"Too solemn," Molly said. "Too self-important. Lulu would have made a joke out of it."

I patted her nice leg, then squeezed it.

The show was a mishmash, nowhere near what Lulu would have done. In fairness, Hergie suffered handicaps. Unlike Lulu, he had not been right there in the room, an eyewitness to Millie's murder. Unlike Lulu, he did not have the use of Millie's house, which both the police and Millie's lawyer had placed off limits, even to Leonard Marsden, after the second murders. Hergie could show only the exterior of the house, along with archival still pictures from the past, including the two nights the Clintons had come to dinner. Most damaging of all, Hergie had nowhere near Lulu's collection of dinner guests from the fatal night. Many turndowns. Perhaps influenced by Bitsy Betsy's theory, not a single woman dared to appear. Too scared. Not many men, either. Maybe they had already endured too much hassle. Maybe both women and men were too busy being famous to give any more of their precious personal time to this subject. But maybe they just didn't want to run the risk of being murdered during the taping, like Lulu and Jane Millhouse.

Because Hergie got only a handful of interviews, he again had to resort to historical footage — a clip from an Elena Bronze movie, a clip from Jiggs Cooley's sitcom, a clip of Jane Millhouse singing the mad scene from *Lucia*, and a heart-breaking clip of the young and lovely Betsy Pope singing and dancing "They Can't Take That Away From Me." When Elena came on, Molly said, "There's Jason's drool." When Hergie showed a snippet of Lulu smiling and joking, she sniffled.

There was excessive footage on the First Family's vacation visits. Here we see the President playing golf. Here we see the President eating an ice cream cone. Here we see the First Lady smiling, smiling, smiling with counterfeit joy.

Given the limitations, I expected Hergie to make much more use of Dirk. So did Dirk, who had spent two long days being interviewed on camera and then a shorter follow-up session to flesh out some points. But because of all the limitations they had to face on the murders, Hergie and ABC were more interested in the Vineyard as "the new Hamptons" and in the celebrity phenomenon. Dirk gave his theory about the murderer's daring character and explained how easy it was to get hold of cyanide. He got to explain, briefly, how anybody at Millie's dinner could have poisoned her Chartreuse. But he had not been present for any of the three murders, and he was not part of the official police investigation. He was also a bit stiff. Not much stopwatch activity.

Instead Hergie gave us a celebrity tour of the Vineyard, not just the guests at Millie's dinner but all the other famous and infamous folks that we have been saddled with. He showed us their faces and their houses. The Island house tour showed all the celebrity palaces and told approximately what each one cost. At the end of this segment Hergie paid special loving attention to the old Waverly place, "the House of Eight Gables" that Chick Bird had bought and was about to tear down. "On the Vineyard," Hergie said, with a carefully straight face, "this is called modernization." The word "alas" was implied, not spoken.

During the commercial break Molly said, "The lawyers must have had fun with that part. Telling him how much he could and couldn't say. They probably even told him what tone of voice and what expression. I bet he'd like to kill that Chick Bird."

"Who wouldn't?" I agreed.

I fixed drinks. Dirk was glum. Molly was pleased that Hergie's special wasn't as good as Lulu's would have been.

The final segment was better. Because he and Hergie were longtime friends and fellow Vineyarders, Everett Munk had agreed to talk about Millie and her work, but he had imposed one condition. He must not be asked about Millie's Very Personal Bequests, where he was on the thousand-dollar "A" list. Furthermore, said Everett, Hergie must not talk about the bequests anywhere else in the show. That meant Hergie couldn't even use Jiggs Cooley's public denial of sexual relations with Millie. It must have been a tough choice: either no mention of the juicy VPBs or no Everett Munk. I thought Hergie made the right choice. Everett's stature and authority and his intelligent appreciation of Millie's writing gave the special some badly needed personal heft. Unfortunately neither he nor Hergie had

147

read Millie's final book, *Celebrity Watch*. A gaping hole. And the only person who had read it, Leonard Marsden, appeared just long enough, seated at his office desk in New York, to explain that he could not discuss it because Okapi Press was defending the book against "the prying eyes of the police." Another gaping hole — actually the same one.

The nice surprise was Dr. Sunbeam. I had never heard him give one of his famous "chats," either on TV or in a lecture hall, but I knew he was a popular speaker. Molly said afterward that Hergie had given him more than two minutes without interruption, a long stretch of straight monologue.

They taped him at his Life Center, the tax-free, domed pink palace he had built on Sengekentocket Pond. For a few seconds he was shown roaming along his bluestone walks and gazing out from his parapet overlooking Sengekentocket, while Hergie explained who he was. As if everybody didn't already know. Then, cheerful and cherubic, with his plump pink hands folded in front of him, Sunny settled down in his white leather office chair to talk.

"I came here for the same reason the Methodists did a century and a half ago, when they started their famous summer camp meetings. Back in 1835 the Methodists thought this was a beautiful place, suitable for worship and contemplation and personal commitment. It still is. I began life as a minister, you know, so I was drawn to a place that offered those opportunities." He leaned forward with a merry smile. "Of course many of our celebrities, such as those at Mildred Silk's unfortunate dinner party, have been drawn here for other reasons. One reason, to be sure, is the chance to spend money in a profligate and ostentatious way — the trophy house. Another is the chance to be with people who have similar tastes, similar notoriety and" — a little wave of one hand — "similar quantities of money.

Kindred spirits, you know. Oh yes, I'm afraid I'm a kind of celebrity myself, thanks to my books. And yes, I did spend a good bit of money on this Life Center, but I remind you that it is a Foundation, not a commercial enterprise. Its purpose is not ostentation but the treatment of my lovely clients in an attractive setting. I have always believed that an attractive setting is an open window that beckons the soul and the spirit."

Sincere! He sounded sincere!

"I'm sure I will be in Mildred Silk's book, and I'm sure she found something unfavorable to say about me. That never bothers me. The world is large enough to support many views and opinions. She was a brilliant writer, although — how shall I put it? — rather negative in her view of the world and the people in it. She, in turn, will be in my next book. I'm writing a book about death" — he smiled into the camera — "from a positive point of view."

After Hergie's wrap-up, Dirk looked at his pad. "Shit," he said. "Eight hundred and twenty dollars."

"Maybe you should let ABC's accounting department figure it out," Molly said. "They're not used to such small numbers. Maybe they'll make a mistake."

Next morning they would both be leaving for New York. Molly had finished cleaning up the debris of Lulu's special and was ready to see what her job possibilities were at CBS or elsewhere. She and I stayed up late in bed saying an affectionate goodbye, until finally Dirk yelled at us to shut up and go to sleep.

After they had gone, Molly by plane, Dirk by car, it felt lonely without them. So I called Elena. I got the butler and gave him my name. I held the phone for a while. Then I held it some more. The butler came back to say that Miss Bronze was "unavailable," but he would tell her I had called.

God damn Dirk, I thought. He should never have confronted Elena at the Yacht Club to ask questions. Obviously she blamed that on me. I guessed I would not get a chance to tell her that Lulu called her "Ole Miss Tits." And I guessed I was not going to get a chance for anything else.

I got out one of the two novels I was working on, the one set in New York, and wrote a few pages. I find it easier to write about a place when I'm away from it, so when I'm on the Vineyard I work on the New York novel, and when I'm in New York I work on the Vineyard novel. A toss-up which one I will finish first, if either.

Armed with the virtue of gainful labor, I climbed up the driveway to pay homage to my parents in the big house on the bluff. If Diane had been there with all her well-behaved children, I might not have gone. Even so, it was not a successful visit. It never is. After parrying a dozen or so of my father's thrusts, I kissed my mother's not-very-welcoming cheek and said goodbye. How sharper than a serpent's tooth, etc.

I spent one more day on the Vineyard before deciding I had important things to do in New York. The police had ordered all of us to notify them of any change in our whereabouts. But when I told Sergeant Kenny Waters of the state police that I was going to New York and could be reached at the following phone number and address, he did not seem very interested. I got the feeling I was not a leading suspect. Perhaps I never had been. I asked him if there was anything new on the case. He said not much. They had all been terribly busy preparing the necessary court papers to get hold of Millie's manuscript.

* * *

Dirk explained to me how the system works. It sounded cumbersome, but then I have never been part of the law enforcement process. Dirk says everything about law enforcement is cumbersome.

Even in a homicide, even in a triple homicide like ours, Massachusetts has no jurisdiction in New York. As publisher, Leonard Marsden and Okapi Press owned Millie's manuscript, and Marsden was not only her publisher but her literary executor as well. Once he had decided not to show the book to Captain Mulvey's team, he had made sure there were no copies of the manuscript in Millie's house to be seized on Massachusetts soil. Neither the Massachusetts police nor the Massachusetts district attorney could seize any evidence in New York State. Only New York could do that. Millie's longtime secretary, Miss Quinn, might have been persuaded to turn over any early copies of what she had typed. Mulvey's team had made the effort. But Miss Quinn had been a good scout, followed orders, kept no copies and sent everything back to Millie. And like many first-class typists, she explained that she never paid the slightest attention to the content of what she was typing. Just bang out the words, it went faster that way. She couldn't remember anything that was useful to the police.

So Captain Mulvey and his crew helped the Massachusetts D.A. prepare an "affadavit of facts" to establish the importance of Millie's manuscript to their homicide investigation. They set forth who was present at Millie's dinner, what Millie and Marsden had said that evening about the contents of her forthcoming book, and how and when the murder took place. Then they produced a similar affidavit of facts concerning the murders of Lulu Waring and Jane Millhouse, along with the attendant circumstances, including even the Dr. Pepper and the smoked turkey sandwich. The affidavit could not state what vital information Millie's manuscript contained since neither the police nor the D.A.'s office had read a word of it. They could only make the case that the manuscript was presumptively crucial to the investigation and should therefore be made available. This lengthy document, almost as rich in speculation as in fact, was forwarded to the office of the New York D.A. for action. According to Dirk, the New York D.A. wouldn't much care what the document said. He would just take it to court and ask for the search warrant.

"We always cooperate," Dirk said, "even when we think the other guy doesn't know what he's doing. After all, it's us against the bad guys."

By the time I got to New York and phoned Dirk, the court had granted the requested search warrant to pick up Millie's manuscript at the Okapi offices. But even then the law required that the New York police, not the Massachusetts police, must execute the warrant and take physical possession. Dirk asked the lieutenant, an old friend from homicide days, if he could come along since he was involved in the case. The lieutenant, who had seen Dirk on television, said sure, why not.

I asked Dirk, "Can I come too? I'm involved."

"Certainly not. You're a civilian."

"So are you."

"Once you've been a cop, you're never a civilian."

"Besides, I've never seen anybody execute a search warrant. Do they really search the place? Look in closets, open all the drawers? Pry up the floorboards?"

"No, they just show Marsden the warrant and tell him to hand over the goods."

"Do they do it at gunpoint?"

"Jason, you're a fucking romantic. No, not at gunpoint."

"Suppose Marsden says no."

"He can't, it's a court order. He'd be in contempt."

"I'd still like to come."

"I'll tell you all about it," Dirk promised.

* * *

Dirk lives on a shady street in Queens in rented rooms. He says nobody on a retired detective's pay can afford to live in Manhattan. Since I can afford to live in Manhattan, I do, but way over between First and Second Avenues in the East Eighties. Pleasant but not gaudy, with no serious view from any of my five windows. Nobody who lives in Manhattan goes to Queens except to get to an airport, so Dirk and I usually meet somewhere in midtown.

When I am just back from the Vineyard, the food I crave most is Chinese, so I offered to buy him dinner at Shun Lee Palace.

"You didn't mention drinks."

"Now that you're a bigtime consultant, you can buy your own."

"No drinkee, no talkee."

So I agreed to throw in the drinks. Over his Scotch and my vodka and a bowl of crisp fried noodles with a fiery mustard dip, we decided that we would have deep-fried shrimp balls, spicy scallops with toasted bean curd and Singapore rice noodles with extra curry. Then he told me about the search warrant fiasco.

Like many book publishers in the last decade, Okapi Press had moved to lower Manhattan, both to get more space and to escape from the high rents in skyscraper midtown. On the sidewalk in front of the converted loft building on West 19th Street, Dirk met his old friend Lieutenant Huggins and a hefty young black officer named Cooper. Cooper looked like the kind of officer who could tear the manuscript out of Marsden's hands if that should be necessary. Both Huggins and Cooper were in uniform, and Dirk was in jacket and tie for this official occasion.

A kind of ordinary shabby old building, Dirk said. Grimy gray blocks of stone that might have been white fifty years ago, or maybe seventy-five. He sounded so disapproving that I reminded him that Okapi was not only a respected publisher but one of the few not owned by the Germans. Under those circumstances the building couldn't be expected to look snappy.

Nobody on duty in the small lobby, which was little more

than an elevator well. One of those black boards with white letters told them that Marsden was on the third floor. They rode up in an elevator that was slow and creaky in spite of being converted to pushbutton automation. They emerged in front of a glass door that said "Okapi Editorial Offices — Ring and Enter," just like a doctor or dentist office.

"Real high-tech security," Cooper said.

Lieutenant Huggins rang and they entered.

A tan linoleum floor, not recently waxed. Rows of head-level-high cubicles were occupied by solitary, serious men and women who did not bother to look up as they walked past. Most of them wore glasses and were surrounded by piles of books and manuscripts. A hushed atmosphere, not a fun place to work, Dirk decided. Marsden's office, at the far end of cubicle row, was guarded by a surprisingly cheerful young secretary, out of place in this solemn setting.

Lieutenant Huggins reached for his wallet to show his credentials, but the secretary said, "Oh, you're the police. Mr. Marsden's expecting you, go right in. Would you like coffee?"

A surprising offer, Dirk thought, but I explained that coffee is the lifeblood of both publishing and writing. Most people in the profession can't talk or think without coffee. Huggins declined and they walked in.

A big office, the size of three or four cubicles put together. The floor-to-ceiling shelves were filled with books, all neatly lined up. Dirk wondered if they could all have been published by Okapi. I thought probably. Okapi was not a publishing giant, but it had been around a long time. Also book publishing is competitive and self-centered. Marsden might have a couple of reference books by other publishers on his shelves, but everything else would be Okapi.

Two men were waiting for them. In a swivel chair behind the

battered wooden desk, surely an antique, sat Leonard Marsden. With his big mustache and grizzled hair he managed to look tweedy and shaggy in spite of a dark blue jacket. Right next to him at the corner of the desk was an extremely dapper gentleman with a bow tie who, Dirk said, had lawyer written all over him. And not a mere house lawyer but somebody more substantial.

Both men stood up.

"Mr. Marsden," Huggins said, presenting the warrant across the desk, "as you know, we're here to —"

Marsden held up his big hand, palm outward, fingers spread wide. "Gentlemen, this is my lawyer, Mr. Astrachan. He has information that makes your warrant invalid."

The lawyer in turn picked up a single sheet from Marsden's desk. "Okapi has filed an appeal against the judgment. Here is the court notice. It suspends your warrant until our appeal is heard." He held out the sheet to Huggins.

Dirk had promised Huggins to keep quiet, but lifetime habit overtook him. "On what grounds?" he asked.

"It's there in the notice. The threat of severe financial damage."

Marsden recognized Dirk. "You're that retired detective, the one on television. What are you doing here?"

Having no plausible explanation, Dirk stared back at him.

Huggins said smoothly, "I asked him to join me because he's familiar with the case. I'm not."

That encouraged Dirk. "You're trying to protect first serial rights?" he asked Marsden.

Marsden opened his mouth to answer, but Astrachan cut in. "We will discuss that in court — with your D.A. Good day, gentlemen."

On their way out the secretary asked if they were sure they wouldn't like some coffee.

* * *

The fact that I was a civilian did not keep me out of the court-room for Marsden's appeal. The press was there in some quantity, not only the tabloid reporters who were covering the appeal as a news story, hoping for yet another Millie Silk sensation, but also representatives of the magazines that were vying for first serial rights to her book. Dirk and I sat next to each other on one of the back benches. He had heard that Okapi was bringing in expert witnesses, both literary agents and magazine editors, to support the appeal.

The courtroom was quite full when Appellate Judge Charles Whipple opened the proceedings. Astrachan and Marsden sat alone at the plaintiff's table, Astrachan dapper in bow tie and dark gray pinstripes, Marsden shaggy in a shapeless suit of nondescript brown. The D.A.'s office had four lawyers at the other table, including one black and one woman, a politically correct quartet.

Tall and lean, Judge Whipple wore horn-rimmed reading glasses way down on the tip of his nose. Instead of peering over his glasses when he looked out at lawyers or witnesses, he pushed them up to the top of his bald head. He began by asking Astrachan why Okapi had not lodged this protest at the original hearing.

The way Astrachan rose to his feet convinced me that he knew what he was doing. Graceful, not too fast, relaxed, confident. "Your Honor," he said, "we thought the issues involved were too important and complex to be resolved at the level of a routine hearing. We sought a ruling at this level." What he was carefully not saying was that the first judge was by-the-book and rubber-stamp, while Judge Whipple was known to be open to interesting argument. He was also known to be informal and outspoken.

"I happen to agree with you," he told Astrachan. "All right, counselor, get on with it."

Astrachan got on with it. Mildred Silk's last book, partly because of the circumstances of her violent death, had attracted enormous interest for prepublication serialization. Serialization in a major magazine, followed by newspaper, radio and television commentary on the disclosures, provided massive advance publicity for the book itself. A substantial sum of money was at stake — very substantial. Okapi, a relatively small independent publisher in a competitive market dominated by conglomerates, could not afford to forgo such revenues.

"Nobody's asking you to forgo anything," Judge Whipple said. "The Commonwealth of Massachusetts just wants to read the book for evidence."

Astrachan smiled at the judge. "Ah, Your Honor, you have put your finger on it. Once the district attorney has our book, the whole Commonwealth of Massachusetts will read it."

Judge Whipple smiled back. "Counselor, I believe you exaggerate."

"Only slightly, sir. May I try to convince you?"

Whipple nodded. "By all means," he said, "but not endlessly."

"Of course not. Although if Your Honor has never been in the magazine business, I think the evidence will be both entertaining and surprising."

"I have never been in the magazine business. Go ahead and surprise me."

Astrachan called two literary agents and two magazine editors. One after the other, telling different war stories, they said the same thing. In first serial publication, exclusivity — total, complete, protected exclusivity — was more important than anything else, certainly much more important than the illusive quality of mere literary excellence. Once a magazine bought exclusive prepublication rights to a hot property, it would go to great lengths to guard that exclusivity until the issue was actually on the newsstands. Conversely, a magazine that had lost out in a bidding war for a hot property would go to great lengths to undercut the winner's exclusivity.

An editor named Stokes told how only three people in his entire organization were allowed to read any part of one hot property he had bought. The three were himself, the trusted editor assigned to excerpt it, and a copy typist who had been with the magazine eighteen years. Every piece of paper and every computer disc related to the project was locked in a safe every night. When the articles were ready for the printer, the trusted editor carried them personally and then stood guard over the printing process. "We were all familiar," Editor Stokes said, "with the famous instance when a magazine bribed a printer to furnish an advance copy of a rival's exclusive story and thus was able to publish what the rival's exclusive story was going to say." When Astrachan asked how that could be done legally, since the rival had bought exclusive rights, Stokes explained, "Oh, that part was easy. You can't quote directly, except for maybe a sentence or two, but you can print the gist of what the other guy is going to run." He did not mention, and the D.A.'s team did not know enough to point out, that the successful briber had been Stokes's own magazine.

A literary agent named Cadwallader testified about the precautions he had taken to protect a hot property. The three magazines who were considered serious bidders were required to sign, in advance, a notarized confidentiality agreement promising not to reveal any of the contents of the manuscript they were about to read. Cadwallader knew it would be difficult to recover damages if they broke their oaths, but at least he could make it extremely embarrassing for them if they did so. The manuscript then had to be read in the agent's office in the presence of the agent himself. No one was allowed to take any notes.

Another literary agent named Smythe testified that when *Time* and *Newsweek* were in combat to win the memoirs of a superstar government official, he did not want to risk letting either magazine read the manuscript in advance. Since all government is a sieve, he feared that the loser, having identified the most headline-worthy parts, would find some roundabout way of getting the same information through other Washington sources and proceed to publish it. At the same time, for business reasons, Smythe felt he had to treat the two newsweeklies equally, since both were important customers. His solution was to invent, in his own mind, an outrageous asking price, then tack on another hundred thousand dollars. He then got the two top editors on line for a conference call and told them his price. "I realize you have to consult your publishers. The first one to call back gets the book." The *Time* managing editor asked a reasonable question. "Don't we get to read anything?" No, Smythe said, you don't. In twelve minutes the *Time* editor called back.

Astrachan's final witness was a magazine editor who had signed a contract with a book publisher to buy first serial rights to a hot property. But before he could publish his excerpts, another magazine and a newspaper got hold of advance copies of the book and published lengthy stories revealing much of the contents. The magazine editor went to court, charged the book publisher with reckless failure to safeguard the magazine's exclusivity and won a decision that the magazine did not have to pay.

"Well, counselor," Judge Whipple said when Astrachan had finished, "you have confirmed my conviction that the more one learns about any profession, the worse it looks. I would like to ask a few questions" — he pulled his glasses down to reading level and looked at his papers — "of Mr. Marsden." He pushed his glasses back to the top of his head.

Astrachan nudged Marsden, who put his hands on the plaintiff's table and pushed himself to his feet.

He stood there, a tough old coot, not intimidated by his surroundings or by the judge. Book publishing is a quiet business, perhaps sedate is not too mild a word, but Marsden had been around a long time and had fought his share of publishing wars. As he liked to boast, he had been trained in a real war. True, he had only been a young army quartermaster in World War II, but he had been stationed in London during the bombing. A ceiling had once fallen on him, and an office building he had been visiting was demolished by a V-2 rocket five minutes after he left. If you've been through that, he liked to say, you don't scare easily.

Facing the judge, he certainly did not look scared.

"Mr. Marsden, what precautions have you taken to protect this manuscript? How many people in your office have read it?"

"I'm the only one who has read it."

"Not even Mr. Astrachan?"

"No, sir. Mildred Silk's murder changed all the normal procedures."

"Normally how many people at Okapi would have read it?"

"Oh, by this time, maybe half a dozen. I always edited her books myself, so no other editor would have seen it. But there would be our lawyer, of course. And the publicist and a copy editor. Fairly late in the game, the advertising manager as well. All would be pledged not to discuss the contents with any outsider."

"How many copies are floating around?"

Marsden was offended by that word, offended enough to snap back at the judge. "They are hardly floating," he said. "There is one floppy disc version and one printout. Both are in a secure place."

The judge was mildly amused by Marsden's vehemence. "The same safe place?"

"Yes, sir."

I could see Marsden thinking that, for maximum security, maybe they should be in separate places.

"And where is that, sir? Under your pillow?"

Laughter in the courtroom, even a smile from Marsden.

"In a safe deposit box."

"And if you release a copy of the manuscript to aid the Massachusetts police in their investigation of three homicides, just what is it you fear?"

Marsden was about to answer, but Astrachan rose to his feet. "If I may, Your Honor, I would like to answer Your Honor's question in Mr. Marsden's behalf?"

"Why? He's doing fine so far."

"Your Honor, my client has had less experience with law enforcement agencies than I have."

"You and I are in a privileged profession, counselor. All right, shoot."

"Your Honor, our witness Mr. Smythe testified a short time ago that — his exact words were — 'All government is a sieve.' In government there is no such thing as a secret. I submit that in my own experience, no part of government is more sievelike than the office of a district attorney — unless perhaps it is a police department. I am sure every reporter and editor in this courtroom could confirm that statement."

When he paused to look at the press section, he was rewarded with several smiles and nods.

"He's right about that," Dirk whispered to me.

"It's fairly obvious why D.A.s are sieves. They are elected politicians. Most of them hope to run for governor. They count on the press for publicity. Good publicity means votes. They profit from being good sources. 'I'll do you a favor, you do me a favor.' The police, on the other hand, are not politicians, but they love to tell the press what the press doesn't know. It's just plain good fun to be a good inside source."

"Counselor, I think that's enough analysis. What's your point?"

"Sir, my point is that if Okapi has to surrender this manuscript to the D.A. and the police, the contents will inevitably become public. And that will destroy the financial value of their exclusivity. The value of first serial rights will plummet. In a word, it will cost Okapi a sum of money that it cannot afford to lose. In addition to Mr. Marsden, Okapi's other investors must be protected. Okapi has been counting on this book for major income."

"So, counselor, what relief do you seek?"

"We request that you vacate the search warrant."

"In a homicide case? With a strong probable cause that the manuscript will aid the investigation?"

"Yes, Your Honor."

Judge Whipple brought his glasses back down to the tip of his nose. In silence he stared down at the papers in front of him on the bench, but I did not think he was reading. He was thinking. The silence went on. Then it went on some more. He made some notes to himself on a sheet of paper. The courtroom was very quiet.

Finally the judge looked up, pushed up his glasses. He glanced at the court stenographer, making sure that her fingers were poised over the keys and that she was not about to run out of paper.

"This is our decision. Despite Okapi's well-reasoned and well-presented appeal, this Court cannot reject the affidavit of facts presented by the District Attorney of New York in behalf of the District Attorney of Massachusetts. Three heinous homicides have been committed. All three homicides appear to be clearly — I repeat that word, clearly — related in some fashion to the manuscript written by Mildred Silk. We do not know what that manuscript contains, but it is not difficult to surmise that it might reveal motivation or other significant evidence. While one might wish that the Massachusetts police had been able to solve these heinous crimes by traditional methods of investigation, that does not seem to be the case. They are, to state it bluntly, stuck."

"Wait till Mulvey reads that!" Dirk whispered.

"This Court is therefore compelled to reject Okapi's appeal and to reaffirm the search warrant for the Mildred Silk manuscript. However, the Court is convinced by this morning's presentation of evidence that the financial damage Okapi might sustain as a result of this decision could be severe. Therefore the reaffirmation of the warrant is accompanied by the following protective order." He picked up his page of notes. "One: Okapi will deliver to the District Attorney of New York for transmission to the District Attorney of Massachusetts a single printed copy of the manuscript. Two: that single copy will not be duplicated by either office." He looked over at the table of four assistant D.A.s. "Is that understood? You all get that?" All four nodded enthusiastically. "Three: the actual substantive contents of the manuscript, having great commercial value to its owner, Okapi Press, will not be revealed to anyone in the media." He stopped and turned to the stenographer. "Miss Tyler, strike that last phrase. It should read 'will not be revealed to anyone except the immediate persons charged with the official investigation of the Silk, Waring and Millhouse homicides. This restriction specifically applies to all members of the media.' Four: if, and only if, the manuscript does contain information that bears directly on any or all of the three homicides, such information — and only such information — may be used in any legal proceedings, including grand jury hearings, depositions and trial. That concludes the Court's ruling."

He turned to Astrachan and Marsden. "That is the best I can do for you, gentlemen. I hope it will give you full protection. This Court is adjourned."

The usual bustle and chatter ensued, especially from reporters rushing over to talk to Leonard Marsden.

Dirk and I got up to go.

"I guess we'll never get to read Millie's book," I said.

"Why not?"

"The judge's restrictions."

"Oh, those," Dirk said. "Don't take those too seriously."

"Why not? They sounded plenty serious to me."

Dirk shrugged. "It just means everybody involved has to be a little more careful. It'll take a little more time. We'll have the book in a week."

One Miss, One Hit

$\mathcal{I}$ DID NOT BELIEVE Dirk's prediction. After Judge Whipple's multiple restrictions, my bet was that we were in for a long, long wait before reading Millie's book, maybe not until magazine serialization. But I wasn't bored while we were waiting because there were two more attempts at cyanide homicide. One in New York, one at the Vineyard.

The murderer showed a certain lack of imagination by continuing to use cyanide, but on the other hand, why switch when you're ahead?

I was still in New York when the first occurred, and I was back on the Vineyard for the second. My proximity to both events improved my standing as a suspect, though not as much as I would have liked.

The day after Judge Whipple's ruling, and the day before he had been ordered to hand over Millie's manuscript, Leonard Marsden returned to his Okapi office after a long literary lunch. The entire book publishing industry once functioned over long literary lunches between editors and authors and agents. This is less true today when so many of them have given up martinis and old-fashioneds in favor of white wine or even Perrier or San Pellegrino. It's a wonder any books ever get written or any deals ever get made. Marsden, however, belonged to the old school. So, therefore, did his editors. They were all expected to have long literary lunches, but warned to watch the expenses, eat in cheap restaurants — not a difficult challenge in that neighborhood. Marsden still believed that this was a gentleman's profession.

As he told the police, he came back from his lunch at the National Arts Club shortly after three o'clock. He went first to the men's room, then walked down between the cubicles to his office. His secretary Maureen was not at her desk, but he thought nothing of it. She might be in the ladies' room, she might be shopping, she might just be having a long lunch herself, though probably not a literary one. Anything was possible, and it didn't much matter. She always got her work done.

Marsden walked into his office, took off his jacket and hung it on the back of the door. Maureen — he assumed it was Maureen — had put his tall glass of black coffee in the center of his desk, right beside the small covered bucket of ice cubes. This was normal. He always had his iced coffee — strong, black Medaglia d'Oro — the first thing when he returned to the office. He found it dissipated the effects of a long lunch and restored his energy for the afternoon's work. Since the exact time of his return was uncertain, given the vagaries of literary lunches, Maureen never put the ice in the coffee, lest it melt and dilute the powerful flavor. So the glass of powerful black coffee was in its usual place in the center of his desk, the bucket of ice cubes a few inches away to the right. The glass was filled well short of the rim in order to leave room for the ice. Same as always.

As he told the police, he removed the cover of the ice bucket with his left hand and picked up two cubes with his right hand. No, he did not use tongs. He didn't like ice tongs — awkward to manage and totally unnecessary. In his opinion, tongs were sissy things. (That's right, Dirk said, sissy is the word he used, it's in the detective's report.)

The cubes were still in his right hand when he noticed something most unusual. The coaster — the thick, round, cardboard coaster with the Okapi logo, a black antelope head against a gold field — was not under the coffee glass. He put the cubes back in the bucket, replaced the cover and lifted the glass.

Sure enough, there was a wet ring on the antique desk, once owned by Maxwell Perkins, bought by Marsden at auction after the great editor's death, religiously preserved ever since. He was furious. He was damn furious. He set the glass in his in-box and wiped at the ring with a Kleenex. That was better, but the outline remained. Maybe it would come off with some special furniture polish. If not, he would have Maureen's head.

But then he thought, no, that is impossible. Maureen had been trained within an inch of her life never to put anything on the Great Desk that might leave a mark. Besides, she was almost as proud of it as he was. He had heard her boast about it to visitors. It was unthinkable that she could have forgotten the coaster. And yet maybe, just this once, if something terribly important was on her mind. . . . He pulled out the top right-hand desk drawer. The coaster was not there in its customary place.

He walked to the door of his office and raised his voice so that all the cubicles could hear. He often communicated with his editorial staff in this way. "Where's Maureen?"

After a moment a voice called back, "She went to the dentist."

He told the police he had forgotten all about her dentist appointment, though she had mentioned it to him first thing this morning. His memory was not as good as it used to be. But that meant somebody else, no doubt with good intentions, had fixed his coffee and made that abominable ring on his desk. That man or that woman was about to be in bad trouble.

"Who fixed my coffee?" he called in the same loud voice.

A longer pause. Then a voice said, "Maureen did. Just before she left."

So it was Maureen. Perhaps distracted by fear of the dentist, she forgot the coaster. Many people were terrified by dentists, especially women. He considered such people soft, weak, lily-livered. (Yes, Dirk said, lily-livered is in the report.) But then where was the coaster itself? If Maureen forgot it, why wasn't it in the drawer?

Oh well, enough of this. He would tell the cleaning woman to get after that ring this very evening. Lemon Pledge or Butcher's Wax would surely remove it. The key was to give the ring quick treatment.

Meantime, work to be done. He sat down in his swivel chair and reached for his coffee and the ice bucket. Then he stopped.

Later, when he explained it, he could only put it down to instinct. Some warning instinct, no doubt provoked by the mysteriously missing coaster, made him stop. The fact that he had recently seen three people die of poisoning was also floating around in the back of his mind. He had no wish to become the fourth. He looked at the glass of coffee. He bent his head down and sniffed at it. He smelled nothing but the rich aroma of strong Italian coffee. He dipped the tip of one finger into the liquid and touched it to his tongue. Nothing. It tasted like strong Italian coffee.

Just the same, where was that coaster? He put the glass back in his in-box and dialed 911.

* * *

When the police lab analyzed the coffee, it turned out to contain more than ten grams of amygdalin, a drug containing cyanide that is used to treat cancer, although many doctors consider it a bogus treatment. It must be administered by injection. It cannot be taken orally because enzymes in the intestine

168

would release the cyanide content. Unlike potassium cyanide, the crystalline powder gave off no telltale odor of bitter almonds when it dissolved in liquids. If Marsden had drunk his coffee, he would have noticed nothing. The amygdalin would have gone down his throat and into and through his stomach, and he still would have noticed nothing. But once it entered his intestine, Marsden would have been, as the lab technician put it, "in very, very bad trouble." It would have killed him.

This time Dirk did not have to persuade Lieutenant Huggins or anybody else that he should be involved. Even though retired, he was the only homicide detective in New York who knew the Mildred Silk case and all its players. He was returned to temporary duty, his per diem based on his final salary. The NYPD much preferred to bring back one of its own rather than accept the offer of expert Massachusetts help that Captain Mulvey offered as soon as he learned of the incident. Mulvey didn't just offer, he suggested, he insisted. From his point of view, this might be the major break. Leonard Marsden had survived and could talk. Now at last Mulvey's team had a live target to interview and analyze and then interview again. But the NYPD position was that Massachusetts had had its crack at solving three homicides and got nowhere. The attempt on Marsden was in New York's jurisdiction, and New York would now show the Bay State how it was done.

The secretary proved unshakable. Maureen Custis had worked at Okapi for three years. Everybody, not just Marsden, liked and trusted her. In every office or organization, Dirk said, there is always one person who knows where everything is and how everything works and just what buttons to push. In any investigation, he said, it is imperative to identify that person as soon as possible. Luckily for this investigation that person was Maureen Custis, not only a central figure but a central figure who knew all the answers.

She was absolutely definite. She had put the coaster under the coffee glass as usual. No, shaking her pretty head, she could not possibly be mistaken. She had taken it out of the drawer, put it on the desk and set the glass of coffee on top of it. Yes, she knew exactly when she had done this. Twenty minutes to two. The reason she was sure was that her dentist appointment was at two, and she had to leave Okapi at quarter to two to get there on time. Fixing Mr. Marsden's coffee was the last thing she did before leaving. The police checked her digital watch to make sure it told correct time. Of course it did.

So that glass of coffee was in place and unpoisoned at twenty to two. Unless, of course, Maureen had popped in the poison on her way out the door. Secretaries have been known to murder their bosses, usually with ample motivation, but Dirk thought Maureen was much too bright to have chosen such a self-incriminating method.

So the cyanide went into the glass between 1:40 at the earliest and approximately 3:20 or 3:25 at the latest, when Marsden came out of the men's room and walked down to his office. Only one hundred minutes, or at most one hundred and five minutes, to account for. That should be a breeze for a professional police force.

My first step would have been to learn which guests at Millie's last dinner party were currently in New York, and exactly where they were during those hundred or so minutes. Eventually it turned out that quite a few of us were in town. Dr. Sunbeam was here to negotiate his contract for *The Sweet Breath of Death*. Jill Klein was taking depositions all week long for her forthcoming defense of a serial rapist, a Harvard man who called himself Beowulf Junior. Everett Munk was delivering a YMCA lecture on his favorite novelist, Nathaniel Hawthorne, and Elena Bronze was attending a high-publicity wedding. None of them could be ruled out by the circumstance of timing.

On the other hand, said Dirk, that doesn't mean quite as much as you might think. Theoretically it's easy enough for anybody to get from the Vineyard to New York and back again in a single day without people knowing you had left the Island. Provided you paid cash for your plane ticket, not credit card or check, and provided you weren't recognized.

"Pretty theoretical," I said.

Dirk shrugged. "Every once in a while something theoretical turns out to be true."

However, the police didn't start where I would have started. That's not how the pros work. They start at the hub and work outward. Their first step was to learn where each Okapi employee was between 1:40 and 3:25. Most of them had been out to lunch or had just got back from lunch. The police would have a long, busy time checking out these stories, establishing not only each employee's presence at each restaurant but also the duration of presence. But, Dirk said, that's the kind of patient routine they like to do and are very good at. It would bore me to death.

Only two employees had stayed in to work the entire time, eating deli sandwiches at their desks. They had ordered from two different delis, so there had been two different delivery boys. Neither editor had noticed any strangers in the office, but both had been absorbed in their manuscripts.

The second step was to determine if it would have been possible for any nonemployee to get in and out of the Okapi offices without being noticed. Was it ever! The lobby on the ground floor was unattended. The elevator was automated. Anyone who didn't fancy the elevator could use the fire stairs. The front door to the third-floor offices had its "Ring and Enter" sign, but anybody could enter without ringing. As for outsider traffic, so much of it passed through all day long that nobody paid any attention. The cubicle walls were high enough to keep the occupants from seeing all the comings and goings. Without bothering to ring, messengers came in to deliver manuscripts or to return them. Authors came in to talk over manuscripts or book ideas with editors. Delivery boys from the neighborhood delis went in and out all the time. Deliveries of stationery and other office supplies arrived from the local Staples, where Okapi kept an open account to ensure that nobody ran out of paper clips or colored editing pens.

"It's not like Tiffany's," Maureen explained. "Once the women lock their purses in their desk drawers, there's nothing to steal. We do lock the doors at night when we close, but that's about it."

Real high-tech security, as Officer Cooper had said.

The source of the poison was another blind alley that would keep the police busy for weeks. Because of its widespread if questionable use in cancer treatment, amygdalin was readily available in many places. It could be bought in its pure state from a chemical supply house for roughly eighty-five dollars an ounce, more than twice the lethal dose found in Marsden's glass of coffee.

"I never heard of it," I told Dirk. "How did the killer know it could be used as a poison?"

"When we catch whoever did it," Dirk said, "we'll ask that question."

Dirk and another detective spent a very long time with Marsden himself, exploring the distinct possibility that the would-be killer had no connection to Millie's book. Suppose somebody with a totally different reason to kill Marsden wanted to make this look like yet another Mildred Silk murder. What better concealment than to mislead the police by using cyanide? It was a perfect opportunity for a copycat crime.

How were his relations with his staff? Had anybody quit recently? Had he fired anybody recently? Where can we find them? What about enemies in the publishing world? After almost fifty years in publishing, he must have some enemies. Rival publishers? Disgruntled agents? Rejected authors? What about the other shareholders in Okapi? Any strong differences of opinion? What about his personal life? Family? Women? Perhaps a discarded lover? ("At my age?") Who had reason to want him dead? Who would benefit from same?

Marsden was patient and thoughtful about answering their questions. Apparently unshaken by his narrow escape, he swigged away at glasses of iced coffee, promptly replenished by Maureen. He admitted — confirmed by everyone on his staff — that he had a temper, was irascible and never hesitated to criticize anyone's performance, sometimes publicly. No doubt he hurt some feelings from time to time — also confirmed by everyone on his staff — but that couldn't be helped. After all, it was his business and his responsibility to make it succeed. He managed to come up with the names of a fair number of people who might wish him ill — although surely not that much ill.

Though cooperative, Marsden told Dirk and the other detective that they were barking up all the wrong trees. "It's the Silk book. Somebody's still trying to stop it."

The attempt on Marsden's life delayed for two days the decreed delivery of Millie's manuscript. Only Marsden had access to the safe deposit box. Only he had authority to print out the single copy that Judge Whipple had ordered Okapi to hand over. He was not about to delegate that authority, no matter how many questions the homicide detectives wanted to ask him. Vigorous statements, both by phone and by fax, kept arriving from Captain Mulvey asking where the hell was his manuscript.

"Suppose Marsden had drunk that coffee," I asked Dirk. "How would you get the book out of the safe deposit box?"

"A court order to open the box," Dirk said. "It's routine but it takes time. The bank always puts up an obligatory fuss over invasion of a client's privacy, especially if the client is dead."

"What do you suppose the banks do in Switzerland? They never tell anybody anything about their clients."

"The Swiss don't poison people," Dirk said, "so the subject probably never comes up."

I myself was interviewed by NYPD homicide, although not by Dirk, of course.

The inquiry was less ardent than I might have wished. Unfortunately Dirk had told his colleagues that the possibility of my guilt was remote. Both the author and the editor had said I wasn't even mentioned in Millie's book, and I had had no dealings with Marsden, professional or personal. I had never even submitted a manuscript.

"Couldn't you have left me a little more slack?" I asked him.

"They don't have as much time to waste as you do."

The two young detectives, obviously not the first team, did come to my apartment, and they did tape my answers. They did not waste a lot of time. Almost the first question they asked was where had I been during the near-fatal one hundred minutes. This immediately undercut any chance I had to arouse their suspicions. I had to confess that I spent almost the entire time having lunch with a Miss Molly Dodge of the late Lulu Waring show. What did we talk about? Well, I told her about the hearing on the Okapi appeal, and she told me about her job interviews, which were extremely promising. We ate in midtown because she had another job interview in Rockefeller Center at three o'clock. We had said goodbye at five minutes to three. Even though they had not asked for it, I gave them Molly's home phone number so they could verify my account. I didn't think they would bother to call her.

They didn't even pursue the possibility, which had certainly occurred to me, that right after saying goodbye to Molly, I might conceivably have jumped in a taxi, caught nothing but green lights all the way down to 19th Street and then two blocks crosstown to the Okapi building, raced up the fire stairs and down the corridor to drop the poison in Marsden's waiting glass of coffee before he got to his desk. Or maybe instant luck on the Sixth Avenue subway, followed by a brisk crosstown sprint. I admit either possibility was a stretch, but I thought they should have explored it. Instead they thanked me for my time, turned off the tape recorder and left.

I had obviously finished my performance as a suspect. I had also finished my New York shopping, and now I needed only one last Chinese fix before returning to the Vineyard. I proposed an exotic farewell expedition to Chinatown, but neither of my guests liked the idea of going all that distance. So Molly and Dirk and I had dinner at Café Evergreen, the best *dim sum* emporium north of Doyle Street. This large, modestly decorated restaurant in the East Sixties is always filled with Chinese, the best possible endorsement for top food at bottom prices.

I wanted to hear all the latest developments in homicide, but first we owed it to Molly to celebrate her new job. Three things to celebrate: better pay, a better title and two free weeks before she had to report to work. She agreed to pay me a visit at the Vineyard. Being a successful alumna of *Celeb/Celeb* had proved to be a huge credential. She had received three definite offers, and a probable fourth offer if she was willing to wait a few days. She wasn't. This afternoon she had accepted the top staff job with Sam Barrabas.

When our drinks came, Dirk and I toasted her and wished her luck.

Then Dirk said, "Tell me something, Molly. Why that job? I mean, you had a couple of alternatives. Was the money that good?"

A fair question. Sam Barrabas was the ungenial host and

loudmouthed tyrant of *Washington Up Close*, the weekly political interview and talk show. Every political figure in Washington hated Barrabas but could not afford to ignore his ratings. The public loved him because he treated politicians like liars and scoundrels, as indeed they were. He was said to be somewhat nicer off screen than on, but I didn't believe it.

"No," Molly said, "the money was almost the same. I guess Barrabas was more of a challenge than the others." She sipped her drink, and I thought that was the full explanation. Then she said, "I decided I didn't want to work for anybody I liked as much as Lulu. If somebody kills Barrabas" — she shrugged and laughed — "who cares?"

"Death to Barrabas!" I said.

"Not yet," Molly said. "I'd like to earn some of his money first."

"Speaking of death," I said to Dirk, "where's the coaster?"

Dirk shook his head. "No idea. We assume the perp took it. But we think we've maybe figured out why. The perp was pouring amygdalin in the coffee, not much time to spare, and maybe spilled some on the coaster. The coaster's wet, right? From the moisture off the glass, right? So now there's this trail of white powder on the coaster. It's wet and it looks like a mess, and the perp is maybe in even more of a hurry now and says, I haven't got time to clean this shit up. Sticks the coaster in a pocket and beats it."

"What's with powder?" I asked. "Doesn't cyanide come in little pills? At least that's how spies used to hide it under a false tooth cap."

"Both ways," Dirk said. "Pellets or white granular powder. In the case of amygdalin, it had to be powder because that's what the perp dropped on the coaster."

"What about Lulu?" Molly asked. She could finally talk about Lulu without crying. "Powder or a pill?"

"Could have been either," Dirk said, "but I'm damn sure it was a pill. Not just for Miss Waring but also for Miss Millhouse and Miss Silk. Much too hard for the killer to pour powder in front of all those folks. Had to be pellets."

"So why suddenly switch to amygdalin when it came to Marsden?"

"Beats me. Maybe the killer ran out of pellets. Maybe it's a copycat killer who had amygdalin crystals instead of cyanide pills. Or what the hell, maybe our whole theory is wrong. That's been known to happen. Maybe the perp just grabbed the coaster as a souvenir."

Our *dim sum* appetizers began to arrive, a parade of little dishes and metal stay-hot containers. Usually four dumplings or portions per dish but sometimes only three. This is one aspect of the Mysterious East that I have never been able to unravel. Why four in this dish and three in that one? Don't bother to ask. All you ever get from a Chinese waiter is a big smile and "Oh, just come that way."

Much competitive chopstick activity as we divided up the various fried and steamed dumplings and the baby ribs and the sliced egg rolls.

"Another thing," Dirk said. "The prints on Marsden's glass. The only prints the lab found were his."

"You mean he tried to poison himself?"

Dirk laughed. "The point is that the secretary's prints weren't on the glass, even though she fixed the coffee. That means whoever poisoned the coffee was careful to wipe the glass."

"Or else wore gloves."

"You're not thinking tonight, Jason." For the second time he helped himself to the final dumpling in a four-dumpling container. "If the perp wore gloves, there'd be no reason to wipe the glass, so Maureen's prints would still be on it."

"Unless Maureen wore gloves too."

177

"Are you suggesting she wore gloves in the summer to go to the dentist?"

"I don't know, just thinking aloud."

"Jason, this town is too much for you to handle. I think you better go back to the Vineyard and rest up."

* * *

It was the first murder in the one-hundred-and-forty-seven-year history of Edgartown's Scrimshaw Inn. High time, I say. How can an inn claim to be "historic" if there has never been a murder or a suicide, and if there are no moaning ghosts roaming the corridors at night?

Eloise Abernathy, proprietor of the Scrimshaw, descended from an unbroken line of Abernathy owners all the way back to whaling days, did not share my view of history. She was outraged. A pretty, stout, white-haired old lady, equal parts charm and greed, she was convinced the murder would damage her splendid profit center. My own guess was that since scandal always attracts attention, and since attention always attracts customers, it would probably be good for her business. Not that her business could get much better. Scrimshaw rooms were sold out in advance for the entire season and heavily booked in the off-season as well. Same for the restaurant. The only way Eloise Abernathy could increase business was to increase prices, which she did with daring frequency.

Eloise was an Island Character and knew it. She was used to being quoted on all Vineyard matters. Since she knew she'd be called when anything interesting happened, she had time to work up a lively quote or two. This time she told the police and the newspapers and the radio and TV reporters that never, never, never, not once in the untarnished, unblemished record of the Scrimshaw Inn, had anything remotely like this ever, ever happened. "I blame it," she said, "on all these newfangled ways and all these terrible new people who are coming to the Vineyard." She did not say that some of the most terrible new people were her celebrity guests at the Scrimshaw Inn, including the one who was murdered.

The inn owed its origin to the nineteenth-century whaling trade — and to the bizarre fact that a sandbar prevented heavily laden ships from entering or leaving Nantucket Harbor. All the great Nantucket whaling ships had to do their final outfitting and loading in Edgartown. And when they returned after their two-year and three-year voyages, filled with heavy barrels of sperm oil, they had to unload in Edgartown before they could sail home into the Nantucket harbor.

Resolvert Abernathy, a foresighted Vineyard businessman, guessed that all those Nantucket whaling captains and mates would prefer to spend their last days before a voyage, and their first homecoming days after a voyage, in a cozy Edgartown inn rather than in cramped quarters aboard their ships. He opened his inn right on the Edgartown waterfront and named it the Scrimshaw, after the whalebone and whale ivory carvings that sailors made during the monotonous voyages. His guess proved accurate. The captains and mates, especially those home from a successful voyage with the certainty of sharing fat profits, were eager to eat, drink and sleep ashore, and to pay well for the luxury. Resolvert, a straitlaced Yankee, would not supply women, leaving that chore to other Edgartown business establishments, but he supplied everything else. His grateful clients often gave him scrimshaw souvenirs, and he bought other scrimshaw pieces from sailors. He kept them all, guessing that someday they might be worth a lot of money.

Once again he guessed right.

Today the inn's lobby, the main sitting rooms, the bar and

the restaurant all display Resolvert's magnificent scrimshaw collection, carefully locked in glass cases.

The inn's logo, a two-inch profile of a sperm whale, is everywhere. On the restaurant china and glassware and napkins. On sheets and pillowcases and towels and soap dishes. On matchbook covers. On the bathrobes and ties and handkerchiefs that you can buy at the front desk as take-home souvenirs. On every sheet of stationery, including your staggering final bill. All of Edgartown is big on whales because of the whaling heritage, but nothing in Edgartown is bigger on whales than the Scrimshaw Inn.

In spite of Eloise Abernathy's prices I have frequently stayed at the Scrimshaw.

After Columbus Day I close my house, drain the pipes and shut off the heat. I always do this myself because I am a first-class amateur plumber. I learned the hard way, from things going wrong when I couldn't get anybody to come fix them. Now I even help friends with leaky faucets and nonfunctioning dishwashers. Once I've closed my house, it's too much trouble to turn everything back on when I come up for a short off-season visit. There are other, cheaper places, but I agree with the whaling captains of long ago. The Scrimshaw is the place to stay.

One of the Scrimshaw traditions is the breakfast tray, which happened to play a central role in the murder. Eloise was driven to invent it in order to save money. The summer employment picture on the Vineyard is tight. Even with the influx of college kids who want to spend a jolly summer working on the Vineyard, every business, every restaurant and inn and hotel, needs extra help and has to pay competitive wages. Eloise kept her restaurant fully staffed for lunch and dinner, since both were extremely profitable, but she hated to waste money on the breakfast staff, since that was her least profitable meal.

In fact, breakfast lost money. She hated to pay the maitre d' just to smile and seat people and hand out menus. She hated to pay all those waiters and waitresses to set the tables, take the orders, serve the food, pour the coffee, make out the checks, then finally clear the tables and reset them. And the kitchen had to be fully staffed with cooks and cooks' helpers to prepare all the different last-minute orders. A nightmare of expense.

Challenge: how to avoid all those wages? Response: close the dining room for breakfast. Challenge: how can the Island's most elegant inn avoid serving breakfast to its guests? Response: serve breakfast on individual trays delivered to each room. Then Eloise would have to pay only the kitchen staff plus one waiter to deliver the trays. Challenge: some guests don't like room service. Response: make it irresistible.

Eloise began with a new breakfast menu, which she christened the Scrumptious Scrimshaw Breakfast. Many wonderful goodies to choose from, and many of them were rarely if ever found on Vineyard breakfast menus. Every kind of egg and omelet, of course, but also blueberry pancakes, French toast with cranberry syrup, kippered herring, flash-frozen shad roe and trout, creamed chip beef, minute steak, corned beef hash with poached egg, bay scallops — once in February, I even had smelts. Hashed brown potatoes, home fried potatoes and, for southern guests, hominy grits. All the usual juices and melons and berries and cereals and rolls and muffins and croissants. The sheer variety was a Vineyard breakthrough.

She decorated each tray with a single flower in a bud vase — a rose, a lily, a peony, a daisy, a chrysanthemum, depending on the season. Since these came from the Scrimshaw garden, they cost her nothing. Each tray also carried a little identifying flag in the shape of a sperm whale, just large enough to carry the guest's name in red crayon. The whales were white plastic so that Eloise could wipe off the crayon and use them over and over again. The guests had to hand in their orders the night before, along with the preferred time for delivery outside their bedroom doors.

Each night when the dining room had been cleared after dinner, the breakfast trays were set up with china and silverware on a large serving table, ready for action at dawn. A sperm whale flag identified each tray. Next morning all the waiter had to do was pop the flower of the day in the bud vase and wait for the cooks to prepare each order, deliver the tray to the right room number, put it on the floor and knock. Then go back downstairs for the next tray.

Because the kitchen knew in advance exactly what to cook and when to cook it, there was less wasted food and less last-minute frenzy. To her delight, Eloise found that at breakfast she could now eliminate one of the cooks and one of the cooks' helpers, along with the entire dining room staff. Money in the bank.

The guests loved it because they thought it was sophisticated. As Eloise discovered, they didn't even mind paying extra. She was not only saving all that money through staff and food economies, but she was also able to do what she liked best, raise prices. A wild success, entirely her inspiration, followed up by perfect execution.

Therefore it came as a deep personal affront when a guest was murdered by means of his own Scrumptious Scrimshaw Breakfast. Although not a southerner, he had ordered hominy grits, and that's where he got it. He apparently died solitary and silent. At least nobody reported hearing anything until noon, when the maid entered to make up the room, discovered the body and screamed her head off. At last the Scrimshaw Inn was truly historic.

* * *

While Eloise Abernathy was understandably upset, many others were not. In fact, you could call it a fairly popular murder, as murders go. The only folks who were really unhappy about the death of Chick Bird were those in the teardown and construction business. They lost buckets of money.

Bird had arrived on the Vineyard two days ago for his final hearing before the Edgartown Zoning Board of Appeals. He had already been through several months of tiresome hearings before the Planning Board and the ZBA, meantime enduring steady editorial attacks for his failure to preserve the Waverly family's House of Eight Gables. His patience, never one of his best qualities, had worn exceeding thin. Now Bird sat there with his lawyer while the Martha's Vineyard Preservation Trust made a last desperate effort to get the Waverly house away from him. The Trust is a private charitable organization that collects, renovates and then merchandises historic Island buildings, renting them out for parties, weddings, dinners, dances. The do-good cost of their work is nicely balanced by a steady flow of income.

Today the Trust's effort was two-pronged, both legal and financial.

On legal grounds the Trust argued that the Town of Edgartown had been remiss in not designating the Waverly house an historic landmark. Had it done so, Eight Gables would have been protected against demolition, regardless of who bought the property. Having failed in that responsibility, the Town should now correct its mistake in the only way possible. It must seize the property by eminent domain.

Nobody, not even the Trust lawyer and officers, thought much of that argument. Bird's lawyer, a heavy hitter from Boston, cited two State Supreme Court rulings to the effect that no town in Massachusetts had any obligation to declare anything a landmark, regardless of popular opinion. That was strictly up to each Town's government. The fact that Edgartown had never got around to declaring the Waverly place a landmark was too bad but irrelevant. The fact that Edgartown had never expected the last remaining Waverlys to put their place on the market was also too bad but equally irrelevant. The only relevant fact was that while everybody else, including the Trust, was trying to figure out how to respond to the Waverlys, Chick Bird just went ahead and bought the property in good faith at the full asking price. It was now his to do with as he liked.

The Zoning Board of Appeals, reluctantly but unanimously, had to agree. On the Vineyard, property rights are sacred. If you buy it, it's yours.

The Trust's financial pitch had more heft. Having dug deep into the pockets of its wealthy board members and into its own substantial assets, the Trust was now prepared to make Chick Bird a juicy offer. It would buy the Waverly place for what he had paid for it, plus a premium of ten percent. In addition it would pay all his architects' fees, all his legal fees and all other reasonable out-of-pocket expenses. As a businessman, surely he could appreciate the generosity of this offer.

Bird and his lawyer conferred. Then the lawyer said, "Mr. Bird would like to know what the Trust means by 'reasonable.' Would that include his living expenses for all his necessary visits to the Scrimshaw Inn during all these hearings?"

The Trust conferred. "Yes."

"And the expenses for flying his plane to and from California?"

The Trust people conferred for quite a long time. The president, a New York City CEO when he wasn't vacationing on the Vineyard, whispered long and low to his lawyer. The lawyer finally said, "It is our assumption that Mr. Bird's plane is a corporate aircraft. It is our further assumption that its entire operation is therefore treated as a fully deductible business expense on the company's tax returns."

Bird and his lawyer conferred again, but only briefly. "Mr. Bird congratulates the Trust on its business acumen. However, he asked his questions solely out of curiosity. He thanks the Trust for its interest, although as a businessman he considers a ten percent premium extremely modest in view of current soaring Vineyard land prices. He does not intend to sell his property. On the contrary, he is eager, after all these unconscionable delays, to remove the old Waverly house and to build his new vacation home." The lawyer turned to the Board of Appeals. "Gentlemen?"

* * *

Afterward there were estimates about how much money the demolition folks could have made from tearing down the old Waverly house and hauling it off to the town dump. These estimates did not vary a great deal because the demolition folks had had a lot of recent experience tearing down big old houses and carting them away to make room for new trophy houses. Then there were estimates about how much it would have cost Bird to put in the airstrip for his jet. Lots of variation on this one because almost nobody on the Vineyard had a large enough property to support a private airstrip, so there wasn't much experience to go on. But the big number, the number that broke every heart in the Vineyard construction business, was the cost of the trophy house that Bird would have built. The excavation! The foundation! The framing! The lumber! The wiring! The plumbing! Endless!

Nobody knew what his estate would now do with the Waverly property. The betting was that the Preservation Trust would eventually wind up with it. After selling off most of the surrounding land, to a conservation buyer if possible, it would completely restore and renovate the House of Eight Gables, carefully preserving every architectural twist and turn and whimsy. Eight Gables would then become some kind of popular and profitable attraction. Perhaps a nightclub? Perhaps a hall for intimate rock concerts? Perhaps a bizarre setting for weddings and receptions?

* * *

Although Eight Gables survived, Captain Andrew Mulvey did not. He had failed to solve any of three celebrity murders, and here was a fourth. The governor (Italian) and the district attorney (Hispanic) and even the United States senator (Irish) agreed that it was time to replace the Irish dynamo. He didn't even get to read the Mildred Silk manuscript when at last it arrived in Boston. That privilege fell to the new chief investigator, Captain Modesto Abbudanza. We Massachusetts residents with keen minds were able to guess that he was of the Italian persuasion, like the governor. According to the media, he was known to the troops as Mo, and he was said to be smart and popular. He had another valuable characteristic. When his appointment was announced, Dirk called from New York to say that he and Mo Abbudanza were old drinking pals from various homicide conventions. He had already congratulated Mo and offered his help.

"Great," I said. "Maybe he'll let you see Millie's manuscript."

"Oh, he can't do that. But don't worry, I have another source for that. Say, Jason, there sure seem to be a lot of murders around you."

"I've noticed that too. But this is the first one I didn't get to see."

"You didn't get to see Mr. Marsden."

"That was just an attempt, not a murder. In my league we only count the successful ones."

"Any news on Mr. Bird? Have you confessed yet?"

"No, but the word is out that he was a very poor tipper. Really stingy, like most celebrities. He gave a flat ten percent on his dinner checks, sometimes less. Maybe a waiter or a waitress decided to teach him a lesson. Are you guys getting anywhere on Marsden?"

"Lot of leads, no results."

"Same here. You know, Dirk, it's not all women victims now. We have an attempt on one man, a hit on another man. Maybe Bitsy Betsy will come back to the Vineyard, now that it's not just females."

"I doubt it. She's so scared, we won't see her again till we nail somebody."

"What do you mean, you have another source for Millie's book?"

"Forget I said it. Listen, what's your FedEx address? I only have your post office box."

I gave it to him. "What are you sending me?"

"A package. Actually it's being sent to me, care of you. Don't open it till I get there."

I couldn't believe what I thought I was hearing. It had to be the manuscript.

"I didn't know you were coming back to the Vineyard. How soon?"

"Couple days. Since Marsden looks like a dead end, I'm being released from temporary duty. Your guest room's available, right?"

"Molly will be here part of the time." She and I had promised each other a very special weekend.

"I can live with that if you're quiet between three and five a.m. Promise me about the package, you won't open it. It's important."

"Why?"

"It's part of the deal."

I promised.

* * *

"Can you come over to the Scrimshaw?" Kenny Waters asked me over the phone.

"Of course." I had expected to be interrogated but not there. "What's up?"

"Captain Abbudanza wants to meet everybody, kind of get the feel of who's who in this case. These cases."

I could tell by his voice that Kenny didn't approve of this informal approach. "Just kicking the tires before he takes off?"

"You could put it that way. Listen, I have to schedule a lot of people. Ten-fifteen for you, if that's convenient. The green parlor."

On the way into the parlor I met Everett Munk on the way out. We said hello. He looked his usual rumpled self.

Mo Abbudanza was as short as Dirk but much thicker. Black hair, black eyebrows, dark brown eyes. A short-sleeved white shirt. Eloise Abernathy had reluctantly lent the Captain the second downstairs sitting room. It contained three cases of Resolvert's scrimshaw collection, but not the finest pieces. Sergeant Waters was there, too, and I said "Hi, Kenny," and he said, "Hello, Jason," an exchange that would not have taken place during Mulvey's regime. Kenny and I were only acquaintances, but when you've shared three murder investigations together, formality tends to evaporate.

Abbudanza and I shook hands. He looked me over, pleasantly enough, but I could see he was measuring me. "I hear you're an old friend of Schultz."

188

"Yes, quite a long time. He's coming up to visit me in a few days."

"So he tells me. Let's get together while he's here. Meantime, would you mind telling Sergeant Waters and me where you were from Tuesday afternoon through Wednesday morning?"

That was more like it! That was the way a suspect should be treated.

I took them through that period. Kenny jotted notes, no tape recorder. I had been alone quite a lot of the time, including all night, what with Molly still in New York and Elena Bronze still sulking, so I didn't have anything approaching a total alibi. That was obvious to all three of us.

When we had finished with that, Abbudanza put his hands behind his head and stretched back in his chair. Pretty casual for a chief investigator. "We'll be asking everybody this," he said. "What did you think of Chick Bird?"

Half a dozen ways to answer that, but why not the truth? "I barely knew him, but I didn't like him at all."

His pleasant expression didn't change. "Why's that?"

"I don't like rich celebrities. Especially on the Vineyard."

"You sure have enough of them."

"They're wrecking the Island. Look what Chick Bird wanted to do to the old Waverly place."

"Haven't been out there yet," Abbudanza said. "I hear it's quite something." He was still stretched back in his chair. "When you say you barely knew Bird, how do you mean?"

"I met him twice, once at Mildred Silk's dinner, where we just shook hands, and again when we were rehearsing for Lulu Waring's TV special. I've seen him a few times at the Yacht Club and sometimes at big parties, but not to talk to."

"Okay, that sure sounds like you barely knew him. Hardly enough to — how did you put it? — not like him at all."

"I didn't like him in principle, because of what he was. But the little I saw of him I didn't much like him in person, either."

"Oh? How come?"

"I thought he was too young to be so arrogant."

Abbudanza nodded. "It happens when you make a fortune right out of the starting gate." He took his hands down from behind his head. "Okay, thanks for coming in. Tell Dirk to call when he gets here."

I left feeling that I was at least a partial suspect, what with an incomplete alibi and an established dislike of the victim. I couldn't wait to tell Dirk that I had been promoted.

And I would have lots to tell Molly when she arrived for the weekend on the late afternoon plane.

As I headed for the front door, Elena Bronze came walking down the corridor straight toward me. I hadn't seen her or spoken to her since the night at the Yacht Club.

She wore a full, loose white shirt like an artist's smock. She was obviously next for a talk with Captain Abbudanza. I wondered how she would greet me.

I stood aside to let her pass, gave her a big smile and said, "Hello, Elena."

She looked at me, a blank look, and simply nodded.

I try not to get angry at beautiful women, but this was far too little from someone with whom I had so recently spent such a long, marvelous night. Suddenly I didn't care who she was or how famous she was.

As she started to pass, I grabbed her shoulder. I stopped her and swung her around to face me.

"Just so you know," I spoke in anger, glaring down at her, "you are a very rude woman. But I'd still rather make love to you again than anything else I can think of."

Her face softened. "Now that's better," she said. She paused to think about something. Then she said, "I'm having some people to cocktails at six. Why don't you come a little early?" Her marvelous wicked smile. "Say three-thirty?"

Because of my enthusiasm for women, I have a tendency to get myself in trouble over arrangements. Molly's plane was arriving at five-thirty for that very special weekend we had promised each other. What could I do? Amend my statement? Tell Elena, "I'd rather make love to you again than anything else I can think of — except meet Molly's plane?" Experience told me this would not go over well. But I could not bear to give up either Elena or Molly.

I made a lightning calculation that would have astonished all my arithmetic teachers. If I drove like mad on Elena's long, wide dirt driveway, I could probably get from her house to the airport in twenty minutes. So I had to leave her house at 5:10. That meant I had to jump out of bed promptly at five to shower and dress. I didn't want to offend Elena by seeming too hasty about leaving, but she too had to get dressed for her cocktail guests arriving at six. Surely an actress would need more time to get ready and to look perfect — hair, makeup, clothes, jewelry, all that. Surely a full hour? If so, five o'clock would suit both of us for jumping out of bed. And if things got really tight, could I be a few minutes late at the airport? Maybe Molly's plane would be a few minutes late, as planes so often are.

"Right!" I said. "Wonderful! Three-thirty."

She touched a finger to my cheek, gave me a naughty smile, then went down the hall for her interview with Abbudanza.

* * *

Wonderful, indeed. It was the most wonderful afternoon of my life — at least until the end. It would be nice and terribly flattering if Elena could say the same, but being very beautiful and famous and having had much more experience, she doubtless had even finer afternoons in her memory bank. Just the same, she had an extremely good time.

We were so joyously occupied that it was, in fact, Elena who suddenly cried, "My God, it's after five!" She jumped out of bed. "I have to get ready for my guests!"

We had already said many loving things to each other, so it didn't matter that neither of us could spare a second for fond goodbyes. Her last and only words as she and the fabled bronzinis vanished into her gold-fauceted bathroom, were, "You can use that bathroom down the hall to your left."

I am not one to dawdle in showers anyway, but this was the fastest shower of my life. When I should have been reliving all those treasured moments with Elena, all I could think of was how late I was, how much trouble I was in. No time for total toweling. I was still half wet as I sprang into my clothes. Ten seconds to comb my hair. Then racing down the stairs two at a time, running through the front hall with just a glimpse at the flash of surprise on the butler's face, then out the door and into my Mustang.

Vroom!!! As they say.

Maybe Molly's plane would be late. But I knew it wouldn't be. I just knew it. If anything, there would be a tailwind to bring her in early. I desperately needed an excuse. Usually excuses occur to me readily, but this time I was caught unprepared. That part of my mind was not functioning.

It was definitely past six when I reached the airport. No time to mess with the parking lot. I left the Mustang right outside the main entrance, where a taxi driver shouted, "Hey, you can't park there!" I waved gaily and hurried inside.

She was sitting there in the back of the waiting room, reading an Edith Wharton paperback. When I called "Molly!" she put it face down in her lap and looked at me. Not a friendly look.

"I'm sorry," I said, coming up to her.

"This is not a good start to our big weekend. I've been sitting here over half an hour."

"I'm sorry I'm late." Okay, here was my best lie, all I could come up with, not wanting to hurt her feelings, which I could see were already hurt. "The police kept asking me questions."

"You've been with the police all this time?" She stood up, disbelief written all over her.

"Yes, they kept thinking up questions to ask. You know how they are. After all, I'm a suspect."

Time to change the subject. I put my arms around her and gave her a big welcoming hug. "Our weekend begins." Then I gave her a light airport kiss.

She wrinkled her nose. Then she sniffed.

"If you've been with the police all afternoon, how come you smell of sex and perfumed soap?"

I couldn't think of an answer.

She threw Edith Wharton at me. "I think that terrific weekend you promised me just got lost in somebody else's bed. That plane's going back to New York in twenty minutes. Thanks a lot."

Millie's Manuscript

So I was alone in the house next morning.

The white truck emblazoned with the big blue "Fed" and the big red "Ex" swung into my parking area at a brisk speed, barely missing my Mustang. Gracie Mayhew, the FedEx driver, left her motor running. Since she is in a hurry all summer long, she has barely missed my car lots of times. She hopped out — tall, long brown hair, blue jeans, pale denim shirt.

She carried a clipboard and a package that looked just about the right size for a book manuscript. One of those big white envelopes, not a cardboard carton. "Hey, Jason."

"Hey, Gracie."

"This time you have to sign for it, receipt signature required. First time ever for you, I think. Who is Susan Finch?"

"I give up. Who is Susan Finch?"

"Not one of your girlfriends? It's addressed to Susan Finch, care of you." She looked puzzled. "You want to refuse delivery? You want me to take it back?"

"No, no, I'll take it. Actually, Gracie, now I do remember. Susan Finch is one of my girlfriends. She slipped my mind for a minute."

"You're losing your grip, Jason." She winked at me. Once last spring when she wasn't so busy, she had stopped long enough to make love. We had stayed friendly. "Sign here please."

She hopped back in her truck and drove off.

I stood there holding the package. The sender's name was illegible, an obfuscation that was surely as deliberate as "Susan Finch." I was holding the key to Mildred Silk's murder, and maybe to the other murders. Most book manuscripts are packed in a cardboard box that once held a ream of bond paper, but there was no box inside this envelope. I could feel that it was just a thick wad of loose pages. I could slide them around. I didn't see why I had to wait to read it. After all, Dirk had guaranteed that I could read it right behind him. Since I was going to read it anyway, why not let Dirk read behind me instead? Actually it would save time in the long run, because I was free to start right now.

Except for my promise to Dirk.

I considered steaming open the envelope, the way they did in the boys' adventure books I used to read, but I had a hunch that I would make a mess of it. Not only a mess steaming it open but a mess sealing it back together, leaving telltale traces of my chicanery. I would just have to wait for Dirk. Since I had no alternative but to wait, I could tell myself that I was behaving well by honoring my promise. Just the same, virtue is not its own reward, the way it's supposed to be. Virtue did not pacify my impatience.

I locked the package in the security closet, where I put my liquor when I close up the house in the fall. I phoned Dirk's apartment in Queens, getting his answering machine.

I left a short message. "Hello, Susan Finch, I've got it. When will you be here?"

* * *

Dirk was as eager as I was. He drove up early the next morning in time to catch the one-fifteen ferry from Woods Hole. This time he wouldn't need my guidance to navigate Five Corners and then drive through Vineyard Haven, but I couldn't sit still at home, wondering whether or not he had caught the ferry. Just before the two o'clock arrival time I drove downtown through a steady summer rain and loitered at the bottom of the A & P parking lot. I kept my motor running and my windshield wipers flipping, trying to look as though I were waiting for a parking slot to open.

Every car coming off the ferry had to pass right in front of me. The black Toyota with the New York plates was the twenty-seventh car. As he went past me, heading for Five Corners, I beeped my horn and swung in behind him. Dirk forced his way through Five Corners as if he had been driving on the Vineyard for years. Of course, the right turn is easier than the left turn or the straight-across, but it was still impressive for a newcomer, a New Yorker with a lifelong reliance on traffic lights. Then he dashed straight through Vineyard Haven's Main Street traffic without any sign of frustration or terror. I was proud of him. From the last line of parked cars at the outer edge of town, it was clear passage out to my house. Dirk drove faster than I. Cops don't worry much about speeding tickets.

By the time I swung into my parking area, Dirk was already out of his Toyota, an old briefcase in his hand, waiting for me.

"Good driving," I said. "Just like a native."

"Stop fucking around. Where is it?"

I started to shake hands, but he grabbed my arm and dragged me into the house. He seemed almost angry in his excitement. All the years I had known him, he might get angry about this or that, like Vineyard traffic, but when it came to his profession, he was cool, polite, orderly. For some reason this case had got to him in a different way. Maybe because it was his first homicide since his retirement, but I thought it was more than that. I remembered how he had acted the day Lulu Waring and Jane Millhouse had been killed before my eyes — before everybody's eyes, except his own.

By the time I had opened my security closet and removed the package, Dirk had cleared my round wooden table. From his briefcase he took lined yellow tablets and ballpoint pens. He had called me from Woods Hole and told me to put on a large pot of coffee because we would be working hard and late.

I held out the package. "Here you are," I said, and added with false pride, "unopened."

Despite his excitement he studied the package to make sure it had not been tampered with, by me or Gracie Mayhew or anybody else in the FedEx complex.

"How did you get hold of this?" I asked.

"Don't ask. Marsden's lawyer was right. Procedures are a little loose in this area."

He tore open the package and removed a fat handful of pages. He looked at the first one. He read aloud, "Celebrity Watch by Mildred Silk. Copyright Okapi Press." He looked at me with a wild grin. "Well, they sent the right book. Let's get to work."

I had envisioned Dirk reading quickly, as I knew he did. I expected him to take occasional notes about clues, then pass the pages on to me in, as the lawyers say, a timely fashion. I would read more slowly because I would want to savor Millie's style, along with clues to the murders. While I disapproved of almost everything Millie wrote, I had always admired the way she wrote it.

But Dirk's reading pace was slow and thoughtful. He spent five minutes absorbing the first page, making a note, rereading the page before he passed it to me. I can't read anything one page at a time except sonnets, so I waited for more.

While I waited, I suggested, "Why don't you let me read first? I can read a lot faster than you can."

Dirk sighed. He neatly replaced page two on top of the pile and looked at me sternly. "Jason," he said, "this is not a speed-reading contest. I'm working. I'm the one who got us this manuscript. I'm the one who is a professional detective. So we are going to do this my way, and you will have to adjust. Now don't interrupt again. Pour me a cup of coffee and shut up."

I poured his coffee. Professional Detective Schultz could read as slowly as he liked and take as many notes as he liked, but I didn't have to sit beside him doing nothing. I put on my yellow slicker, pulled up the hood and went for a walk. While waiting to read Millie's book, I would visit her house.

This was one of those ugly summer days that the Vineyard produces, much to the despair of first-time renters and day-trippers. Gray clouds and steady rain, with now and then a burst of cold wind. Sometimes this goes on for three straight days. My parents and many other parents with young children designed a program to confront three consecutive days of bad Vineyard weather. The first day, which could be viewed almost cheerfully as a relief from the usual swimming, sailing and tennis, was devoted to indoor games and jigsaw puzzles, with parents par-ticipating as a show of good will. Yes, it's raining, but aren't we all having fun playing games together? The second day was an expedition to Oak Bluffs to ride the Flying Horses, the oldest functioning carousel in America. It is so antique that the outer-ring horses don't even move up and down. The Preservation Trust saved and restored it, then turned it into a profit center. Many rides and much grasping for brass rings, followed by pop-corn and salt water taffy. Every parent and every child hoped that the bad weather would end after the second day. When it didn't, we had to visit the State Lobster Hatchery, where we peered into bubbling tanks of water occupied by lobsters of every size, starting with half-inch babies and moving progres-sively upward to full-grown critters. Wall charts told more than children wanted to know about the habits of lobsters and why some lobsters are blue. No known program covers a fourth day of bad Island weather.

In the rain I walked up to West Chop, the northern tip of the Island, past the lighthouse and around the sweeping bend of gigantic old shingled houses, created long ago by wealthy Bostonians. In its early days back in the nineteenth century, West Chop was so elegant and so isolated from the rest of the Vineyard that it had its own pier and steamer and hotel, even its own tiny post office. The post office survives today. Open only during the summer months, it is the smallest, cutest post office I have ever seen.

West Chop is no longer isolated. It still claims elegance, although its exclusive image has been severely damaged by interlopers, Millie and husband Harry Harkness among them. Years ago, a man who built shopping malls could not be a proper West Chopper. On the other hand, a Boston banker who loaned money to a man who built shopping malls could be the perfect West Chopper. But that distinction is long gone.

Millie's house, no longer a crime scene, stood deserted and blank in the steady rain. No lights. No open windows. No car in the gravel driveway. No "For Sale" sign on the front lawn. The West Chop Association did not favor such gross commercialism. Everybody knew it was for sale, so why mention it? If anybody wanted to buy it, he could readily learn that the person to call was real estate broker Bebe Cone, former acquaintance of Mildred Silk, now self-promoted to close friend.

Although Millie had expanded and modernized the old MacCaulay place, she had the taste and the shrewdness to keep it looking as though it still belonged in West Chop, even if her husband didn't. Just another West Chop mansion, although now the most notorious. I stood in the rain looking at her forlorn, empty house before walking home.

When I got back and took off my dripping slicker, Dirk didn't look up from his reading and note taking. He was on his third page of notes, and a respectable pile of pages was available for me to read.

"More coffee," he said.

I filled his cup, poured one for myself and sat down beside him. I picked up my pile of manuscript pages and began to read.

The introductory chapter was called "It Takes One to Know One." It was a sociological essay on celebrities, and it was Millie at her best: intelligent, witty, savage, self-serving and irresponsible. Of all Millie's books that I had read, this opening chapter convinced me that here was the best possible melding of author, style and subject matter.

She began with an anecdote, treasured in the annals of New York City's Players Club, of which Millie admitted that she herself was "one of the very earliest women members." Mark Twain, an even earlier member, always sat at the big round table, reserved by custom for the Club's most celebrated men. One day at lunch he offered this opinion to his illustrious companions. "I would rather go to bed with Lillian Russell stark naked than with General Grant in full dress uniform."

This, said Millie, is the epitome of the finest celebrity style. A great celebrity makes a celebrated remark about two other celebrities to a table full of celebrities. "It takes one to know one," she wrote. "And it takes a celebrity to appreciate and, when necessary, to deplore other celebrities."

Without even a minimal bow to modesty she explained why she alone was equipped to describe and to evaluate the celebrities of Martha's Vineyard. She was not just some grubbing journalist. She was not just some scandal monger peeking through windows. She was both a serious writer and a central player in the drama. She knew them all and had known them for years. They had been guests at her renowned cocktail parties and dinners. They had clustered together under her microscope. Now she was ready to divulge everything that she had seen, identified and classified. Much of it would be ugly, she promised, as is often the case when an interested and intelligent observer peers closely at her slides.

Alas, she warned, licking her lips, her book would contain no superb writer like Twain, no superb sex queen like Lillian Russell, no superb war hero like General Grant. The celebrity level had, in her opinion, deteriorated steeply since that far-off time. She dismissed Princess Diana in a parenthesis, payback for not letting Millie give her a dinner party: "(Anyone who spends only one week on the Island and spends that in seclusion hardly qualifies as a Vineyard celebrity.)" As for the rest, many a celebrity today was, in Falstaff's phrase, "little better than one of the wicked." Still, she trusted that her readers would enjoy what she was about to dish up. She was fully prepared to bite every hand that she had ever fed.

I could hardly wait. "This is marvelous," I told Dirk.

"Depends on your point of view," he said. "Try not to interrupt."

The second chapter, "Hooray for Hollywood," dealt with the invasion of the Vineyard by movie folks — actors, actresses, producers, directors. "This event," Millie said, "is on a smaller scale than the invasion of the Roman Empire by the Visigoths, but more vicious and more destructive." The trouble with movie people was that they did not know how to conceal the fact that they were disgustingly rich. Movie stars like Jack Nicholson and Robert De Niro had rented waterfront palaces in the price range of one hundred thousand dollars for the month of August. This drove up rental prices everywhere and made everybody else feel jealous. Still, said Millie, this was minor depredation compared to what happened when Hollywood people built houses rather than rented them.

This was where she would stick it to Elena.

Millie told good stories, with names and addresses. The

Hollywood couple who bought a landmark house, tore out and rebuilt the insides, then shipped vans of furniture and Oriental rugs and paintings and sculptures and antiques all the way from California. Although I had never been invited to that house since the vans arrived, I took Millie's word for it that not a single item bore any esthetic relationship to the Vineyard. And the Hollywood producer who shipped full-grown trees from New Hampshire to his new Vineyard home because he certainly wasn't going to waste any of his precious time waiting for trees to grow. He wanted to see them full grown right now. And the Hollywood studio mogul who was even more impatient. On the day of his housewarming party, attended by every celebrity on the Island, his driveway was lined on both sides with a mature fruit orchard, transplanted from Connecticut. Ripe apples, pears and peaches hung from the branches, ready for plucking. Millie quoted George S. Kaufman's line: "It just shows what God could do if He had money." She had malicious fun with them all — their excesses, their squandering, their indifference to what suited the Island.

Then she came to Elena Bronze.

I find it irresistible to read the dirt on someone I know, even someone I like as much as I do Elena. In fact, perhaps especially about someone I like. I knew I would enjoy passing on Millie's digs to the target herself, tidbit by juicy tidbit. Elena would be amused by some, angry at some, furious at others. It would be a fascinating conversation, which we would surely have in bed.

But as I read the pages, I kept looking in vain for Millie's shiv.

"Elena Bronze built her waterfront mansion while she was looking the other way. She returned from making a movie in Australia (*Outback Outrage*) to find that her architect and contractor had done her wrong. . . . Her house looks as though it had escaped from a second-rate Bauhaus. . . . She has a California butler straight out of the Erich Von Stroheim role in *Sunset Boulevard*. . . . But unlike most Hollywood homes on the Vineyard, her house is better on the inside than on the outside. . . . Her New England antiques suit the Vineyard. . . . As a barebreasted film star, she may be getting a little long in the nipple, but she has that Best Actress Oscar and Best Supporting Actress Oscar to prove that it's more than just the profligate baring of bosoms. . . ."

This was beneath Millie's minimum standard for venom. I tried to remember what Elena had told me about Millie's mean personal comments. It was that first evening when we were driving in her convertible, and she abruptly told me what she had refused to tell the police. I remembered being flattered. All right, but what had she said? Elena's pride had been hurt, I remembered that. Oh yes, it was something about breast-lifts. Like face-lifts. That was it. Millie asked Elena how many breast-lifts she had had. But that hadn't been all, there was another jibe about Elena's age. It snapped in, the way memory sometimes does. Isn't it about time you became a character actress?

I went back and reread the Elena pages. Something felt wrong. Millie didn't call her a liar about being away when the architect and contractor made her house look so wrong for the Vineyard. She didn't even imply that Elena might have been lying. And then, "Her house is better on the inside than on the outside." Almost a compliment. "Her antiques suit the Vineyard" — an unmistakable compliment. And "a little long in the nipple" was milder and kinder than asking how many breast lifts she had had. But even if one took that crack as criticism, then came the immediate mention of Elena's Oscars.

Was this the Mildred Silk we all knew and loved? Millie was nicer to Elena on paper than she had been in person. Could there have been some sexual attraction? After all, Jane Millhouse had made Millie's "A" list, and Elena was more attractive than the vast soprano. Maybe Elena's physical appeal, perhaps subconscious on Millie's part, had blunted the author's dagger?

I put my questions aside because Dirk had cleared another chapter for me to read. It was called "The Presidential Pestilence."

Millie loved sweeping generalities that she didn't have to prove. This time she opened with the claim that no President in modern times had chosen a vacation home with more destructive impact than Bill Clinton. Harry Truman vacationed in his hometown of Independence, where everybody was used to him. Jack Kennedy went home to the Hyannisport compound. Lyndon Johnson went back to his ranch in Texas. Jimmy Carter went back to Plains, Georgia, to watch the peanuts grow. Reagan was already a familiar California neighbor — movie star, governor and all that — when he picked Santa Barbara. Bush had been vacationing in Kennebunkport for years. True, when all these men took vacations, the press and Secret Service followed them, but at least the Presidents were returning to places where they were already well known and accepted. No big deal, no excitement, a minimum of disruption. Their homecomings were not news to their neighbors and therefore not much trouble.

But Bill Clinton had zero experience of the Vineyard — and vice versa. The Vineyard wasn't used to Presidents. None had visited since Ulysses Grant in 1874. Half the Vineyard was delighted that the President had chosen to come here, but the other half was horrified. The second half, Millie proclaimed, was right.

Because, Millie said, Clinton was not the only one to discover the Vineyard. So did many of the media and, through them, so did the rest of the world. If the President had picked the Vineyard, it must be a very special place. Unfortunately, from the time of the Clinton family's first visit in 1993 and through every succeeding visit, the Vineyard got extensive coverage in newspapers, magazines and television. The colored cliffs of Gay Head, the picturesque fishing village of Menemsha, the ferry boats coming and going through the harbors crowded with pretty sailboats — all received admiring attention from the cameras and the voices. Old Vineyard celebrities, including Millie, were trotted out for inspection and comment. Newcomer celebrities gushed about how wonderful the Island was and what a great time they had last night at the birthday clambake for the President. The Vineyard was compared to the Hamptons, mostly to the Vineyard's credit because the Hamptons were old hat and the Vineyard was new.

"After several summers of this," wrote Millie, "only outstandingly gifted dolts could fail to realize that Martha's Vineyard was IN-IN-IN. The rush of the lemmings followed."

As I myself had written for the *Globe* on the occasion of the First Family's first vacation, "There Goes the Neighborhood."

Millie described her negotiations with the President's close buddy Vernon Jordan over the guest lists for the two dinner parties she gave for the Clintons. Jordan, a regular summer visitor for years, was as familiar with the available showcase celebrities as she was. She held firm and won the basic points: the dinner must be limited to her traditional twenty-two people seated at three tables. No, she would not accept more because everybody would then accuse her of pandering to the President. No, Chelsea would have have to go to a movie or watch television, because Millie refused to invite a teenager to a formal dinner. But yes, she would make an exception and seat herself and the President at an eight-person table rather than her customary six-person table, because that would give two more people dinnertime exposure to him.

Jordan told her the President had a few political guests that he would like to include. A Wampanoag tribal leader, to show his solidarity with Native Americans, and a black selectman from Oak Bluffs, to show his solidarity with African Americans.

"Vernon," she said, "since we already have you, we don't need another black."

"Two blacks would still be only ten percent," he argued, smiling that big Jordan smile. "Just about right to represent the national population."

"Vernon," she said, "I am not going to let politics wreck my dinner party. I will accept one token Indian and one token black — and you're the token black."

Both dinners were a great success, Millie wrote, because the President had been more charming and interesting than expected, and because Millie herself had been brilliant. Hillary and the other guests were barely mentioned.

Dirk was only halfway through the next chapter, "Boobs from the Tube." That would give us, from Millie's final dinner party, Lulu Waring, Jiggs Cooley, Mary Hergesheimer and, because he had canceled at the last minute, Bob Hergesheimer. None of those was actually a boob, but Millie gave herself literary license to write anything she felt like writing. Besides, the Vineyard was endowed with enough real celebrity boobs from TV to justify her chapter title.

Dirk had been taking a lot of notes on this chapter, so it would be a while before I got to read it.

"How about a drink?" I suggested.

"Coffee," he said, without looking up.

"Man cannot live by coffee alone. I'm going to have vodka." No answer.

I got up and poured my drink. The tinkle of ice cubes got to him. "All right. A Scotch."

"Great detective crumbles under pressure." I poured his drink. "What do you think so far? Who did it?"

Dirk stretched way back in his chair, then leaned forward and took a hearty swig of Scotch. "So far," he said, "nobody is really pinned down. A lot of ugly things to follow up on, though. That Miss Silk is not a very nice person."

"Like I told you all along."

"Reading this, I can understand why some people might like to get rid of her."

"A lot of people. But she's a good writer."

"I'm not reading this to enjoy the writing."

"Didn't you like what she wrote about Clinton wrecking the Island?"

"He's not a suspect."

"Presidents don't have to be present in person to commit murder. They can assign somebody from the CIA."

"What's his motive?"

"Millie refused to invite Chelsea."

"Jason, with a little training you could be a detective." He straightened the pile of manuscript pages. "Let's take a break from this and talk about what you're going to feed me for dinner."

* * *

We did only a little more reading but a lot more drinking and talking that night. The next morning brought a second day of wind and rain, so we had total immersion in the manuscript. I finally persuaded Dirk that I could read chapters in the back of the book, make my own notes and stick the pages back in his pile. I promised not to lose or misplace any pages. He was extraordinarily methodical — slow reading, with notes and notes and notes, facts to check on, accusations to check on.

My notes were different. Whatever chapter I was in, I found myself especially intrigued by how Millie described the guests at her last dinner party, one of whom had killed her. The book was filled with many other names and anecdotes and jibes and slashes. But in one chapter or another she dealt with everyone who was there that final night. Except me, of course, the last-minute, noncelebrity substitute for Bob Hergesheimer. I have already told what she wrote about Elena Bronze.

Here are my notes on some of the others.

JIGGS COOLEY: "His smart-ass sit-com character appeals to the juvenile audience, ages fifteen to forty-five.... Puerile humor supported by the loudest laugh track ever.... Slightly more winsome in person than on television. One could almost warm to this curly-headed child if he had not committed an epic atrocity of Vineyard house-building. With taste that could have been honed only in the sit-com world, he pulverized a new, perfectly good and perfectly tasteful house to make way for a monstrous California hacienda with a red tile roof...."

Note to self: No mention of homosexuality? Millie's physical description rather favorable. Did she make a pass at him and get nowhere? Is that why he was on her "B" list?

JILL KLEIN: "If your crime is vicious enough, especially if it is sexually kooky enough, Klein will get you off.... Ask not for justice, ask only for victory.... At cocktail parties or for that matter even at the Community Services Auction or Edgartown's Fourth of July parade, Klein's bright black eyes roam the crowd, looking for clients. Not that she needs the money. She needs the action.... No giant Vineyard client as yet, but mark my words...."

Note: No mention of jury tampering in the Lyman case? That's almost public domain, and surely one could write around any charge of libel..

LULU WARING: "She has been a famous TV figure for so long that nobody remembers how she got there. A young Georgia girl with great ambition and intelligence but without a *soupçon* of beauty, she came up the hard way. Starting as a page girl, the lowest rung, she became the uncrowned queen of studio fellatio. She serviced every mid-level and top-level executive she could get her mouth on. . . . As her fame and ability grew, so did opportunity until, finally, a grateful executive gave her a tiny role on the local news show. Her charm and her drawl and her sharp intelligence did the rest. She never again looked back — or down."

Note: Pure Millie! Wow, if true.

SAM AND BEBE CONE: "Many marriages are made in hell, but this one belongs in Dante's Seventh Circle. . . . Bebe got the trophy house, but Sam got the trophy mistress straight out of the British peerage. . . ."

Note: Come on, Millie. Everybody knows it's the Duchess of Casteldowne. Even the Duke admits it. And where's the story of the ruby necklaces?

EVERETT MUNK: "He thinks he's the best writer on the Vineyard. . . . He longs for financial triumph the way he longs for bourbon. After half a dozen highly respected novels, mere critical triumph tastes to him no better than soda water. . . . He is fiercely and protectively jealous of his third wife Nancy, who is cute and flirtatious. . . ."

Note: And dumb! And sexy! And available!

DR. SUNBEAM: "Born Matthew Smeck, he has wisely abandoned that moniker. . . . A salesman of immense superfical charm, on the page and on the platform and on the tube. . . . He writes for and appeals to Mencken's 'booboisie.' Consequently he has cleaned up financially in a way that poor Everett Munk never will. . . . Dr. Sunbeam's Life Center on Sengekentocket Pond is a perfect replica of a huge pink plaster cunt. . . ."

Note: Very amusing, Millie, but what about the fact that it's a tax-free cheat? And why "salesman" when you always called him charlatan?

BETSY POPE: "A sad has-been . . . She followed the Clintons to the Vineyard. Hardly surprising, since all entertainers except Charlton Heston are knee-jerk Democrats. . . . One of those instantly recognizable voices, like Sinatra, and she still makes an occasional recording with that unforgettable, unmistakable voice." (Followed by a quote from "Ozymandias") "'Nothing beside remains. Round the decay of that colossal wreck, boundless and bare the lone and level sands stretch far away.'"

Note: Very apt, a colossal wreck indeed. But nothing about Bitsy's widely reported lifestyle? The drugs, the orgies, etc.?

CHICK BIRD: . . .

Note: Too boring for comment. Like everybody else, Millie deplores his buying Eight Gables, but she doesn't even mention the bimbo.

But then —

JANE MILLHOUSE: I didn't take notes because they would have filled pages. Also because it was much too sensational for notes. It was the finest, most breathtaking piece of Millie's writing that I had ever read — vivid, erotic, intimate, immediate, astonishing. Without blushing or bragging or apologizing, Millie told the full story of her love affair with the great soprano. She told how, as a high-level Patron of the Metropolitan Opera, she had approached the diva in her dressing room after a superb performance of *Lucia*. She requested an at-home interview. As Millie intended, Millhouse assumed it was for an article, and they set a time to meet at her apartment.

Millie claimed she had dressed for the appointment "modestly," but I thought that unlikely. She told how, "taking my whole life and career and pride in my hands and throwing them on her coffee table like beads," she made a straight-out, flat-out proposition. She, Millie, had never in her life, at least not since meaningless boarding school shenanigans, had a physical experience with another woman. Many men, yes, but no woman. She now felt certain that she had missed something important, that her life was incomplete. She was now determined to have that experience, but it must not be with just anybody. It must be with someone of great value and beauty and significance. "So I am asking you to be that person."

The diva sat quietly through Millie's speech, her dark face impassive, inscrutable. She listened closely. Even after Millie finished, she continued sitting there, motionless. At last she stood up, rising to her full majestic height, towering over Millie, still no expression. After a long moment she put her great hands on Millie's shoulders. Then she smiled and, "in her smoldering voice," said, "Let's both find out."

I'm not sure I believe it began exactly that way. But I believe what Millie wrote about the affair itself. She described the exploration, the growing desire, the initial embarrassment, the experiments, and then eventually true lust and perhaps something like love. It lasted over several months, much of it at the Vineyard and in both their homes. I found some of the physical details shocking but, because of Millie's perfect taste and her skill in writing, never prurient. I was fascinated — and, I have to admit, deeply moved. How could the woman who wrote this remarkably frank, this painfully honest account — ?

I stopped.

I looked back over all my notes. I thought back over the book. I thought back over Millie's other books. I thought back about Millie herself.

I realized what must have happened.

* * *

"Dirk," I said, "this is not Millie's book."

"Yeah? So whose book is it?"

"It's not the book that Millie wrote. It's only partly what she wrote."

"How do you know that?"

"I know it. Believe me, no mistake."

"I'm sorry, Jason, but why should I believe you?"

"Because I knew Millie. And I know her writing. I know her style. And I know quite a lot about the people she was writing about. There are too many things that ought to be in this manuscript that aren't there."

"Like what?"

"Too many to explain." I could see disbelief in Dirk's eyes. "Well, for instance, take Jill Klein."

"No thanks," Dirk laughed. "You can keep her."

"I'm serious."

"All right then, what about Jill Klein?" He was trying to be patient with me.

"You remember at the Yacht Club when you brought up her jury tampering in the Lyman case?"

"Sure."

"Did you notice the Lyman case isn't even mentioned in Millie's book?"

"Listen, Jason, I'm trying to solve some murders. I'm interested in what Miss Silk wrote that might give us evidence or motive. I'm not interested in what isn't there."

"You have to be. As you told Jill Klein, the suspicion of tampering was in the press. Practically public domain. But Millie doesn't mention it."

"Maybe she was afraid of libel."

"Millie was a high-risk writer. The daring old girl on the flying trapeze. She would have found a way to write around any possible libel, and besides, the Okapi lawyers would have protected her. But there is no way Millie could have written about Jill Klein and left that out."

"Maybe."

"No maybe. And then Sam and Bebe Cone. I've seen pictures of Sam Cone with his mistress the Duchess of Casteldowne, pictures with identifying captions. For God's sake, the Duke himself has acknowledged the affair, but Millie doesn't name her. And she doesn't tell the story of the ruby necklaces."

"What story is that?"

"Too long to explain, but it's not a story that Millie, with her fetish for big jewelry, would leave out. And Dr. Sunbeam. She doesn't even mention the fact that his Life Center is a tax-free cheat."

"All right, but what does this have to do with murder?"

"Everything. And Betsy Pope. Remember I told you about Betsy trying to buy a house in that north shore enclave, and the association refused to let her in? Because of her druggy lifestyle and famous orgies? Not mentioned."

"Maybe she felt sorry for Miss Pope. She practically said so."

"Yes, she called her 'a sad has-been.' But that wouldn't stop Millie from sticking it to Betsy. Or to Elena Bronze. Or to Chick Bird. Malice was Millie's stock-in-trade. She would never have missed all those chances. Never. Don't you see the pattern?"

I could see that I was at last getting to Dirk. He liked patterns.

"Yeah," he said, "all right, but there are places where she really cuts loose. Like Lulu Waring."

"Yes, and Jane Millhouse. Those are terrific. Savagely funny about Lulu and then shockingly, beautifully intimate about her affair with Millhouse."

"I didn't care much for some of that stuff with Miss Millhouse."

"You don't have to, but it's vivid, splendid writing."

"Okay, I admit it's pretty juicy."

"More than that. Better than that. The Lulu Waring and Jane Millhouse sections are extraordinary. Millie at her peak."

"I suppose so."

"No question. And tell me, Dirk, what do these two women, Lulu Waring and Jane Millhouse, have in common?"

"Oh."

"Yes. They're both dead."

* * *

Dirk was phoning his friend Mo Abbudanza in Boston. I was on the bedroom extension but under orders not to say a word. Dirk had to talk his way through three underlings before he finally reached the captain.

After they said hello, Dirk asked, "How come you're back in Boston instead of down here on the Vineyard? In New York we like to work where the murders actually took place."

In the same note of raillery Abbudanza said, "Oh, you big city detectives are so smart. We sure could learn a lot from you."

"So why aren't you here?"

"Because, my friend, we've got a whole expert team right here sifting through the Silk manuscript line by line."

"Been a long wait. Are you finding out anything?"

"Buckets. What can I do for you?"

"Well, I had an idea I'd kind of like to look into. I assume you have all of Miss Silk's legal papers?"

"Sure, from her lawyer. Copies, anyway. What are you looking for?"

"Not much, probably, but I'd like to see her book contract. The one with Okapi for this last book."

"Yeah, we have that. At least I think we have it. No, I know we have it, I remember it listed in the documents. What's your fax number down there?"

"Just a second," Dirk said.

I put down the phone and hurried into my living room and wrote my fax number on Dirk's pad. He read it slowly to Abbudanza. Abbudanza read it slowly back to make sure he had it right. That's how cops are.

"Okay, it may take them a little while to find it, but I'll have them send it to you. If you learn anything useful, let me know."

"Sure thing. Many thanks, Mo."

They hung up.

We waited just over two hours before the fax phone rang and the first page of Millie's contract began to print out. It took a long time because the contract was nine pages long, single-spaced. Most of it was book publisher boilerplate dealing with the royalty schedule and the ownership of paperback rights and foreign rights and subsidiary rights.

The information we were looking for was clause 27(a). It read:

"No changes, deletions or additions will be made in the text without the Author's express approval and consent, which shall not be unreasonably withheld."

I felt a tingle of triumph. I knew I was right.

"I guess," Dirk said, "we need to talk to Mr. Marsden."

In for a Penny

"Of course she'll remember me," Dirk said. "That woman remembers everything."

Once again he was on the living room phone and I was on the bedroom phone. He dialed Leonard Marsden's private extension at Okapi.

"Okapi Publishing, Mr. Marsden's office," the familiar voice answered.

"Hi, Maureen. This is Detective Schultz."

"Oh hi, Dirk." Maureen was on a first-name basis with all the investigating officers. "Have you learned anything?"

Dirk and I had discussed whether or not he had to tell Maureen Custis that he was no longer officially investigating the attempted poisoning of her boss. We decided he did not have to tell her unless she asked.

Dirk did not answer her question. "I want to make a date to ask Mr. Marsden another question or two. How's his schedule? I'm up in the Vineyard, but I could come down whenever he's available."

"You don't have to. He's up there now in Miss Silk's house. Working on her papers. Just give him a call."

After a little more friendly chatter with Maureen, Dirk hung up. I joined him in the living room.

"That's a break," I said. "Let's call him."

Dirk shook his head. "I think it might work better if we just dropped in, no warning."

"Then let's go." Dirk had promised me, because of what I had spotted in Millie's book, that I deserved to be present if he could possibly arrange it.

Dirk shook his head again. "I think for this one we need official standing."

He picked up the phone and dialed Abbudanza's office in Boston. I went back in the bedroom and picked up. Because Dirk had complained about how long it took to get through the underlings, he now had Abbudanza's direct line.

"Mo, it's Dirk. I think I'm on to something after all, but I need your help."

"Right off, that sounds suspicious."

"Yeah, I suppose so. Well actually, Mo, it is suspicious. But if anything comes of it, you're going to be really pleased. And I mean really — no shit — pleased."

"What do I have to do?"

"I'm a licensed detective, right?"

"A former licensed detective."

"I want you to deputize me."

"For what? What do you have in mind, a posse? You going to go out and hang somebody? Lynch somebody? Frontier justice?"

"I want to be a deputy for twenty-four hours. On the Mildred Silk homicide case. Actually, Mildred Silk homicide et al."

"Preposterous."

"Listen, Mo, if it works, you're going to be the happiest investigative homicide captain in Massachusetts. If it doesn't work, no harm done."

"I'll send an officer with you. Then whatever you have in mind, you won't need to be deputized."

"Actually I was going to ask for some help. While you're deputizing me, how about adding my colleague Jason Arnold?"

"Jason Arnold? You want me to deputize somebody who's a suspect in the Bird homicide? How's that going to look if it turns out he did it?"

"I withdraw it, I won't need him. Twenty-four hours, Mo. I wouldn't ask if I didn't have something going."

"Whatever you get, you'll give it to me first?"

"Of course. Absolutely."

A long pause at the other end of the telephone. Finally Abbudanza said, "Twelve hours. Go see the state police in Oak Bluffs. I'll arrange it."

"Great. Thanks."

"Dirk, don't screw me on this."

"Scout's honor."

"It better be good."

"Fighting chance, Mo."

When they had hung up, I said to Dirk, "What do you mean, you don't need me? You promised I could be in on it."

"I don't need you to be a deputy. You can just come along. Like a writer, or something."

He told me to bring my notes on the manuscript. He got his tape recorder and two reels of tape.

The weather had turned bright and sunny after two days of rain and wind. None of the kids would have to visit the lobster hatchery. We drove over to the state police station in Oak Bluffs. Because of Abbudanza's comment about me, Dirk thought I better wait outside, so I didn't get to see him be sworn in and promise faithfully to uphold the laws of the Commonwealth of Massachusetts. It took half an hour. I expected him to emerge wearing some kind of badge, like a silver star, but they just gave him a plastic ID card to carry.

He was excited when he climbed into the front seat beside me, his dark eyes bright and eager. "Let's go get him," he said.

* * *

I pulled into the gravel driveway at Millie's house and parked behind a rental red Buick. As we walked to the front door, Dirk said, "Leave all this first part to me. Don't say anything till I ask you to."

He knocked on the door. We waited. No sound of footsteps. He knocked again, louder, longer. He waited a few seconds and then started knocking again.

An annoyed baritone voice said, "Yes, yes. Coming."

Now we could hear footsteps. The door opened, and Leonard Marsden stood there. He wore a rumpled long-sleeved blue shirt with the cuffs flipped back. Equally rumpled tan slacks. Maybe he had slept in his clothes. If so, he must have slept badly because he looked tired. And he had not shaved. Bristly gray whiskers sprouted around his bushy guardsman's mustache. I had filed him away as tall, shaggy and impressive, but today he was mainly tall and shaggy.

He glared at Dirk, then at me, then back at Dirk. He recognized both of us. "What's this?" he said.

"I want to ask you some questions," Dirk said. His voice was cold, professional. "Can we come in?"

"No. I've answered everything a dozen times to every cop in New York, including you. Besides, I'm working."

"It's not about your attempted poisoning," Dirk said. "It's about Miss Silk's murder. Can we come in?"

"You're not Massachusetts police."

Dirk took out his deputy ID and showed it to him. "Can we come in?"

"What about him? Arnold?"

"He's helping me."

"I told you, I'm working."

Dirk stood still, saying nothing.

Marsden finally shrugged. "I suppose it's better than going over old papers."

He stood aside to let us enter. "In her office."

He led the way, then sat down heavily behind Millie's desk. He waved us to a couple of chairs. Every flat space in the office was covered by old manila file folders. A huge cardboard carton was half filled with discarded papers. When he saw us looking at the mess and mass of paper, he said, "This is the last time I will ever agree to be a literary executor. What do you want to know?"

Dirk took his time. I admired the methodical way he handled it. He took out his tape recorder, opened it, inserted a reel of tape and closed it. He carefully placed it on the edge of the desk. He pretended to fiddle a bit, getting it set just right. Then he pushed the record button. "I am taping this conversation with Leonard Marsden," he told the machine. He gave the date, the time and the location. He wasn't even looking at Marsden. He was looking at and talking to the machine.

Now Dirk looked at Marsden, took out a small white card and said, "I am going to read you your Miranda rights." He had once told me that of course he knew them by heart, but reading them from the card was more intimidating. It also eliminated any possible later claim that he had left out something. He read aloud the fact that Marsden had the right to remain silent, the right to have a lawyer, and so on.

Marsden heard Dirk through before he said, "Okapi once published a book attacking the Miranda rights. A scholarly book. It sold reasonably well." He thought for a moment, remembering back. "Mostly to law school libraries," he added.

"Then you understand your rights," Dirk said. He returned

the card to his pocket. "At the end of this conversation I am going to charge you with the murder of Miss Mildred Silk. I thought you might want to discuss it first."

Marsden did not seem upset. He was leaning forward, his elbows on Millie's desk, his chin resting on his fists. I could not see any change in his expression.

"Why would I do that?" he asked. His deep voice held no inflection.

"Because you couldn't publish the book the way Miss Silk wrote it."

"Oh? You've seen what she wrote?"

"I don't have to. For the record, where is her original manuscript? Her original handwritten manuscript?"

"For the record, Lieutenant, I have no idea. She must have destroyed it. It's not in her papers."

This was impossible, but Dirk did not know it. Millie had given all her original manuscripts, one after the other, to Wellesley, a source of pride to both Millie and her college. I longed to point this out but obeyed orders to keep quiet until spoken to.

"On the contrary, Mr. Marsden, you destroyed it."

Marsden took his elbows off the desk and leaned back in his chair — Millie's chair. He might have been enjoying himself. "Why would I do that?"

"Because you changed what she wrote."

Marsden spread his hands in innocence. "My good fellow, I'm an editor. That's what editors do. I have spent my life changing what authors wrote in order to improve their books. That's my job."

"Not with Miss Silk. I read her contract with Okapi. No changes allowed."

Marsden was silent for a good ten seconds. No expression. Then he said, "Without approval."

"Without express approval and consent," Dirk amended.

"Which shall not unreasonably be withheld," Marsden amended further. "Don't try to educate me about my own contracts, Lieutenant. I've signed thousands of them."

"With that clause?"

This time Marsden's silence lasted fifteen seconds . . . twenty seconds . . . thirty seconds. I could see he was close to the edge. A sigh. "Not often."

"Exactly." Dirk turned to me. "I believe Mr. Arnold has a comment."

I started to clear my throat but just in time recalled Dirk's instructions. Don't clear your throat. Don't be nervous. He's the one who's nervous. I spoke my rehearsed opening line.

"Mr. Marsden, your editing of Millie's book is an outrage. It is a disaster. It is a crime in itself."

This time the pause was endless. And this time his face did reflect his feelings.

He was a lifelong professional editor. He was wounded. Worse than wounded, he was stricken.

Finally, with a note of despair, he said, "You've read it then."

I nodded. Don't talk when you don't have to.

"Is it that obvious?"

I nodded again.

He sighed again and shook his head. "Under the circumstances," he said, "I did the best I could."

During the next hour both Dirk and I inserted questions. Dirk's questions were mostly about specific crime details. Mine were about Millie's manuscript. These are Marsden's words, taken from the tape.

* * *

The same clause was in her last contract, but then it was no problem. That book was a collection of her essays, almost all of them previously published in magazines, so there were virtually no changes beyond an occasional footnote of explanation. Yes, the clause was put in at her request. She was our most distinguished and most valuable author, and we had done seven books together before *Celebrity*. She was entitled to special privileges. Besides, she was a very clean writer. A beautiful writer, very intelligent. I seldom had to suggest anything more than minor changes. The publishing world would be much simpler, as well as more profitable, if more authors were like Millie. She was a dream. As well as a full-fledged bitch. And, in fairness, a very nice bed partner. Oh yes, many times. I was pleased but not flabbergasted to find myself on her "A" list for Very Personal Bequests.

She and I had many preliminary talks about *Celebrity Watch*. Some authors are leery about discussing their next book, not quite sure where they are going, but Millie had total confidence. It was a perfect subject for her, and during the years she was writing, the Vineyard started getting more and more publicity and attention. As a result, more and more celebrities. I couldn't wait to publish the book and cash in on the Vineyard's new notoriety. Every book of Millie's was important and successful, but this one promised to be more than successful. I thought it might make a great deal of money.

Money. That was crucial to Okapi. Because we are privately owned, with a limited number of investors . . . I have never had to say this publicly, but we were desperate for a major success. As a small publishing house surrounded by more and more conglomerate giants, we had little to support us beyond our reputation for excellence.

Excellence. I have spent my life in search of excellent books, hoping that at least some of them would make money. Not necessarily a fortune. Just enough to support what I believed in, which was good books. Millie's writing had that rare combination of excellence and profitability. Long-term profitability. Every one of her books that we published is still in print and still selling on our back list.

While I waited for *Celebrity Watch*, I was aware that if Okapi did not soon have a marked financial improvement, we would probably have to sell out to the Germans. The fucking Germans. I thought when we defeated them in World War II, that was surely the end of that. But here they come again. Also the fucking Japs. I thought we defeated them too.

Millie's book was my great hope. I couldn't bear that she was taking so long to finish it, although of course while Okapi's finances were going down, the value of the Vineyard as a book subject kept going up. Celebrities, the Clintons, Princess Diana, magazine stories, all that free publicity. If we could just hang on, Millie and the Vineyard might save us. So I thought.

Then Millie sent me the first six chapters. You saw *Apollo 13*? "Houston, we have a problem." She was always a venomous writer, it was part of her charm. I have read every word she ever wrote for publication, and those first six chapters were some of her very best writing. But unpublishable. Libelous, malicious, invasive of privacy. At first I thought she was teasing me. With her long and controversial writing experience, she had a pretty good idea of what she could get away with and what was out of bounds. Naturally, as a writer, she liked to push the bounds as far as possible. Our libel lawyer and our libel insurance company occasionally had hot arguments with her. But I found myself, more often than not, taking Millie's side. In my profession, freedom of speech is worth a mass. If you can't risk a little libel suit now and then, you should get out of publishing and go to work for a hardware chain.

Still, there are limits, and this time I had to blow the whistle. But as well as I knew her, I had to be careful. An editor's relationship with a successful author, even a longtime relationship, is fragile. Six other publishing houses are dying to steal her away from you. They are eager to offer her more money, a longer multi-book contract, a car and driver, all kinds of blandishments and bonuses. An unhappy author is like a free agent in baseball or football: "What's the offer?" Loyalty is not a factor.

Of course I had several substantial holds over Millie. We worked well together, her books had been successful, both critically and financially, and Okapi's reputation for excellence was solid. Perhaps most important of all, at Okapi she was the acknowledged star, the jewel in the crown. That would not be true at some of the bigger houses that would gladly have given her huge advances. Millie had her husband's fortune, so money alone would not be a sufficient lure.

With all this in mind, I took her out to lunch at her favorite literary show-off place, the Grill Room of the Four Seasons. Over our drinks I told her how great the writing was, never better. She agreed. She was always a staunch admirer of her own work. But, I said, much as I enjoyed her pyrotechnics, she must realize that a number of things in this first draft would have to come out, or at least be softened.

Now I knew from long experience that what she had showed me was anything but a first draft. She did all her writing in longhand, gave it to her secretary for typing, reworked the typescript, sometimes making extensive changes, then had it retyped. All copies returned to Millie. This process might be repeated several times before she was satisfied. But I thought if I called it a first draft, it would be easier for her to accept the fact that she was going to have to make a lot of changes. I was wrong.

"Lenny," she said, narrowing her eyes, jutting her chin out, "this is not a first draft. This is the final draft. You had better adjust."

Well, it all came out over our very long lunch, a lunch that was mostly drinks. No guarantees, she said, but this was probably her last book. She did not intend to dribble on and on, publishing inferior late work like Hemingway or Maugham or even Faulkner, just to prove she was still alive. She was determined to make this last book her best. That meant writing exactly what she thought, saying exactly what she meant about everybody. Let the chips fall. Most of these celebrities were frightful people, and by God she was going to let them have it, right smack in the kisser. A few of them were not so frightful, one or two were even on the cusp of being admirable, but she was going to tell the absolute truth about them, nothing held back. This would be her last testament, and it would be as good and blunt and wicked as she could possibly make it.

So of course I asked her, what about libel, what about invasion of privacy.

"That, dear Lenny, is your problem."

I told her it was a problem for both of us, but she shook her head and gave me her best savage smile. Her contract specified no changes without her agreement, and this time, for the first time and the last time, she was not going to agree to anything. Unless, of course, in the unlikely event that I could point out a misspelling or a grammatical error. She knew that Okapi, like all publishers, carried libel insurance and suggested that I be prepared to invoke it. She also said that as I knew perfectly well, public figures are virtually libelproof, thanks to the *Times v. Sullivan* Supreme Court decision. That would protect Okapi against Clinton, pursuer of young women, and also against Senator Washburn, pursuer of even younger women, lowest age limit not yet established. As for celebrities in general, courts hold them to a higher standard of proof for libel because they have ready access to the media to defend themselves against any and all damaging statements.

All this was true, but I had visions of a succession of libel suits that would drain our resources far beyond the limits of our insurance and eat up the profits from the book.

I would have to spend the next three or four years dealing with lawyers rather than with authors. A bleak and desperate prospect. As a last resort I reminded Millie that her contract specified that her approval of changes could not be unreasonably withheld.

She gave me the straight, hard stare. "So cancel my contract," she said. "I think I can find another publisher."

"Don't be silly," I said, and called for the check.

When I got back to the office, I told my secretary no calls and no interruptions and closed the door to think. I will spare you my ruminations, but here is where I came out. I desperately needed Millie's book. I desperately needed the profits from Millie's book. I needed many changes in Millie's book before I could publish it. But once she completed her manuscript, I didn't need Millie herself. She probably wasn't going to write any more books, so this was the only one I needed. I didn't need her. In fact, I concluded, I needed to get rid of her in order to accomplish everything else.

Oh yes, cold-blooded, I agree. I learned that valuable trait during the war, when I worked for Wild Bill Donovan in OSS — Office of Strategic Services, forerunner of the CIA. If you bothered to look up my service record, as I suppose somebody did, it said that I was an Army quartermaster stationed in London. Donovan was very good at arranging that kind of thing — or any other kind of thing, for that matter. He thought his team should have what he called protective coloration. So my service record gives the impression that I was in charge of boots and underwear and helmets and fatigue clothing. That was one of Donovan's little jokes, because in real life I did handle supplies for OSS agents. Including, among other things, cyanide pills.

Yes, yes, that's right, we really did give them to agents in the field so that they could eliminate themselves immediately if captured. Cold-blooded but practical. Kinder and quicker than torture, and the final result is the same. Yes indeed, concealed under false tooth caps, although some agents hid them in various other places. You may never have heard this, but do you know what the British espionage services called them?

They called them L-tablets. L for lethal. So quaint and dainty. So British.

I had a good deal of time to think about disposing of Millie while she finished her manuscript, but I never seriously considered anything except cyanide. It's so easy to carry around, and the results are instantaneous and infallible. Actually at the end of the war I took home a full bottle of cyanide pills. They were in a dark-glass bottle because cyanide deteriorates in light. It was a wonderful war, so we all took home souvenirs. When it came time to think about Millie, I realized that my World War II pills, even in a dark bottle, might no longer be effective. I couldn't find any reliable chemical evidence about the shelf life of cyanide, but fifty years struck me as a long time. So I got a fresh supply. No, I'm sorry, I see no compelling reason to compromise my source.

After Millie's unfortunate demise, I had to work fast on the manuscript. Much faster than I like to work. Book publishing is, after all, a leisurely business. I knew the police would insist on reading the manuscript for possible clues, so I had to make sure that the version they eventually read was the version I intended to publish. I had to get rid of Millie's handwritten manuscript and make sure no other versions were tucked away in her papers. And I had to make sure that the secretary, Miss Quinn, had followed Millie's instructions and kept nothing, as indeed was the case. No paper trail anywhere except for the one computer printout. I had to take the final computer disk version and edit out all the libelous material that I didn't dare risk publishing. I couldn't give that job to anybody else. I had to do it myself and at top speed. No doubt I erred on the side of caution. With no time to spare, when I was in doubt, I softened Millie's wording or just cut out the passage altogether. If I had had the time, I could have done better. I regret Mr. Arnold's judgment on the result. It is a judgment I have rarely heard on any book I've edited.

Yes, you have guessed it. I could not bear to give up either the Lulu Waring or the Jane Millhouse passages. Both were headline material — and best-seller material. Also, if one respects good writing, they were marvelous. Lulu practicing fellatio on the network staff, vivid and hilarious. Those sex scenes between Millie and Jane Millhouse. The images — images that stick with you. "That gorgeous glistening pink against the brutal black." I couldn't give up those scenes. Those passages had to be preserved. But at the same time they were blatantly libelous and invasive. If Waring or Millhouse chose to sue, the cases would be basically indefensible. One would have to negotiate a whopping out-of-court settlement, or face a jury trial with the risk of monstrous monetary damages. Obviously Lulu and Jane had to go.

Oh well, in for a penny —

Lieutenant, I resent that. There was not the faintest danger of a mishap. Lulu Waring's glass was labeled with a big red LULU, and she had been drinking out of it all morning. In the highly unlikely event that someone else picked up the glass to drink from it, I was close enough to clumsily knock it out of that person's hand. Unless the person had been Jane Millhouse, in which case I would probably have let it ride. And then, in all the post-Lulu confusion, it was easy to slip a pill in the smoked turkey sandwich. That, too, was clearly labeled. And again, I kept my eye on the sandwich platter, and again I was close enough to take remedial action if someone else picked up the smoked turkey. I guarantee there was no chance of an accident. I consider that charge insulting.

Well sure, I'm sorry. I had nothing personal against either woman. But *ars longa, vita brevis.* And as Mr. Faulkner once said, "Ode on a Grecian Urn" is worth any number of old ladies.

No, the heirs of Lulu Waring and Jane Millhouse could not have sued over the book's contents. You cannot libel the dead, except in the rare instance when you accuse them of having a serious mental disability, which might be inherited by their offspring. Or which might lead people to think the offspring had inherited it. If you call a dead person crazy, the family can sue. Otherwise not.

So now I didn't have to fiddle with those marvelous passages about Lulu Waring and Jane Millhouse. But I still needed time to finish editing everything else, and I was racing against all those demands to release the manuscript. I'm too old to be comfortable with computers, so I really had to struggle with the word processor. I found it much easier and quicker to delete than to rewrite. I suppose that affected my judgment.

Jiggs Cooley? Well, I don't follow the sit-com world too closely. I thought I had heard that he was gay, but I wasn't sure that he himself had ever come out and said so. I had no time to do research. I just took it out. No, Millie didn't write anything about having a sexual experience with Cooley, so I don't know if she went after him or not. Millie was quite an imp about sex. I never knew who she would go after next, but there was always a lot of action. For all I know, she may have left a few names off her VPB list. Some of them were a long time ago, and she might have forgotten. But sorry, I just don't know about Cooley.

On Jill Klein, I deleted Millie's savage page about her jury tampering in the Lyman case. Millie treated it as established fact. If I had had more time, I could have saved some of it. After all, there was a good deal of speculation at the time of the verdict. But I couldn't even consult our libel lawyer about what was all right to publish and what wasn't. The last person I wanted to take on in a libel suit was a courtroom litigant of Miss Klein's caliber. Safer to take it out.

On Betsy Pope, I thought I'd better delete what Millie wrote about her frightful way of life. Of course, other people had published many gamy details, although I didn't have time to go back and check which of Millie's charges had already been printed and which hadn't. I suppose I could safely have published some of it. But I remembered that Pope had come close to suing the association that kept her from buying the north shore house. If she wanted to sue about that, she might sue about anything. Frankly, I was also worried about letting Millie say that Betsy Pope is "a colossal wreck," though that's what she is. I decided — rather daringly, I may say — that those weren't Millie's words, they were Percy Bysshe Shelley's. Let her sue Shelley.

I had to exercise great caution about Sam Cone's affair with the Duchess of Casteldowne. Millie had great fun with her. She christened her "Doris, the Open Door Duchess," and then she played around quite wittily with Doris's open door policy. But British libel laws are much tougher than ours, so I just took all that out. Yes, I hated to lose the ruby necklaces. Millie had tracked down the whole story. She even talked to the Paris jeweler who sold that monumentally expensive ruby necklace to Sam Cone so that he could give it to Doris. According to Millie, the necklace was so fabulous that even the Duke of Casteldowne was pleased that his wife owned it, regardless of how she earned it. When Bebe saw the color picture in *Vanity Fair* of Doris wearing the superb necklace above her superb cleavage, and when she heard from her closest and dearest friends that Sam had given it to Doris, she told Sam that unless she got her own matching ruby necklace, she would never agree to a divorce. Sam paid the jeweler to make an exact duplicate. Bebe wore it on every possible occasion but then reneged on the divorce. Grounds for murder, in my opinion. You might want to keep an eye on the Cones. No wonder they hated each other. Well, I couldn't risk printing all that. I could be sued by Doris, by the Duke, by Bebe, by Sam and, for all I knew, by the Paris jeweler. I practically wore out the DELETE key.

When Judge Whipple ruled that I had to turn over Millie's manuscript to the district attorney, I still needed more time to finish sanitizing what Millie wrote. So I staged my own poisoning to gain a couple of days. Rather well, don't you think? I thought the whole business of the missing Okapi coaster was quite ingenious. Damn ingenious, if I do say so. Worthy of Wild Bill Donovan himself.

But perhaps I was even more ingenious to come up with amygdalin instead of potassium cyanide pills. If my "murderer" had used one of the old-fashioned L-tablets, to use the British designation, it might well have dissolved before I got back to my office, creating the famous bitter almond odor. Naturally, once I walked into my office and smelled that, I would never drink the concoction. So that would have been a patently unconvincing attempt to kill me. Instead, my "murderer" had to use a form of cyanide that was odorless when it dissolved. Hence amygdalin.

Actually, Lieutenant, even experts in your profession might not be aware that some people are physically unable to detect the odor of cyanide. It's a genetic condition like color blindness and, like color blindness, it almost invariably occurs in males. It's a gender specific abnormality. True, the problem does not arise very often, but imagine that one of your autopsy surgeons had this abnormality. He might open the corpse of a cyanide victim and never smell the deadly telltale odor. Your surgeon could conceivably die from the fumes — or at least feel pretty damned sick. An amusing possibility. However, it would have been far too complicated for me to claim to be one of that handful of genetic abnormalities who can't smell cyanide. That's why I came up with amygdalin instead of potassium cyanide. Damned ingenious, don't you think?

Of course after my attempted murder, I had to spend all those hours and hours answering your tiresome questions about who might have reason to kill me. But, with the help of strong black coffee and stay-awake pills, I managed to finish my editing. I gained the final swatch of time I needed. At last I had one master computer disk and two master printouts, one for Okapi, one for the district attorney.

The coaster? It's in my office in the bookshelf. Second row from the top, fourth book from the right, one of our less successful ventures called *Origins of African Art*. I can't remember now just why we decided to publish it. Nobody bought it at the time, so I figured nobody would look at it now. Anyway, that's where the coaster is, tucked between the pages. After you finish with it, you might consider giving it to Maureen as a souvenir.

Chick Bird? Gentlemen, you have me. I have no idea who killed him, but I didn't. Millie had written very little about him. Like me, she was not interested in computers or in the computer business. She believed that writers should write by hand. She describes her theory in one of her essays. She believed that the direct physical contact between the hand and the pen and the paper imparts an emotional immediacy that cannot be achieved in any other way. She admitted the usefulness of the typewriter, and of course she had all her handwritten work typed up by her secretary, but she personally did not own one. Same feeling about the computer. A celebrity like Chick Bird, whose whole world was computer software, was not worth much of her attention. As you read, she deplored his purchase of the House of Eight Gables, but that was perfectly safe because everybody else had deplored it, both in print and over the air. And she pointed out the extravagance of his coast-to-coast trips in his own jet, but what else is new? What you see is what she wrote, word for word. I didn't have to delete anything, including Mr. Bird himself.

So where does that leave us? In splendid shape, I think. Millie's book, in spite of all my hasty deletions, is still a valuable property. Very valuable. It will make a great deal of money for Okapi and sell forever. The additional publicity stemming from what I have told you today will add to the bonfire. Murder has its rewards. Everybody will have to buy the book. Okapi will not have to be sold to the Germans. Thanks to the keen judgment of Millie's literary executor, myself, plans are already afoot to publish a matched, boxed set of her complete works. It will sell handsomely. Also a deluxe edition bound in leather that will sell out at a fantastic price. I have left full instructions for my successor.

As for myself, I am satisfied. I have had a long, distinguished career in the best of professions. I have published many outstanding books of which I have every right to be proud. Okapi will not only survive but will perhaps flourish. So no sad songs for me, and no regrets.

Nonsense, Lieutenant. I have not the slightest intention of enduring an expensive and humiliating trial, followed by interminable abject appeals. I do not have to submit to that pointless torture.

Observe. With thumb and forefinger I can readily remove this cap from my upper-left molar. And behold, what have we here?

Goodbye, gentlemen.

Eight Gables

$\mathcal{9}$T'S LUCKY we got it all on tape," Dirk said. "Otherwise Mo would have had my ass. Yours too."

"Well, you finally got to see one."

"A suicide, not a homicide. It's not the same."

We were sitting on my small deck, Dirk with a big Scotch, I with a big vodka. We were weary but exultant after our long, long day with the police and the medical examiner and the pathologist. Because of Dirk's promise to give everything to Mo Abbudanza, we did not talk to the press, an adventure that I hated to miss. Mo, who arrived dramatically on Millie's lawn by police helicopter from Boston, took all the bows. Privately he was very grateful to us, although he suggested that if he, Mo, had been there, Leonard Marsden would never have managed to get that pill into his mouth.

"Listen," Dirk told him, "we not only solved all the homicides for you. We saved you and the D.A. a lot of trouble. No arraignment, no trial, no appeal, no hassle, no nothing. Just a body bag."

"Yeah," Abbudanza said, "great with me, but the D.A. doesn't think so. He would have loved that trial. He says it would have been big ammunition for the governor's race."

Regardless of the D.A.'s disappointment, Abbudanza was happy. Several times he shook my hand vigorously. When Dirk turned in his deputy I D card, Mo cuffed him on the shoulder and said he hadn't even needed his full twelve hours as a deputy to wrap up the whole thing.

Now it was over, and we could enjoy a good stiff drink in the twilight. Maybe two or three stiff drinks in the twilight. A reward to ourselves of precooked cold lobsters awaited in the refrigerator. These were a present from Dirk because of my contribution to the case.

A day of triumph.

"I had a terrific time," I said. "I can't say I want to see any more people die of cyanide, but everything else was terrific. The chase was terrific, everything I had imagined it could be."

"Yeah, it was," Dirk agreed. "I didn't realize how much I'd missed it."

"Thinking of going back on the force?"

"No thanks. I had enough years and enough rules and regulations. I'd rather be retired. But it was good to have another shot. Good to prove I hadn't lost my touch. And I even made a little money out of the Hergesheimer special."

Maybe that's why he felt he could afford the lobsters. He was not what I would call a reckless spender.

We drank in companionable silence. The twilight turned darker.

"What do you think about that Chick Bird business?" Dirk said.

"I don't think much of anything. I think Marsden probably felt guilty about all the people he told us he'd killed. Three is a lot. Maybe he decided not to admit to the fourth."

"He didn't sound like he felt guilty. I thought he sounded proud of himself. I think if he had killed Bird, he would have said so and boasted about how he did it. Why keep anything back? He knew he had just a few more minutes to live."

"Maybe Bitsy Betsy's theory was right. Maybe he was comfortable killing women celebrities but was a little ashamed about killing a man."

"Yeah, I guess that could be. But Miss Silk hadn't written anything bad about Mr. Bird. Marsden hadn't had to delete anything. So he had no reason to kill him."

"Maybe you're right. I don't know, maybe it was Hergie. Remember what he had to say about Bird on his special?"

"Hergie was in New York when Bird was killed."

"Oh. Well, then maybe it was one of the waiters or waitresses. Teaching Bird a lesson for being such a cheap tipper."

Dirk was quiet for a bit, long enough to take a couple of swallows. "Well, Jason, I've been thinking about it quite a lot. I think you killed him."

"Me?"

"You."

"Why would I do that?"

"I think you had a romantic notion of saving that crazy old house. That House of Eight Gables. I admit the house is pretty special, in a weird kind of way. Once the town board ruled in Bird's favor, that house was doomed. I think you knew that was coming, or anyway you thought it was likely. I think when you were down in New York, you picked up some cyanide from somewhere, to be ready just in case."

"Where was I supposed to get it? The corner drugstore?"

"How do I know? A chemical supply house? A hospital lab? A medical school? It's not all that hard to come by. Maybe you stole some from Marsden. He seemed to have an ample supply."

"Very funny."

"Yes, well here is how I see it. You had stayed at the Scrimshaw Inn a number of times, so you were completely familiar with the breakfast drill. You knew all the guests had to fill out their order cards the night before and leave them at the front desk. You could easily have got an advance look at the orders. If you did, you saw that Mr. Bird had ordered hominy grits. That's just the kind of dish that would appeal to your sense of humor. Also it's white, like potassium cyanide. Sprinkle, sprinkle, sprinkle. If I was handling the case, I'd run a big check on whether or not you were seen at the Scrimshaw that night. Maybe for drinks? Maybe for dinner? Maybe just hanging around? If you were there, somebody probably saw you. And you knew all the breakfast trays were set up in the dining room. You knew that in the morning there was only one waiter to deliver all the trays to the rooms, one by one. Each time he went off to deliver a tray, the dining room was empty for at least a couple of minutes. You were hiding — I picked out two possible spots — where you could see the white whale flags with the names on them. When Bird's tray was ready, you just slipped out from whichever place you were hiding, dosed his hominy grits, then slipped right out again and drove home. Maybe somebody saw you leaving? I'd run a big check."

"All that just to save a house that didn't even belong to me?"

"You thought it belonged to the Vineyard."

"It did."

"I'm not saying it didn't. It would have been a shame to lose it. But also, Jason, I've known you a long time. You've always been fascinated by homicide. I think that on top of the wish to save that old house from becoming one more celebrity tear-down, you may have seen the whole thing as a sporting proposition. You were wondering, can I pull it off?"

I laughed. "Dirk, that is very far-fetched."

Dirk said nothing. He went inside to refill our drinks.

When he came back and handed me mine, I said, "Is this safe to drink?"

"You're asking me?"

I laughed again. I took a hearty swallow. "So this wild theory of yours," I said. "What are you going to do about it?"

It was getting dark, but I could just see Dirk's smile. "Nothing. Why should I do anything? I'm retired. I'm not even a deputy anymore."

"What does Mo Abbudanza think about your theory?"

"I haven't discussed it with him."

"Then what does he think happened?"

"He thinks Marsden was deranged. Brink of death, didn't know what he was saying. Mo says of course Marsden killed Bird, just like he killed all the others. Mo considers the case closed."

"Then I guess it is."

"I guess it is."

Suddenly I felt starved. "How about starting on your lobsters?"

ACKNOWLEDGMENTS

Whenever I write about legal matters, I start with my colleague and counsel at Time Inc., E. Gabriel Perle. He answers my questions and then tells me whom to consult for further expert knowledge. On this book he educated me on interstate subpoenas and search warrants and courtroom procedure. He also read the manuscript for a pre-press legal review, and in the process protected me against half a dozen typos.

Whenever I write about crime or police action, I start with Thomas Reppetto, president of the Citizens Crime Commission of New York and a former detective. He answers questions and tells me whom to consult.

About cyanide, I consulted Dr. Lawrence Kobilinsky, John Jay Professor of Biology and Immunology, and Dr. Morris S, Zedeck, Pharmacologist / Toxicologist and chairman of the Zedeck Advisory Group Inc., New York. Both were very instructive about the intricate chemical facts of cyanide poisoning and were wonderfully creative about suggesting plot ideas.

Sergeant Jim Plath, homicide detective of the Massachusetts State Police, explained police procedures in the event of a cyanide poisoning at the Vineyard.

Alex Gigante, house counsel at Putnam, advised me about the ground rules on libel and libel insurance at a publishing house.

Janis Klein and Nick O'Gorman of CBS took me through the procedure, the personnel and the equipment that would be required to create a TV special at the Vineyard.

As usual, Ann Nelson, owner of the Bunch of Grapes bookstore in Vineyard Haven, gave me advice before, during and after the writing of the book. And also, as usual, whenever I write about the Vineyard, I rely on Eulalie Regan, librarian of the *Vineyard Gazette*.

My thirty-five years at Time Inc., mostly at *Life* magazine, contributed a great deal of personal experience about serial rights, libel and editing. One of the literary agents from whom I sometimes bought first serial rights was my old friend, Sterling Lord, who represented this book.

If, in my writing enthusiasm, I have accidentally committed any factual errors, none of the above people is guilty.

I am grateful to my son William Parish for thinking up the title.

CHAMPAGNE KISSES, CYANIDE DREAMS

was set in a digital version of Electra, a type originally designed by William Addison Dwiggins for the Mergenthaler Linotype Company and first made available in 1935. Notable for its clean and elegant lines, Electra is impossible to classify as either "modern" or "old style." It is not based on any historical model nor does it reflect any particular period or style. In the interest of increased legibility, Dwiggins reduced the contrast between thick and thin elements that characterizes most modern faces, creating a face that was free from idiosyncracies that could distract the eye from reading.

Design and composition by Carl W. Scarbrough